THE DREAMS

Vicious, weird, and horrifying, they haunted Sabra Narman and made her life a living hell. Hoping to escape them, Sabra and her family moved to a quiet country town.

THE TERROR

Little did the Narmans know that tiny Cascade harbored a threat far more deadly than mere visions—an imprisoned spirit whose wrath would wreak unbelievable havoc once released.

THE CURSE

Slowly, insidiously, the centuries-old evil crept into the Narman's home, working its spell, destroying the family. Only Sabra had the power to save her husband and children...if she could master the very hallucinations that had nearly driven her insane.

THE JOHN TIGGES CURSE

LEISURE BOOKS   NEW YORK CITY

A LEISURE BOOK®

February 1993

Published by

Dorchester Publishing Co., Inc.
276 Fifth Avenue
New York, NY 10001

Printed in the United States of America.

For:
The Shredders: Allan, Brad, Katie, Pam, Rose, and Suellen.

The Irregulars: Audrey, Corinne, Jan, Kris, Marta, Megan, Pat, and Shirley S.

The Students: Al, Ann, Carol, Chris, Jane, Joanne, Karen, Linnea, Muriel, Shirley M., and Vi.

PART I

*IT SHALL BE OPENED
SEPTEMBER 3 TO
SEPTEMBER 10*

Chapter One

Sabra Narman stared through the car window at the passing landscape. Cool air, dampened with moisture from Lake Champlain, flowed into the car. From the appearance of the leaves, autumn would be early, she thought.

She glanced toward the back seat and found her children content to look at the surrounding countryside or like Curt, her ten year old, lose themselves in a book. Her husband, Bart, concentrated on driving and watching for their exit which she hoped would be coming up soon. It seemed an age had passed since they had gotten in the car, bound for their new home.

It was almost unreal that they were moving to upstate New York on the advice of her psychologist, Rose Allan. Rose had suggested the move to get Sabra into a new environment. But after living their entire married life of sixteen years in Yonkers, New York, Sabra and Bart agreed that moving to a community as small as Cascade would be a challenge. Still, there was something appealing about the prospect. All the stories they'd heard about life in a small town would be put on the line, and they would soon know if they would be accepted or rejected by their neighbors. Still, moving from a city of over 200,000 to a town of less than 1000 might prove to be unnerving, she thought.

Cascade had appealed to her almost immediately, and that was odd. She still wondered about that. Why had she virtually fallen in love with Cascade? Her first and only negative thought had been that it would be as quiet as her three years in the convent, when she had prepared to be a nun. For whatever reason, she had "come to her senses," as she put it later, and had left before taking her final vows.

Certainly their standard of living would climb considerably. Bart would continue operating his computerized traffic analysis business and retain all of his clientele through the same computer line he had utilized in Yonkers. The cost of living would be lower in Cascade as would taxes and all other expenses. Most of their shopping would be done in Plattsburgh, which wasn't that far away, and she had seen some nice shops in Schuyler Falls, which was also close to Cascade.

The Curse

Sabra thought they would be happy, and that was all she wanted. Her own situation had become almost unbearable during the last year. Consulting a psychologist had been Bart's suggestion and for that she was grateful. Rose had been wonderful.

For several years, Sabra had thought she was losing her mind. The wild thoughts, the fantastic dreams and peculiar feelings she had experienced for almost her entire lifetime had paled to insignificance once the terrifying visions started. She could easily go into a trance-like state and witness bizarre events. She thought she heard voices, some happy, others crying pitifully. She'd seen bizarre monsters that defied description.

Sabra had wondered more than once if she would have considered going to a psychologist like Rose if Bart hadn't been pushed to the brink and asked for a divorce. She had to admit that had sobered her and brought her around to a clearer way of thinking. She passionately loved Bart, and she had felt he loved her in a similar way.

She glanced at her husband and smiled to herself. Bart, who stood six-feet-two, was muscular from having attended an exercise and health spa. He had not tried body building as such, but had established a well-rounded exercise program that would help him maintain a healthy body. When they started going together, she joined the same spa and developed the same passion for exercise as Bart.

As Bart ran a hand through his dark brown hair, she watched him out of the corner of her eye. His dark good looks and brown eyes contrasted sharply with her own blond fairness that might have been taken for Scandinavian but actually came from her German mother.

Sabra thought of their three children, none of whom resembled Bart in the least when it came to coloring. Marcy, Curt and Ginger were all as blond as she, although Curt had Bart's features while the girls were close copies of Sabra.

They had a good marriage for the most part, and the threat of divorce had been made only to snap Sabra back to her senses. Her strange behavior had almost cost him a client, and she shuddered mentally at the memory.

Sabra fingered the crucifix that hung from a gold chain around her neck and turned to Bart when he slowed the car.

"Our exit?"

"Mm-hmmm." He signaled and continued slowing.

"How far, Daddy?" Ginger asked from the back.

Sabra turned to look at her eight year old. "Just a short way, darling."

"Is Cascade the next town, Daddy?" Curt asked, putting aside his book.

"We have to go through Peru and Schuyler Falls and then we'll get to Cascade," Bart said. He braked to a halt and turned left after making certain the road was clear in both directions. They passed under the interstate and wound their way along the two lane county highway.

Sabra sat back and relaxed. Despite having grown up in a large metropolitan area, she found herself easily adapting to the peacefulness and beauty of the countryside.

"You did remember to bring our transcripts for school, didn't you?" Marcy asked.

Sabra turned in her seat again. "I have them, so don't worry."

Sabra faced the front again. Marcy was a good student, and while she was in her sophomore year in high school, she had remained the same level-headed person she had been in grade school. For a while, Sabra had thought that Marcy might become like other high school students she'd known. She had breathed a sigh of relief when Marcy did not become boy crazy, did not begin wearing clothing like Madonna and had opted more to stay at home at night than go out. If Sabra had to describe her 15-year-old daughter, she would have to say she was a good, sensible girl.

Her other daughter, Ginger, was a junior-size reflection of Marcy, with her long yellow hair parted on the opposite side. With that exception, the girls were virtually identical despite their differences in age.

Sabra snapped out of her thoughts. "Was that Peru?"

"Yeah," Bart said, running a hand through his

straight brown hair. "It won't be long now. I only hope the movers get there this afternoon."

"They promised they'd be there right after lunch, and it's almost noon now." Sabra turned away and looked through the window. She wondered if Bart might be questioning her ability to get the job done where the movers were concerned. No, that wasn't fair to Bart. He was only making a statement. She had to stop thinking that every word he said was clouded with doubt.

She reached up and played with the crucifix again. She really didn't blame Bart for having suggested a divorce. Rose had explained—and Bart had echoed her explanation—that he had done so to get Sabra's attention when her visions and dreams began to take over her waking hours. At least now the visions had stopped during the daytime, but she couldn't control her dreams. It had really been the daytime visions that had almost brought their lives together to an abrupt halt.

On occasion, Sabra would help Bart in his work. But when her body would go rigid, that terrified look would cross her face and she'd scream. Then it happened that she wound up screaming into the telephone while talking with their biggest client, and Bart had almost struck her.

"You've got to get some sort of help for this, Sabra. If you don't, I . . . I'm afraid I'll have to leave you. I'll divorce you. I can't stand this anymore, and certainly I can't have you doing crazy things to my clients."

Sabra stared at him, uncertain as to what she should say next.

"Why do you do it? Do you know? What are you thinking of when your so-called visions happen? You've got to get help."

She looked up at him. "Bart, would you really leave me? Walk away from everything? The children? The house? Me?"

He stared intensely at her, his brown eyes narrowed. "Will you get help?"

Having no choice, she called Rose Allan. Her sessions with Rose went well right from the beginning, but the visions continued unabated. Rose had felt that Sabra was in no real danger from them. The psychologist felt that at worst it was nothing but Sabra's imagination taking over and controlling the moment. Rose, along with Bart and eventually Sabra, believed that the consequences of the visions, not the visions themselves, were the big concern.

When they didn't subside along with the dreams, Rose suggested a change of locale, a change of lifestyle that would virtually force Sabra to face even simple things in a new environment.

Refocusing her attention on where they were, Sabra turned to Bart. "Is this Schuyler Falls?"

Bart snapped his head toward her. "Schuyler . . . ? Are you all right? This is Cascade. We went through Schuyler Falls twenty minutes ago." He studied her and then said, "You aren't having one of those visions, are you?"

Confused, Sabra shook her head. "No, I was just lost in thought. I don't remember going through Schuyler Falls. You know I haven't had any problems in quite a while now."

"How long has it been?" Bart applied the brakes when they came to a right angle turn and started down Main Street. Steep hills rose on either side, holding the little town in a gentle, sylvan grasp.

"Months. Ever since we decided to relocate." She reached out with her left hand and laid it on his thigh. "I'm all right. Really. I'm just excited and thinking about a lot of things." She wanted to put him at ease about the visions. She'd lie to keep him happy. "I guess I was thinking of the things we have to do before we can consider ourselves as being truly settled."

An apologetic look crossed Bart's face. "I'm sorry, darling. I really am. That was unkind of me. You have a lot of work ahead of you, don't you?"

"It goes with the territory of moving, I guess."

Again they fell silent, for which Sabra was thankful. This time she wanted to watch her new town pass by as they drove through it. She didn't want to think about anything other than where she would shop. Several majestic homes lined Main Street at this end of town, and she stared in awe, as though she hadn't really looked the first time, which she hadn't. They were magnificent. One in particular, a Queen Anne mansion, stood out over the others. Its small balcony above the front porch held her attention until the house was out of sight.

Shops that had once been grocery stores now either stood vacant or housed antique shops and boutiques of various sorts. She liked antiquing, and although their house was nowhere near as elegant as the mansions they'd just passed, it would be fun to hunt for different antique pieces that would go well with their home.

They passed a small restaurant that offered home-cooked meals and a dress shop housed in the same building. A hotel, probably the largest building in town, had a club and restaurant on the first floor, next to the lobby. Hardware, plumbing and electrical shops nestled together along one side of the street that made up the beginning of the business district. A computer store, an office supply company and a video rental shop were on the opposite side. A theater that offered movies only on the weekend, a good-sized supermarket and a drugstore were interspersed with more antique shops. A Welcome Booth for tourists was next to a fast food outlet, followed by a service station and garage. Bart continued through the last intersection into the northern residential area. They passed over a bridge that spanned a small river. To one side of the bridge, a waterfall dropped the level of the river by four or five feet.

"I forgot how far out of town our house is," Marcy said, as the buildings became fewer and farther between.

"It's only a mile and a half," Bart said. "It'll be good exercise to run into town for a loaf of bread."

"Oh, Daddy," Marcy sighed and sat back.

Minutes later, he braked and turned the station wagon into their driveway. The house sat to the left of the drive, almost against the small hill that rose abruptly to a height of 25 feet next to their home. He pulled up close to the garage and turned off the motor.

They got out and the children ran ahead after asking Sabra for the key. Marcy unlocked the door, and they disappeared inside.

"Want help with the suitcases?" Sabra asked, without taking her eyes off the house. It was as she remembered it, and it still seemed to beckon to her.

"No problem. I'll take these and get the rest later," Bart said, hefting one bag under his arm and then picking up a third with his free hand.

Sabra strolled toward the house and held the door open for Bart who hurried through.

Sabra smiled. She liked the house. It was an old farmhouse that had been modernized, and she felt that its full potential had not yet been reached. She would have fun decorating and acquiring new pieces of furniture for it. She walked through the long, narrow kitchen. It was not to her liking, but remodeling it into a galley-style and putting a new door into the dining room would work wonders for it.

The dining room was square and had a large window that looked out over the front yard and road beyond it. A window opened onto the back of the house where she could see the green of the small hill that was too close. A built-in cupboard with glass doors dominated the wall next to the kitchen, and access was available to the shelves from the kitchen as well. The opposite wall had three doors. One to the left opened onto what could have been a nursery at one time or a fifth bedroom. Bart had said he would like it for his office and computers, and she had agreed without reservation. The room was large and would allow him to expand somewhat since the room he had used in their Yonkers home had been much smaller.

Next stood the door to the stairway that led to the second floor, and to the right huge swinging doors opened onto the living room. She entered the living room and turned around. A large window looked out over the front yard, and there were windows in the wall to her left. Another doorway gave access to the front porch that also had a door to the dining room.

The house was big, and she felt it would be fun to make their new home livable.

Bart came down the steps, followed by the children. Minutes later, each child carried a suitcase, and Bart brought up the rear with three more.

"The van's here, Sabra. Will you go out and meet them? I'll be right down." He started up the steps without waiting for an answer.

"Hurry down," she said in way of agreeing and left the living room.

Soon the movers were trooping into the house, and Sabra was directing them where to put the furniture while Bart and the children helped by getting in everyone's way.

"I have an idea," Bart said, pulling Sabra aside.

"What's that?"

"Why don't I take the kids and go into town and register them? That way you won't have to, and you'll get your furniture placed exactly where you want it. We can kill two birds with one stone."

"Sounds good to me," Sabra said. "I'll get their transcripts."

While she fumbled through her purse, pulling out the three envelopes, Bart said, "We might even be able to spend the night here. I really thought the movers would goof and come in real late or even tomorrow. This is pretty good service."

She handed him the envelopes.

"No motel for us tonight," he said. "Come on, kids. Time to go to school and get you registered."

"Aw, do we have to?" Curt answered. "I was

just unloading my Nintendo."

"You can do that when we get home," Bart said.

Bart pecked Sabra on the cheek and left, following the children through the kitchen. His well-conditioned body allowed him to move with the grace of a professional athlete.

One of the movers came into the dining room carrying a wingbacked occasional chair. "This is the last piece of furniture, ma'am. Where does it go?"

"That goes in the living room," she said, pointing as if the man didn't know where it was by now. When she realized what she was doing, she felt embarrassed.

"Dishes, ma'am," another man said from the doorway of the kitchen. "Where do you want them?"

"Put them here in the dining room. Those are some antique cups and saucers and a collection of bells that go in that curio cabinet." Sabra pointed toward the tall thin cabinet with glass walls and doors. "By the way, the exercise equipment can be put in the garage."

Nodding, the man placed the box next to the cabinet and left the room. She knew everything else was marked, and they would have no trouble putting the boxes where they belonged. She crossed to the porch and stepped outside. The screen door squeaked when she opened it. She jumped, laughing at herself when it banged against its frame. What was wrong with her? She felt nervous, jittery.

She walked toward the back of the house, where the hill rose up. Bart had contracted with a landscaper who said the hill could be leveled. It wasn't that high, and its absence would make the yard that much nicer. He wanted to install an outdoor gym for the children and a small gym for their exercise equipment. With the regime of workouts that Bart imposed on himself and that the children had picked up on, the family was in good physical shape.

Sabra looked down and kicked at a pebble that lay in the grass. How healthy was *she?* Would *she* be all right? Was Rose right in suggesting they pull up stakes and move?

Sabra thought for a moment. She hadn't had a vision since Rose first had suggested the move. Maybe it would work. She recalled the last apparition she had suffered. She had been talking with her family during their favorite TV program, *Jeopardy,* when the room seemed to simply disappear and she was suddenly standing in the middle of a throng of people—strange people, yelling and screaming in a language she didn't understand at all. Their costumes were heavy, dark woolens that hung to the ground. Men were dressed like women, and children ran about, disturbed and screaming out their terror. At least she felt it had been terror. All the other times, she had felt like an invisible intruder since there was never any reaction from the people to her presence. That had always been true until the last vision. That time, a man had run right up to her and grabbed her. She had felt his rough hands on her arms. And he had shaken her so vigorously, she thought for a moment that he'd injure her.

But the thing that had frightened her the most had been the look on his face. Sabra could not describe the absolute terror scratched onto his pock-marked features. He had screamed something at her—and then she was back in her own living room in Yonkers, New York. Bart had shaken her, and when he told her that she had screamed, she wept and wondered if she were going insane.

Sabra trembled from the memory and walked to a fallen tree. Its trunk still desperately clinging to the earth, the tree had been blown down in some long forgotten windstorm, but the roots that had not been torn from the ground were not enough to sustain it.

Once she had sat down, Sabra looked at the back of their new home. It was an old house and a good house. Bart had had a carpenter check out the construction, and other servicemen had checked out the wiring and the plumbing. All seemed in extraordinary condition.

The one thing she had to do was stop thinking about the reason why they had moved to Cascade. They'd be happy here. They'd be happy anyplace because their family had a special something going. She didn't know if it was because she had been an only child that she insisted her three siblings get along well or if they really did enjoy one another that much. She hoped it was the latter since it would be genuine if that was the case.

"When I get through with you, old house, you're going to be beautiful," she said softly.

"Ma'am?" a voice said from her right.

Sabra jumped and got to her feet.

"I'm sorry. I didn't mean to startle you. Were you talking to me?"

Sabra fixed her attention on the man, one of the movers. She felt her face flush. "I'm sorry. I didn't hear you walk up. Is something wrong?"

"No, ma'am. We've finished. If you'd like to check the number of cartons against the invoice here and sign the receipt, we'll be on our way." He smiled and turned back toward the house.

Sabra followed.

When the van pulled out of the yard, Bart and the children still had not returned. Sabra stared at the boxes but decided not to tackle them until her family returned.

She wandered outside again and returned to the fallen tree. Reclaiming her seat, she grinned at what the mover must have thought when he walked up and heard her talking to herself. What difference did that make? She was talking to her new house, and she didn't care what the man thought.

She liked the house and remembered the first

time she had seen it. It had been rather strange how it had happened. When they came to the junction south of Cascade she had told Bart to turn. She wanted to see the town of Cascade, but nothing had appealed to her. In fact, at first she had found herself turned off by the town. They had gone all the way through and were looking at the north side of town when she saw the "For Sale" sign in front of the house. She suddenly felt an overwhelming urge to see the interior.

It had almost been as if the house had been a magnet and she a bit of iron filing. She was simply attracted to it. After looking through it and admiring the six acres on which it was situated, they made a tentative offer based on reports from plumbers, electricians and carpenters and contingent to the sale of their Yonkers property.

When they retraced their path through Cascade, Sabra found the whole town as appealing as the house had been. She had wondered about it then but had never said anything to Bart. She didn't want him thinking that she had developed another mental problem. If that were the case and they were living in a town such as Cascade, where could they go for such help? Surely Rose Allen was too far away for steady consultations. Could she work with someone else? Someone who was closer?

She played with the end of her braid for a moment and then flipped it over her shoulder. Instinctively reaching for her crucifix, she touched it and smiled. She was happy. Everyone in the family liked their new home, she hadn't had a vision in quite some time, and everything was going to work out fine.

Sabra gave the back of the house one more quick perusal and then stood. She walked toward the back entrance and its little entryway and summer kitchen. She thought she could find some good use for that extra kitchen room and—

Her eyes suddenly filled with tears, the house and yard wavering in her impaired vision. Crumbling to her knees, she wept. Bowing down until her head touched the ground, she cried uncontrollably, her body shaking from deep racking sobs.

Chapter Two

While his three children roamed about the hallway outside the principal's office, Bart sat opposite Sister Rita Brent who appeared to be in her late thirties and was dressed in a flowered blouse and blue slacks. She typed information from Marcy's transcript, which was the last, into her computer.

"I'm certainly impressed with your children's performances, Mr. Narman," she said.

"Thank you, Sister. We've been very proud of them."

Sister Rita looked up and, when she saw that they were alone, said, "And I can't recall seeing three such handsome and beautiful children." She suddenly looked away and then refocused her attention on Bart. "I don't want you to think that I'm trying to flatter you, because I'm not. I don't believe I've ever said anything like that to a parent before. I'm just stating a fact. They are very good-looking."

"Thank you, Sister," Bart said, feeling somewhat uncomfortable. He ran a hand over his square jaw. What was she trying to say? He studied her for a moment and found her to be an attractive woman herself. She was tall and had light chestnut-colored hair. Her face was more square than oval, and a pert, turned-up nose lent an air of mischievousness to the nun's otherwise dignified appearance.

He and Sabra had found it highly unusual to find a four-year Catholic high school coupled with a grade school in, of all places, Cascade, New York. In Yonkers, they had had to send their children to the public schools because where they lived was too inconvenient to drive them to the Catholic schools every day.

He winced mentally. Why Sabra didn't practice her faith anymore bothered him in some ways. And in other ways, he didn't really care. He wasn't that religious himself, and as long as they led an upright life, he felt that the example they set for their children was a good one. Bart and Sabra wanted them to have a good Catholic education and a sound footing in religious upbringing. For that reason, he went to church almost every Sunday and took the children. But Sabra no longer went to Mass.

The Curse

He found that particular aspect of his wife's makeup confusing and contradictory at best. She had almost become a nun in a cloistered convent which had required an undying dedication. Now that she was married and a mother, for all practical purposes she had abandoned her faith and religion. No—not her faith. From what Bart could gather without openly questioning her, Sabra still believed in God and all the tenets of the Roman Catholic Church. It was just that she would not go to Mass on Sunday for some reason.

"We'll install Marcy, Curt and Ginger in our 'A' track, Mr. Narman. They should do very well there. We have some advanced programing for gifted children, and I believe yours belong there."

"That's good to know, Sister," Bart said, fixing his attention on the nun.

"If you'd like, we can take the children around and show them their home rooms." Sister Rita stood and walked to the office door. "As far as the children being bussed is concerned, I'm afraid it will be several days, perhaps even a week, before we can alter the route to have them picked up. Will it be a problem to bring them?"

"No problem at all, Sister."

By the time they reached Marcy's home room, it was almost time for the students to be excused for the day. Marcy was introduced by Sister Rita, and Bart noticed several of the boys eyeing his daughter in a way that brought goose bumps to his arms. He wouldn't fight it. It was natural. He'd done the same sort of thing himself. He trusted Marcy and knew she'd stick by her own code of behavior, which was a very mature one.

When they left the room, Bart followed Sister Rita and could not help noticing that her bobbed hair bounced with each step. When he had gone to high school, the nuns were just coming out of their strict way of life, wearing knee-length habits and short veils. Now, one would be hard pressed to tell a nun from other women in public.

"Why don't you guys go on ahead to the car," he said when they reached the front entrance. "I want to visit with Sister Rita for a moment."

"Okay, Daddy," Marcy said and led her younger brother and sister toward the station wagon.

"When will the tuition be due, Sister?"

"I'll have a bill prepared and mail it to you, Mr. Narman."

Bart looked at her closely and said, "I don't mean to be nosy, Sister, but what order do you belong to? It seems that it's impossible to tell these days since habits are no longer worn."

Sister Rita laughed, the sound coming out almost musically. "I understand where you're coming from, Mr. Narman. A lot has changed since Vatican II. We are members of The Sisters of the Divine Jesus."

Bart frowned. He'd never heard of them.

As if reading his mind, she continued. "I don't imagine you've heard of us. We're primarily a teaching order and are centered more in Ohio and Indiana. This is the farthest east and north that we're located. By the way, don't believe it when your children come home from school and tell you that we are Sisters of the Disc Jockey. SDJs have a sense of humor, and I believe we've adjusted to modern times better than any other order. But we are still Sisters of the Divine Jesus."

Bart chuckled at the joke.

Just then, the front door of the school opened and a priest entered, his carrot-colored hair reflecting the afternoon sun.

"Oh, here's Father Wisdom," Sister Rita said. "He's pastor of Holy Martyr's Church. You and your family will be attending there, I assume. He also teaches religion classes here at Saint Boniface."

The priest strode up to them, a broad smile on his face. "Hello, Sister. How are you today?"

"I'm fine, Father. Father, this is Mr. Bart Narman. I've just enrolled his children in school. Mr. Narman, this is Father Paul Wisdom."

"I'm happy to meet you, Mr. Narman." He took Bart's hand in a firm grip and vigorously shook it.

"I'm glad to meet you, Father." Bart noted the wisp of gray in his hair and the fading freckles, estimating the priest's age at around 55 or 60.

"I suppose I'll be seeing you and yours in church on Sunday."

Bart hesitated for a moment. In Christ the King Church where they attended Mass in Yonkers, the congregation was so large that Sabra's absence wasn't noticed by anyone. Here in Cascade, it would probably be a very different matter. This priest could probably take a mental roll call from the pulpit and know who was missing from Mass on any given Sunday. He might just as well tell him now and get it over with.

"You'll probably see me and the children, Father."

Wisdom cocked an eyebrow. "Your wife isn't . . . ?"

Bart waited for a second or two to see if the priest was going to finish the question. When nothing was forthcoming, Bart cleared his throat. "Sabra—ah, my wife—doesn't go to church very regularly."

"Is she Catholic?" Wisdom asked.

Bart nodded. Should he tell him and the nun that Sabra had almost become a nun? That might be akin to betraying his wife or telling tales out of school, so to speak. He couldn't really tell them the reason because he didn't know it himself. In fact, he wasn't certain if Sabra knew why. She seemed to have no argument with the Church or with God in any way.

Wisdom said, "Well, maybe we can get her in the groove where going to church is concerned. I've got to get going or I'll be late for my class. I'll see you in church, Mr. Narman." He threw out a hand and smiled broadly once more.

Bart took his hand, grinning at the phrase the priest had used.

"I'll see you around, Sister," Wisdom called over his shoulder and ran up the steps, two at a time.

Bart mentally shook his head, marveling at the priest's agility, and turned to Sister Rita. "Well, Sister, it's been a pleasure meeting you and seeing your school. I'm very happy that there's a Catholic high school in the area. By the way, where do the children who aren't Catholic attend school?"

"They're bussed to Schuyler Falls to a consolidated high school there."

"I have to ask this, Sister. I don't imagine there's any sort of athletic program here at Saint Boniface, is there?"

Sister Rita shook her head. "I'm afraid we're too small for that. You probably noticed that the class your daughter will be in numbered only about thirty. Each of the high school classes is about that size. It would be impossible to put together a basketball team much less a football or baseball team. Of course, if we had five Michael Jordans in school, we could probably pound anybody, couldn't we?"

Bart did a double take.

Sister Rita grinned. "I'm a sports nut myself, Mr. Narman. We do have a gym period every day, and each class gets there at least twice a week. It's not the best answer, but under the circumstances it'll have to do."

Bart shook his head. "How can you operate this way? How much is the tuition?"

"It's high—very high, but because we have half a dozen nuns teaching here along with the lay faculty, we do manage somehow. Father Wisdom helps out, and Father Duane Richards is on the faculty full time. He teaches science and math to the high school students."

Bart wondered just how "high—very high" the tuition was. No matter how much, he knew he'd be able to swing it. He'd been very fortunate in starting his traffic business when computers hadn't yet swamped the work place. When he bought one, he was one of the first traffic analysts to be computerized and had a lock on some very lucrative clients. There were times when he was almost ashamed of the money he made. It seemed obscene for one man to be making the kind of money he was. He had sufficient funds put aside for the children's college education, and his own tax-sheltered funds easily would take care of retirement, when he was ready for it. He was thankful that he'd been able to keep his feet on the ground where money was concerned. He and Sabra had never splurged, but they weren't lacking for anything.

"Well, I must be going, Sister." Bart turned and walked toward the front entrance.

"Wait a minute, Mr. Narman." Sister Rita reached out, placing a cool hand on his arm to keep him from leaving.

"Yes, Sister?"

"About the tuition. If it proves to be too high, let me know. There are scholarship funds available from the Pendergard Estate. Josiah Pendergard was a meat packing plant owner who went to Saint Boniface years ago. He believed in Catholic education, and as a result we never have to turn anyone away who might have financial problems. The last living Pendergard is his grandnephew, Jerome Pendergard, a retired college professor who lives in Cascade."

"I'm sorry if you got that idea that money might be a problem, Sister. Actually, there'll be no problem. Again, I must be going. It was good meeting you. Should you ever have any problems with any of our children, just give us a call."

"Good-bye, Mr. Narman." Sister Rita turned and walked toward the staircase.

Bart went outside into the warm afternoon sunshine and got into the station wagon. "Enjoy the sunshine, kids," he said pulling out of the parking lot. "Tomorrow you start the old rat race again."

Bart smiled to himself. He loved his kids and wife so much that at times he had trouble comprehending how people could fight and have quarrels and get divorced.

Divorced!

He hadn't thought of the threat he'd made to Sabra since he had actually made it. He recalled how angry he'd gotten when he had entered his office and found Sabra on the phone, placing a call to one of his biggest clients. When he stepped through the doorway, she suddenly had gone rigid, her eyes filled with terror, and began screaming as though someone was about to kill her. He had no problem straightening out the client, after which Sabra's actions quickly became his chief concern. Screaming on the phone was the final straw. If she wanted to have visions and dreams and talk about wild, crazy things, she'd have to do it alone. For all he knew, she might prove to be dangerous in time— not only to herself but to the children.

He had to do something, but nothing he said seemed to register. Then he threatened divorce, and Sabra suddenly understood that she had a serious problem. When he suggested consulting a psychiatrist or psychologist she readily agreed.

Ever since Rose Allen had suggested the move, things had been pretty normal, and for that he was thankful. There had been no more instances of Sabra claiming to have had visions, and her sleep had gone undisturbed. She wasn't nervous any longer, and he felt he had the same beautiful bride back.

There was no way he could ever consider divorcing Sabra and breaking up his family.

"Hey, you kids want a Coke or something before I make a stop on the way home?"

"Can I have ice cream?" Ginger asked.

"And I want a malted milk," Curt said, leaning over the front seat.

"What about you, Marcy?" Bart asked.

"Huh? Oh, I'll have a Coke, Daddy."

Bart pulled into a drive-in.

Sabra got to her feet and, still weeping, stood swaying dizzily for a moment. What was wrong with her? Why was she crying?

Then it struck her. Something was wrong here—but what? What was so wrong that it would make her cry like that? Yet the feeling she had was something more than just wrong. It was as if a totally evil person was nearby or even standing right next to her.

That was the word. Evil! Something very evil was—was what? Nearby? In the house? Where? Where was something so evil that it would make her break down and cry in her own yard? She reached for her crucifix and fingered it.

Might she be imagining that it was something like that? Could it be something inside her? Not something evil but something from her visions or dreams?

"Oh, God!" she cried. "Help me. Don't let the dreams or visions start again. Not here. I couldn't stand it. Rose is too far away. Help me!"

The sensation of evil dissipated, not unlike sweat evaporating off an overheated arm or forehead.

Sabra stood for an instant and then hurried toward the house. She'd love to shower but there wasn't time. Bart and the children would soon be home and she'd have no explanation for taking a shower in the middle of the afternoon, especially since none of the cartons had been unpacked yet.

She went to the first floor bathroom and splashed cold water on her face, thanking the foresight that Bart had shown when he called the day before and had the water and electricity turned on. The telephone was another matter, but right now she didn't want to call anyone. She was fearful of looking closely at her eyes. What if they were red and bloodshot? Considering her blue-white irises, her eyes always looked spectacular whenever they were bloodshot. She looked closely. Thank goodness. The whites weren't even pink, which was unusual considering how hard she had wept.

She dried her face on a paper towel and threw the crumpled bit of paper into a plastic garbage bag. The sound of a car pulling into the driveway sent her hurrying to the window. It was Bart and the children. She raced back to the bathroom to make one final check. Should she tell Bart what had happened? What would he say if she told him she started crying for no reason at all and thought there was something inherently evil about their house or its grounds or the area or the town, something so evil that she thought she could actually touch it?

Bart and the children trooped into the house.

"Hi," she managed. Had she said that in a normal voice? Had it been too high-pitched? When no one said anything, she felt it had been all right.

"I stopped at the landscaper's office and talked with Jim Recton. He's going to start right after Labor Day."

"You're going to do that now—this fall?"

"Why not? If it's done now, sod can be put in and we won't have a mess next spring. He said he'd stop by this afternoon."

"Well, I suppose the sooner we get started the quicker the yard will be the way we want it."

"You're beginning to understand efficiency, Sabra," he said teasingly and kissed her on the cheek.

"All right, you kids," she said. "Up to your rooms and start unpacking your clothes. Tomorrow is school." She turned to Bart. "Right? No problem there?"

"Everything went smoother than silk." He told her about Sister Rita and Father Wisom and everything he'd learned about the school. "You know," he said, "it might be the smartest thing we ever did. If the school is half as good as I've been led to believe, the children are going to profit tremendously from this."

The rest of the afternoon was spent unpacking cartons and putting away dishes and canned food. Clothing was hung up and furniture placed properly.

When Jim Recton arrived, Bart went outside with him, and by the time the landscaper left, it was time to eat. They opted to go to a drive-in, after which the Narman family fell into bed before ten o'clock, exhausted.

Sabra closed her eyes and heard Bart snoring gently. In seconds she fell asleep. Clouds of exhaustion slipped by her, scudding to the left and right. She came to the edge of a cliff and fell over the lip.

Sabra jerked in bed, awakening for a split second. She hated to awaken like that. She was too tired. Was everyone in the family reacting the same way? Had Bart jumped like that? If he did, she hadn't felt it.

She turned over on her side and closed her eyes. She drifted off to sleep and moved ever so slightly when a voice in her dreams whispered hoarsely, *"It will be opened."*

The next morning, while Bart took the children to school, Sabra continued her task to make the new house into a home as quickly as possible. According to what Bart had said, the landscaper would be ready to attack the hill on Tuesday. It would take the better part of two or three weeks to finish the job and get the sod down and bushes and shrubs planted.

Happy to be settling into her new home, she didn't think about the weeping episode the day before in the backyard.

When Bart returned from taking the children to school, he set to work putting together his computer desks and stands. When the furniture was in place, he began unpacking equipment. Copier, fax machine, typewriter, consoles and keyboards were connected and adjusted. After he wrestled a filing cabinet into place, he came out of the office and found Sabra on her hands and knees scrubbing the kitchen floor.

"We should have had the kitchen redone before we moved in," she said, straightening up when Bart entered the room.

"You have a point. It'll be a mess, won't it?"

"If you want to eat three times a day, it'll be a pain in the neck." She got to her feet.

Bart started for the door. "I'm leaving now. I want to stop at the computer store and see what they carry in stock before I pick up the kids."

Sabra looked at the wall clock. "There's a list on top of the fridge. Can you stop by the store on your way home and get some stuff?"

Bart picked up the list and skimmed it. "Yeah, no problem. Marcy can help."

"What time is school out?"

"Around three. It's one-thirty now. I guess we'll be home no later than four with the bacon for the table. See you."

"No kiss?"

He crossed the room and took her in his arms. Their lips touched, and then his tongue flicked into her mouth.

When they parted, she smiled. "All this passion so early in the afternoon? I'm not sure if I can take it. Save some for tonight."

"That's a date." He turned and left.

An unusual stillness closed over the house when the sound of the station wagon died away. She wished the stereo equipment was hooked up so she could play some music. Well, why not the radio?

She fumbled with the dial and found a soft rock station. That was much better she decided when the music filtered through the air.

When she finished the floor, she took the bucket and put it in the summer kitchen after emptying it. The extra space would serve well to keep the cleaning equipment since there was no broom closet in the kitchen itself. When she stepped into the entryway, she froze when she heard a car engine in the driveway. Who could that be?

She went to the screen door and, standing to one side to keep hidden from view, she peered at the white Toyota Camry parked in the drive. A man dressed in black got out. The priest. Could it be the same one Bart had mentioned?

She didn't want to talk to him.

A knock came at the kitchen door, which was closest to the drive.

Another knock sounded.

She went to the stairway and pulled the door after her. The only light came from the top of the steps where a window on the north side of the house stood open to the warm September afternoon air.

She listened intently. No more knocks came and she relaxed. She'd wait a few minutes and then go about her work.

Reaching out she grabbed the knob after two full minutes had passed and almost screamed when another knock sounded, this time from the porch door. It had to be that priest, but she couldn't risk opening the door a crack to see.

"Please, God, let him go away. I can't talk with him now."

The sound of the screen door squeaking and slamming shut brought instant relief, but she waited for a full ten minutes before leaving the safety of the stairway.

Why had she behaved that way? From what Bart had said, Father Wisdom was a nice man. Why had she acted as if he might be an emissary from hell?

What had Rose said about opening up? Don't be afraid of anyone. They don't know about your visions and dreams. Most people are just as insecure the first time they meet someone as you are. Open up.

"Open up," Sabra said and swung open the door.

Then her face clouded. Open up! Something was going to be opened up. Where did she get that idea? Had she heard it someplace? If she had, where? What was going to be opened?

She had no idea.

Chapter Three

Jim Recton arrived shortly after eight o'clock Tuesday morning, and the sounds of the bulldozer and backhoe filled the air. The backhoe swung downward, taking large bites of earth and emptying them into a waiting dump truck.

Inside the house, Sabra found herself alone. Bart had taken the children to school and was stopping to order some office supplies from the computer store. Sabra had promised him she would arrange his office the way it had been laid out in their former home.

The weekend had been fun and relaxing, even though they had worked most of the time. The final result was that the house was in order with the exception of the window treatments.

The Curse

She was going to search out a seamstress who could make draperies and curtains. For the time being, shades would have to do.

Walking past the window that looked out over that part of the yard that was being torn apart, she could see the men working. She marveled at how much of the hill was already gone. The backhoe swung through the air and emptied its load into the dump truck, and the driver got into the cab to haul away the first load of dirt.

In some ways, she loved the isolation of their new home, and in others, she wished that there were neighboring houses she could see. The nearest one, as far as she knew, was about a half mile away, right at the edge of town. She had no idea as to the closest one in the opposite directions.

After Bart returned, he went to his office and closed the door. The one good bit of news he brought along was that an installation man had agreed to come out that afternoon and hook up the telephone.

Sabra poured a cup of coffee for herself and sat down at the dining room table. Absently stirring the coffee, she listened to the roar of the machines working outside. So why did it feel too quiet?

She perused the room once more. Everything was in place except the curtains. Then what was wrong?

She had nothing to do. That was it. Just what was her lot in life? Her children were not any problem, at least while they were in school. Being the typical mother, she worried about them and wanted to do things for them when they were around. But for the most part, they got along very well without her during much of their waking hours.

She could help Bart but right now he didn't need any help. If he did he would have come out and asked her. And she couldn't put on a pair of old jeans and go outside to volunteer help to the contractor.

At 42, she was washed up and worthless. Nothing to do.

A broad grin suddenly crossed her lips. Why not? She had minored in art. She could start painting. That was it. And since she had majored in English, she could just as easily write. She had no pressures of any kind, and with that thought in mind, she went to the kitchen and made a list of what she would need from the computer shop. She hoped they would have sketch pads. If they didn't and there weren't any in town, she'd have to order some pads and pencils and charcoal. Sketching would be relaxing, and she might very easily open up a whole new world to herself.

Open up!

There was that phrase again. She hadn't thought about it since last Friday when the priest showed up, unannounced at the door. She had actually hidden to keep from having to meet with him. That was awful—inexcusable.

The Curse

She was glad she hadn't told Bart or the children. She would have felt the fool if she had told them. They, in turn, would have wondered what was happening to her. Bart would believe the visions would return next. Certainly her behavior last Friday had been totally out of character and downright juvenile.

She jumped when the knock came at the door, and she suddenly realized the machinery had fallen silent. When she went to the kitchen door, Jim Recton stood in the way of the sun, blocking out most of the light. His huge shoulders stood at right angles to his neck, and his chest tapered down to a nonexistent waist and hips. He yanked off his hard hat and coughed.

"Sorry to disturb you, ma'am," he said and stepped back several feet. "We've uncovered something out here that maybe you and your husband should take a look at."

Her curiosity piqued, Sabra said, "What did you find?"

"It's an old dump."

Sabra couldn't help but laugh. "A dump? What's so important about that?"

"Is your husband home?" he asked without cracking a smile.

She could tell it was no laughing matter to the landscaper, and she turned to call Bart. "Yes, he is. I'll call him." Walking through the dining room, toward Bart's office, she wondered what could be so important about an old dump.

In seconds, Bart hurried through the kitchen

and went outside with Recton. Sabra followed.

"A dump?" Bart said when he saw where Recton pointed. "I don't understand."

"Well, there's been a lot of excavating done in old neighborhoods and on farms searching for just such dump sites. It tells historians and people like that what went on way back, how people lived."

"I see. Go on," Bart said, narrowing his eyes as if expecting bad news would come next.

Sabra had read about the same thing herself in *Time* or *Newsweek*. There were a lot of hidden aspects of the past that might very easily have been lost except for such excavations.

"Well, it's your land and your hill and your dump. If you want some college guys running around here with little picks and soft brushes removing your hill, say so and I'll stop. Otherwise, I'll get on with it and get your hill the hell outta here."

"What have you found?" Bart asked.

"Nothing much," Recton said and walked over to the open area. "There's some old bottles that date back fifty years or so. Some old broken crockery and bent kitchen utensils. Even an old apple corer that's all rusted."

"Is it worth anything?" Bart asked.

"Damned if I know. It might be to a museum or those college guys. I can't rightly say. Maybe an antique dealer or bottle collector could tell you."

Bart turned to Sabra. "What do you think,

Sabra? Should we postpone our yard and gym setup in the interests of science, or should we go ahead with it?"

Sabra thought for a moment. It would be all right to help out science, but where were the scientists and historians going to come from? How long would they have to look before she and Bart found a school or foundation interested? In the meantime, their backyard would be a potential quagmire every time it rained.

She voiced her thoughts and looked from her husband to Recton.

"Good point, hon," Bart said. He turned back to the landscaper. "Get it finished. I'm sure there's nothing in there of any intrinsic value, and history will not be slighted if we don't notify the colleges."

"I thought you might say that," Recton said and turned, walking away.

The backhoe coughed to life and the boom swung toward the hill. It took another gouging bite from the earth and threw it up into the dump truck that had returned.

"I've got to get back to work," Bart said.

"I'm going to stay out here and watch for a while." Sabra walked with him to the kitchen door and sat down on the step. When Bart disappeared inside, she fixed her attention on the workers as they dug into the side of the hill. More bottles fell from their burial grounds. Some had turned bluish-purple from the passing years, while rusty cans, some with faded labels still attached, and other misshapen items were unearthed and dumped into the truck. A small doll, covered with dirt, fell from the bucket and landed near the garage.

Tired of watching, she got up and went to the kitchen to check over her list of art supplies.

For the next few hours, the backhoe continued annihilating the hill, the men too busy to watch what was being unearthed. Nothing more was uncovered for several hours until an old kettle, its lid intact, fell into the yard and rolled away to rest against the wall of the garage.

Inside the house, Sabra checked her list of supplies once more and stopped, looking up. The sense of something evil suddenly filled the room, overwhelming her, and she fought the urge to cry. What was causing such swings of moods? As quickly as the feeling had enveloped her, it left and she relaxed. What would Bart have thought if he'd have walked in and found her weeping uncontrollably the way she had in the backyard that first day?

She could hear the backhoe running in the yard and she walked over to look through the window. The yellow arm and its hungry bucket dipped into the waning hillside once more and dropped its load into the waiting dump truck.

Toward 2:30 that afternoon, Sabra left to pick up the children. She stopped at the computer store and learned they didn't carry art supplies, but a boutique four doors away did. Excited with her purchases and looking forward to sketching some of the scenes around their new home, she went to the school and picked up her children.

"How was school today?" Sabra asked.

"It was fun," Ginger said. "I got to finger-paint."

"It was okay," Curt said and opened his lunch box. "My apple was rotten. Yuck. Look."

"Why didn't you throw it away?" Sabra asked.

"I don't know. I guess I wanted to show it to you."

"That's gross," Marcy said.

"What did you do all day, Mommy?" Ginger asked.

"I watched the landscapers tear down the hill."

"Is it all gone?" Curt asked. "Darn, I wanted to see that."

"No. But it won't be too long." Sabra picked up speed as they headed along the stretch leading to their home.

"What's that?" Curt asked, pointing toward a yellow truck pulling out of their yard.

"Rosenspahn Lumber Company" was emblazoned on the truck doors.

"I don't know," Sabra said, slowing down. "Maybe Mr. Recton, the landscaper, had them deliver something."

She pulled into the yard, and the children jumped out of the car and ran for the house. Sabra followed but stopped when she saw Bart in the front yard, struggling with some lumber.

"What in the world?" she said, walking up to him.

"Last Friday when I was in town I ordered a backyard gym for the kids to play on. They just delivered it." He picked up six two-by-fours and carried them around the corner of the house to the north side.

Sabra followed. "Is this where you're going to put it?"

"I thought I'd build most of it here and then move it around to the west side of the house once Recton and his crew are finished."

Sabra thought it looked like a huge jigsaw puzzle waiting to be put together, which was exactly what it was. "Will you need help?"

"Curt can help me a little. It's really not a hard job, not as bad as it looks. The plans are quite simple and easy to follow."

Sabra turned to go to the house. "I'll send him out."

"Okay, hon." Bart set about bringing the rest of the wooden pieces to the spot he'd chosen to start the work.

Sabra entered the kitchen and went to the stairway door which stood wide open. "Curt?"

"What?"

"Your dad would like you to help him put the outdoor gym set together."

"Outdoor gym set? Oh, wow. Great. When will it be ready?"

"You'll have to talk about that with your father," Sabra said.

In seconds Curt came bounding down the steps.

"Don't run, young man." Sabra fixed a motherly yet warning stare on her son.

Curt forced himself to walk across the dining room and out through the kitchen. Then the back door slammed shut and she could see his blond mop bounce past the window in the dining room.

Sabra smiled to herself.

"Hey, Dad? When'd you get the jungle gym?" Curt yelled when he saw his father hunched over the plans.

"Here. Take a look. What do you think?"

Curt looked at the plans and pointed to a picture of the completed gym. "Is this what it'll look like?"

Bart nodded.

"Oh, wow. That's great. Let's get going. What do we have to do first?"

Before Bart could answer, Jim Recton turned the corner of the house and walked up to them. "Say, Mr. Narman, I think I overestimated the time it's going to take to level your hill."

"Really? How come?" Bart stood up to face the huge man.

"Well, sir, when I looked at the job, I figured there might be some rock to contend with but we ain't run into nothing. Oh, some loose boulders and rocks a while ago but nothing real solid. It's just pure dirt for the most part. 'Course we ran into that dump but that didn't slow us down none."

"Well, that's good news. How long do you think it'll take you now?"

"Probably eight, ten days at the most."

"What made you think there'd be rock in the hill?"

"Just the layout of the land around these parts. I don't rightly understand it 'cause I ain't a geologist, but it seems to me like that hill was made by somebody. Not Mother Nature."

"You mean Indians could have built that hill? Is it a burial mound?"

Recton shook his head. "We didn't run into anything like arrowheads or stuff. Besides, from what I know, this isn't the right part of the country for mound builders. If it is, I ain't never heard about any mounds being discovered. Stuff like that usually makes the paper. You know what I mean?"

Bart grinned and nodded. "I understand. Well, no matter who built that hill, I own it— or should I say owned it, since it's mostly gone now? I guess I can do with it what I want to. Right, Mr. Recton?"

"Right you are, Mr. Narman. By the way, you can call me Jim. At any rate, we're going to knock off for the day. We'll be back here tomorrow morning bright and early."

"I'll see you then, Jim."

Recton turned and walked off.

Bart frowned. That was certainly a strange

turn of events. He wondered for a moment as to who might have built the hill. Of course, Jim Recton was only speculating about the possibility that someone might have pushed the dirt together. He considered the height, which had been close to 25 feet or so. Then there were the tall trees that had sat on top of the hill. Whoever built it had done so a long time ago.

"Come on, Dad," Curt said from behind him, breaking into his thoughts, "let's get to work. We'll never get the gym built if you just stand around."

Bart turned to face his impatient son. "Right you are, Curt. Sorry. I got daydreaming there for a minute." He picked up the plans and studied them again. "See if you can find a piece numbered A-21."

Curt started examining the ends of the pieces of lumber, happy to get started.

"Can I go outside and play, Mommy?" Ginger asked.

"Do you have much homework?"

"I've got three worksheets to do. That's all. I won't have any trouble with them."

"You're sure about that?" Sabra asked, looking down at her daughter.

"Positive. Please?"

"Oh, all right. But stay away from that machinery. Do you hear me?"

"Yes, Mommy. I won't go anywhere near it. Can Curt play with me?"

"Curt's helping your father build the gym."

"That's no fun. Well, I'll go see what I can find." She turned and headed for the back door.

"Just stay away from the machinery, Ginger."

"Okay," she called over her shoulder and slammed the screen door.

Ginger stood on the back step for a long moment, looking at the backhoe and the bulldozer. She was supposed to stay away from there and she would.

She looked at the work site and walked toward it. Even though they had only lived here a few days, she thought the missing part of the hill looked strange. From what she overheard her parents talking about it, the hill was going to be taken out completely. It might have been fun to explore the hill first but now it was too late.

When she stood at the mouth of the excavation, she looked up and then to either side. She wished she could stay home from school and watch the men work. It must really be something to see them tear the hill down with those big machines.

Then she saw the head and hurried over to it. One eye stared at her blankly.

"You poor thing." She bent down to pick up the dirty doll. "What ever happened to you?" She brushed off the earth that had encased the doll for countless years and held up the small body for inspection. The hair was colorless and matched the colorless fat cheeks. One eye was missing, while the other fixed its unseeing stare on her. The cloth body was stained from the dirt, and the hands and feet dangled from cloth arms and legs.

"My goodness, you're sick." Ginger squeezed the doll sympathizing with it. "What can I call you? I'll have to think of a good name for you. I wonder if Mommy can clean you up. I hope so 'cause you'll be my very own doll, the one I found. You'll be special 'cause Santa Claus won't be the one who gave you to me. You'll be mine. Come on."

Ginger dragged the doll by one arm, its feet bumping along the ground, its head lolling to one side, and walked toward the garage. The door stood open and she peered inside. The exercise equipment that Mommy and Daddy used was in there. No fun in there at all. Turning away from the open doors, she walked along the side farthest from the house.

Thinking about the doll she'd found and con-centrating more on the adventure she wanted to have in their new yard than on where she was going, she tripped and fell. The doll sprawled to her side.

"I'm sorry. Did I hurt you?" She picked up the doll and scooting around on her fanny, saw the kettle.

Intrigued, she lay the doll aside and got on her hands and knees to crawl over to the kettle. Pushing it, it tumbled to an upright position and settled onto the four feet that protruded from the bottom. The handle curved over the top and appeared rusty and fragile.

Ginger reached out, grabbed the loop handle and pulled back in surprise when it crumbled in her hand. Heavy cast handles on either side were held rigidly in place by caked earth.

She moved closer. The little markings that covered both pot and lid caught her curiosity, and she peered intently at them. The lid had a cast handle on it, but when she tried to lift it, it stuck fast.

Ginger ran her hand over the outside, half-expecting the brownish color to wipe away. When it didn't, she concluded that brown was the normal color of the kettle.

She wanted to show it to someone and stood up and tried to lift it, but it was too heavy. She wondered if her parents knew about the pot. What if they didn't want her to have it? It would be nice to play with and pretend she was making big kettles of soup for her sick doll.

Maybe Curt could help her move it.

After much begging and wheedling, she got her brother away from constructing the jungle gym.

Curt followed Ginger, and when they rounded the corner of the garage, she stopped and pointed proudly at the doll and kettle.

"What's that stuff?" he asked.

"My new things. Will you help me move the kettle? It's awful heavy."

"That's nothing but junk."

Ginger fought back the tears. "It's not junk. I

found them, and the poor dolly needs help. She's blind in one eye and—"

"—can't see outta the other." Curt laughed.

Ginger slapped at her brother's arm. "Stop laughing. She can so see. It's just that she's so dirty and—well, you can help me move the kettle. Please?"

"Where do you want it?" Curt walked over to it and bent down, taking the pot by the side handles. He heaved and barely got it off the ground. "Hey, that thing's pretty heavy. Where'd you find it? Right here?"

Ginger nodded.

Curt studied the problem of moving the kettle for a minute. "I think the best way of doing it is to put it on its side and roll it. If we had a wagon, there'd be no problem. Come on, let's try it."

Ginger ran to his side and watched as he pulled on the pot and made it tumble to its side. The curvature of the pot made it readily easy to roll.

When they were hidden by the trees and away from the prying eyes of their family, they stopped and set the kettle upright. Curt studied the lid.

"Maybe we should open it."

"I tried but it won't budge."

"You're only a girl, Ginger. Let a man do it."

Curt straddled the pot and bent down to grab the lid's handle. He pulled with all his might and managed only to lift the kettle a few inches off the ground. He lowered it and grunted.

"What's the matter?" Ginger asked, an innocent tone to her voice. It was not like her to poke fun at Curt because he couldn't do something.

"The lid's on too tight or something. I guess we'll have to ask Dad to help us open it."

"Do we have to? I wanted to keep it a secret."

"If you want it opened, you'll . . . Wait a minute. Maybe we can knock it off with a hammer."

"Could you, Curt? Could you do it? Please?"

Curt nodded and walked away. In minutes, he returned, carrying his father's hammer. The boy knelt down next to the kettle and examined the lid. There seemed to be strange indentations on it, but they were filled for the most part with dirt.

"Stand back, Ginger." Curt brought the claw hammer back over his shoulder and swung with all his might. The steel head glanced off the lid, creating a spark at the same time.

"Gosh, Curt, did you see that?" Ginger's voice sounded breathless at the sight of the spark.

"Yeah. That happens, I guess."

He wound up again and struck the lid of the kettle, creating another spark. He prepared to strike it again. "This time, I'm going to come down on top of it." Swinging the hammer, he struck the head flush on the lid. This time there was no spark, but the force of the blow dislodged some of the dirt from the indentations.

Curt brushed off the loosened dirt and tried the lid. It was on tight as ever. "Aw, this is just a dumb old pot and it ain't never going to open."

The Curse

Ginger pouted. "I so wanted to have it opened. Oh, well." Her voice trailed off, and she got to her feet.

Curt picked up the hammer and started to walk away. He stopped and bent down. When he straightened up, he held a rusty nail in his hand.

"Hey, look at this, Ginger. It's a square nail. I've never seen one like this before."

Ginger glanced at the nail and walked past Curt. "Come on, Curt."

"Okay," he said and threw the nail at the sealed kettle. The nail ricocheted off the lid, flying into the tall grass and weeds.

The children headed for the house.

When they were out of sight, a low-pitched, gloating laugh filtered through the air. The doll, which lay near the pot, suddenly stirred, and a lopsided grin crossed the frozen expression of the slightly open mouth.

Sabra turned on the faucet and picked up her paring knife to peel potatoes. After skinning the first one, she dropped it in a pan of water, then picked up a second and began peeling it.

Her hands began trembling and shaking until she dropped the potato, half-peeled, the sharp blade of the knife running over the forefinger of her left hand.

She stared at the blood pouring from the wound while it mixed with water. It spread over her hand and dripped into the pan of potatoes.

The sensation of evil again overpowered her, and tears filled her eyes.

She stood rigid by the sink, her shoulders convulsing as she sobbed.

Chapter Four

Sabra watched her husband and oldest daughter washing the dishes from their evening meal. She glanced down at her bandaged left forefinger. She still felt herself lucky in more ways than one. Bart had thought she was crying because of the wound in her finger. He had found her standing at the sink, weeping, her shoulders and whole body trembling—not from the cut in her finger but because of the suffocating sensation of overwhelming evil that had enveloped her once more. When he saw the blood gushing from her finger, he had taken charge and said nothing about her crying. She had made herself stop when he finished cleaning and bandaging the cut.

She looked through the window at the rapidly dying day. In an hour or so it would be almost dark, and she felt more than anxious about going to bed. Despite the fact that Bart would be lying next to her, she still didn't relish the idea of retiring for the night. Her guard would be down while she slept. What would happen if she suddenly experienced that same feeling of filthy evil crushing her the way she had at the sink? What would Bart think if his wife suddenly burst into convulsive sobs?

What was wrong with her? She wasn't experiencing visions or dreams. Might she be entering her change of life? She had heard of women going through the change in their early forties, but why wasn't she experiencing sleepless nights or hot and cold flashes if that were the case? All she felt whenever the crying jags struck her had been the all-encompassing sense of evil. While she should have felt some degree of fear, she hadn't, other than her immediate reaction to her own crying. The first time it had frightened her, not knowing what was causing it. And while she still felt concern and apprehension wherein the crying was concerned, it was not a fear-provoking crying that had scared her. It was the eternal, damnable question— why? Why was she crying like that?

"I can hardly wait until we have a dishwasher installed," Marcy said as she hung the dish towel on a peg next to the counter that held the sink.

The Curse

"Patience, my daughter," Bart said, half-laughing. "All things come to those who wait."

"But Daddy, this is a drag. Isn't it, Mom?"

Sabra focused her attention on her daughter, half-aware as to what they had been talking about. "You mean . . . ?"

"Washing dishes by hand. Look at my hands. They're red."

Sabra held out her hand for her daughter's.

Marcy laid her hands in her mother's. "See how red they are?"

"They're not even pink, sweetheart. Don't worry. I'll be able to do dishes again in a day or two." Sabra smiled up at her daughter.

Bart turned off the light above the sink. "You'll go back to washing dishes when old Doc Bart says you can. That was a nasty cut. It must have hurt like hell to have you crying like you were."

Sabra swallowed and forced a smile for her husband's sake. There was no use in telling him anything right then. Otherwise, he'd have her back to a psychiatrist or psychologist, and she didn't want to go through that anymore. It was like going to confession in an open room to a person who had no business knowing her innermost thoughts.

"It hurt pretty bad, all right." She held up her left hand and wiggled her wounded finger. "I was lucky I didn't cut a tendon or anything like that."

"Considering how deep it was, you can consider yourself darn lucky that you didn't." Bart crossed the room and took her hand in his. "Still hurt?"

"Not really, doctor. Shall I take two of something and call you in the morning?"

"That won't be necessary," he said, stepping to one side to allow Marcy to enter the dining room. "I'll just stay over with my favorite patient and sleep with her to make certain all goes well."

Sabra batted her eyelids. "Why, that sounds positively promising."

"Just don't worry about doing dishes until the bandage comes off."

"I hope you and the others will appreciate me more now that you have to do the dishes."

"Dumb accidents can louse up everybody's schedule, but we'll manage."

"It wasn't a dumb accident. It was just an accident."

"All accidents are dumb to some degree. After all, you didn't plan on cutting your finger, did you?"

Sabra stood. "As a matter of fact, I did. Just so I could get out of washing dishes by hand."

The outside screen door that opened onto the small entryway that serviced the kitchen and the summer kitchen slammed shut, and Ginger stomped into the room, crying.

"What's the matter, Ginger?" Bart asked.

The child sidestepped her father and went to her mother. "Curt's upstairs playing Nintendo. I haven't anybody to play with."

Sabra crouched and hugged her daughter. "Bart, will you call Curt?"

Bart left the room, and Sabra smiled at Ginger. "You aren't lonesome for our old house, are you?"

She shook her head. "No, I like it here. I just want dumb Curt to play with me for a while, that's all."

"Shh. Don't call your brother dumb."

Seconds later Curt entered the kitchen, followed by Bart who stood in the doorway.

"What are you doing right now, Curt?" Sabra asked.

"I'm playing 'Tetris.' "

"Can you go outside and play with Ginger until it's dark?"

Curt dropped his steady gaze to the floor, a surly look clouding his handsome features. "Do I have to?"

"It would be a nice thing for a brother to do." Sabra stood up.

"Besides," Bart said, "if you remember the terms of the Nintendo games, you can play with them only when your homework and other chores are finished and you have done some exercise. A little running around will do you good. Once we get your yard gym set up and the exercise equipment housed in its own little gym, you can get into a better routine of exercise. All of us can."

Curt looked up at his father and then his mother, a look of hopeless resignation crossing his face. "Okay. Come on, Ginger."

Ginger, a triumphant smile on her face, followed her brother to the back door.

Sabra turned off the overhead light and followed her husband to the living room. He dropped into an easy chair and picked up the newspaper. She sat at the end of the couch and studied him for a long moment. She couldn't tell Bart about her feelings of evil being around their new home. He'd think she'd flipped out. Besides, she wasn't that certain the feeling *was* evil. She was almost sure it was, but it could be something else—something she was misinterpreting.

Nor could she tell him about her reactions to the sensation of evil. Her crying could easily be taken as depression by a psychologist, and she didn't want to or need to get involved with something like that. She had read enough about depression to know that that was not the reason she was crying.

If it happened again—if she felt the evil again and she cried—she would have to figure out some way to tell Bart. Right now, she didn't want to tell him anything. She was tired. Once they got the children tucked in for the night, she wanted to go to bed herself.

The entryway door slammed shut and Curt turned to face his sister. "What do you want to do?"

"Let's go find my doll." Ginger started running toward the trees on the north side of the house.

Curt took off after her and in a few strides passed her. "Come on. I'll race you."

He reached the trees several seconds ahead of Ginger. When she caught up, she hugged herself. "It's cold out. Maybe we should have stayed inside and watched TV."

Curt looked around. It hadn't been cold when they had come outside. "Just a minute," he said and retraced his steps to beyond the limit of the trees. The air was warmer outside the trees. It was probably because the grove itself was sheltered so much by the trees that it felt colder in there.

He retraced his steps to Ginger's side. "What do you want to do?"

"I don't know. It's too cold to do anything."

Curt glared at his sister. "Look, Ginger, you made it so I had to come outside. I wanted to play 'Tetris,' but *you* had to have your way. We're going to play outside until it's dark. Mom and Dad said we had to. Now, what do you want to do?"

Ginger shrugged.

"Come on," Curt snapped and grabbed her hand. They walked deeper into the trees and in seconds found themselves standing over the old kettle they had rolled away from the garage earlier that afternoon.

"I'm sorry," Ginger said, her voice sweet and loving.

"Huh?" Curt turned around to find his sister picking up the old doll she had found.

"I'm sorry. I forgot all about you." The child hugged the doll and swung it back and forth in her tight embrace.

Curt looked at her and the doll. A disgusted scowl crossed his face, and he imitated the pouty open-mouth expression on the doll's face. "It feels colder right here, don't it, Ginger?"

Ginger stopped her swaying hug. "It *is* colder."

When she went back to paying attention to the doll, Curt looked around the trees. It was darker inside the grove than it was outside. It was almost gloomy. He wanted something to do—but what?

He turned his attention to the pot and then crouched down next to it. He reached out a tentative hand and touched it. The metal seemed even colder than the air in the trees. He caressed it several times and stood.

A peculiar feeling overcame him, and his face twisted into a peculiar mask. He reached down and undid the belt around his waist. "Hey, Ginger."

"What?" She didn't look at him and continued giving her attention to the doll.

"I'll show you mine if you'll show me yours." He opened the belt and undid the top button of his jeans.

"What?" This time Ginger turned to find him standing near the kettle, unzipping his pants. She walked over to him, dropping the doll when she got near him.

Ginger blanched at the sight of her brother opening his pants and then smiled almost seductively. "Okay." She opened the top button of her jeans and started to unzip the fly when the roar surged through the trees.

It reverberated in an eerie way, and the children stood transfixed, staring at one another, their hands at their waists, frozen in the motion of unzipping their jeans.

The roar came again, even louder, snapping them out of their trance-like state. Curt and Ginger bolted from the grove, desperately trying to close their pants and run at the same time. Curt succeeded first and dashed on ahead.

He couldn't abandon Ginger, so he stopped and turned. Ginger was gaining on him, and she suddenly ran faster when she got the top button together. When she passed Curt, he waited for a moment and stared at the trees. What kind of animal was in there? His hands shook, and he had a desperate need to urinate.

Turning, he ran after the quickly disappearing figure of his younger sister.

"It was a lion." Curt swallowed while his breath slowed.

"Was not. It was a monster!" Ginger nodded, emphasizing the point she was trying to make for her parents.

Sabra looked at her husband who shrugged. "There, there, Ginger. Calm down." She smoothed her daughter's hair back in place.

Bart crouched down by Curt. "I seriously doubt if it was a lion or anything else, son."

"But Dad, I heard it. I know what a lion or tiger sounds like. I've heard them enough on TV. It sounded exactly like a lion or even a bear. Yeah, it could've been a bear. A grizzly bear."

"Not in this part of the country, Curt. You should know that."

Curt frowned. He turned to Ginger who was looking at him, and an unspoken agreement passed between the youngsters—one that said they were right and knew what it was that they had heard.

"Come on, kids," Bart said. "Let's watch a little TV before it's bedtime."

"Good night, Curt," Sabra said, pulling the light blanket up over her son's shoulders.

"Good night, son," Bart said, reaching out to wiggle Curt's foot.

"G'night, Mom. G'night, Dad."

"Sleep tight." Sabra moved toward the door.

"It was a bear." Curt pulled the covers up and then turned over.

Sabra spun on her heel and returned to the side of the bed. "I thought you might have forgotten that by now. Now I'm concerned you'll dream about whatever it was you heard."

"Why won't you believe me? Ginger heard it, too, you know."

"We know she did. She said she did. But how do we know that you didn't hear something that is quite common and thought it was something else? Maybe Ginger heard it differently, but because you were so excited by what you thought was something else, she became convinced that she heard exactly what you heard." Sabra crouched down next to Curt's head. She'd picked up enough psychology over the years from Rose Allan to know that a child such as Ginger could be led purposely or accidentally to believe just about anything.

"I didn't say anything to her about it being a bear, Mom. Honest. You believe me, don't you, Dad?"

Bart moved around from the foot of the bed to stand behind his wife as if backing her up not only physically but mentally and emotionally as well. "As I said downstairs, son, I believe you believe you heard something that sounded like a bear or whatever. What did you do when you heard it?"

"Better yet," Sabra said, "what were you *doing* when you heard it?"

Curt frowned. What had they been doing? Ginger was hugging that dumb old dirty doll. But what was he doing? He couldn't remember. Oh, yes. He'd gotten down close to that old kettle and had . . . Why couldn't he remember? He had to tell his parents something to satisfy them.

He coughed and cleared his throat. "We were just standing there talking, I guess. Then it roared."

"What did you do?" Bart asked, turning to sit on the edge of the bed.

Curt thought for a moment. What had they done? He remembered his hands were doing something, or better still, he was doing something with his hands—but what? What *had* he and Ginger been doing? Had they been too scared to move? Was that it?

"I don't think we did anything. We were too scared."

"Too scared?" Sabra said, echoing his last two words.

"Yeah." Curt propped himself up on an elbow. "It was only when the roar roared again that we ran. Gosh, we were scared. We ran as hard as we could."

"Well, you're safe now, aren't you?" Bart stood up and stretched.

"I . . . I guess so." Curt lay back and nodded.

"You know Ginger isn't making near the fuss about this that you are, Curt." Sabra leaned over to brush a blond lock of hair out of her son's face.

"She's only a kid. What's she know?"

"Now, let's not get nasty, Curt." Sabra stood after pecking him on the cheek for the second time. "Remember, you were a kid yourself once."

"I guess," he said, turning onto his side once more. If they weren't going to worry about a monstrous bear breaking into the house and killing all of them, then why should he?

"Good night again, Curt," Sabra said from the door and turned off the ceiling light. A night light, plugged into a wall outlet, went on automatically.

"G'night." He pulled the covers over his head.

The door was closed but not shut tightly. A sliver of light from the hall outlined the door on three sides.

Curt rolled onto his back. His penis jerked, and he lay still. What was causing that to happen? He'd experienced it a couple of times in the past but for some reason tonight it felt different.

He slid his hand under the covers and inside his pajama pants. What had happened to it? It felt monstrous—huge. This had never happened before. Whenever he had checked it out when it moved by itself like that, he had found it to be a little more stiff than usual, sort of spongy, but this time it felt like . . . like . . . It was hard, hard as a rock and standing straight up.

He reached out and turned on the nightstand light. The soft light made him blink, and he threw back the covers, fearful of what he would find. His eyes grew wide when he saw his erection poking through the fly of his pajama bottom. Good God! Would it stay like that forever? What would people think he had in his pants whenever he stood up? He thought for a moment. Had he ever seen anyone like that with a huge bulge in the front of his pants? He couldn't remember.

He sat up and threw his legs over the edge of the bed. "Go away," he said quietly. Maybe if he treated it roughly it would wither back to its natural state. Was this what he'd heard bigger boys in school talking about when they said they'd had a hard-on or something like that?

Footsteps in the hallway brought him up short, and he didn't move. Whoever it was better not look in his room. He peered at the door that stood open a crack and caught a glimpse of Marcy's bright red robe flit by. He relaxed. She'd been studying in the big bedroom she and Ginger shared. Probably she was going down to get a snack or something before going to bed.

He returned his attention to his swollen penis. If he treated it rough, what would happen? He batted at his penis, and it flopped from side to side eventually standing upright once more. The peculiar feeling that shot through his lower body and legs felt good. Grabbing his penis in his hand he began rubbing it between his open palms. The sensation intensified, and he felt weak as it continued growing. He thought he wouldn't be able to stand it, but the more he rubbed his swollen penis between his hands, the better it felt. The results amazed him. The warmth continued to grow and mount in its tingling way, and when he thought he couldn't stand it any longer, his penis began spitting out a creamy, white substance. He felt super-relaxed and stared at the stuff he had ejaculated. His feeling of little shocks continued but in an abating way, as the climax passed. Spiraling downward, the feeling lessened and lessened until he knew everything was all right. His penis lay limp in one hand, and he turned to look at the mess he'd made on his bed clothes. Had any gone on the floor? He checked and found the damage for the most part confined to his sheets.

Curt jumped out of bed and went to the dresser where he found a box of tissues. Wiping up the spots from the sheets and those he found on his pajama pants, he threw the used tissues into his wastebasket.

He made his way to the door and peered into the hall. His parents were going to retire early that night and hopefully they were asleep already. Marcy was in the kitchen, stuffing her face. He tiptoed down the hall toward the girl's room. Was Ginger still awake?

Now he remembered what they were doing in the trees when they heard the roar. He smiled wickedly and continued toward the girls' bedroom. He found a soft night light on and could make out the form of his little sister under the covers.

He eased the door closed behind him and went to Ginger's bed. "Pssst. Ginger? You sleeping?"

She turned over and yawned. "No. What are you doing here?"

"Remember what we were going to do when we heard the roar?"

She puckered her lips for a moment and then smiled. "Yeah."

"Want to now?"

"Why?"

"Why not?"

Ginger thought for a moment before shrugging. She threw back the covers.

"Where do you think you're going at this hour?" Marcy said from the doorway.

"Huh?" Ginger grunted. "I . . . we . . ."

"We were going to talk for a minute," Curt said.

"Not now. It's pretty late. You'd better get back to your room before Mom or Dad hear you." Marcy went to her bed and slipped off her robe. She wore a shortie gown and crawled into bed.

Curt stood by Ginger's bed. Why was he in the girls' room? He should be in bed. He had been in bed, but now here he was, standing next to Ginger, not really knowing why he had gotten up.

Curt turned and walked toward the door. After opening it, he turned and said, "G'night. See you in the morning."

"G'night, Curt," Ginger said, recovering herself.

"Good night, Curt." Marcy reached over and turned out her lamp.

Curt padded down the hallway toward his own room. He could hear his father snoring, and he turned out the hall light. When he got to his room, he slipped between the sheets, not noticing the spots that had almost dried. Reaching out, he turned off his light and turned over. In seconds, he was asleep.

A tiny moan came from the sealed kettle, rising in volume and intensity until a mighty roar filled the grove, fading into nothingness a few feet from the edge of the outermost trees.

Chapter Five

Sabra looked up and stopped pouring the last glass of orange juice when the door to the stairway opened. Curt walked in, a passive expression on his face. "Good morning, Curt."

"Morning, Mom." He sat down heavily at his place and played with a spoon.

"What's the matter this morning?"

"Nothing."

"Did you sleep all right?"

"I guess."

"Feeling out of sorts?"

He looked up at his mother and shrugged as if to say, "What's that mean?"

Catching the wondering look on his face,

Sabra said, "I mean, do you feel all right this morning?"

"Yeah. I'm—"

Bart entered just then from the kitchen, carrying the coffeepot. The door to the stairs opened at the same time, and the two girls entered the dining room. Everyone took their seats and bowed their heads as they said their individual prayers of thanksgiving.

When Bart raised his head, everyone else followed suit, and he took some toast before passing it to Marcy on his right. She, in turn, passed the plate to Sabra, and when Curt got it from his mother, he took a slice. He handed it to Ginger who took the plate and then swung out at her brother's arm, striking it with her open palm.

"Ow! Mom! She hit me."

"I did not," Ginger cried.

"You did, too." Curt rubbed his arm as if it had been struck heavily.

"I saw you do it, Ginger," Bart said, a puzzled expression on his face.

"Well, I ain't going to take it." Curt turned in his seat and kicked at Ginger who lithely jumped from her seat. Curt's foot struck the edge of the chair, and he howled as the pain telegraphed itself to his brain.

Ginger stood next to her father, laughing at Curt's discomfort.

"Quiet!" Bart stood and threw his napkin onto the table. "That's quite enough. What's wrong with you two this morning?"

Sabra sat at her end of the table transfixed by the scene. She'd never seen such a thing happen with her children before. What could be wrong? Why had Curt come down to the dining room with a sullen look on his face? At first, she hadn't really defined it, but now, witnessing the spat going on between her two youngest children, she drew the conclusion that her son had come into the room appearing as if he might be looking for a fight. Still, it had been Ginger who had struck out at him first.

"Marcy, you stay at the table. Ginger, you and Curt come with your mother and me to the living room." Bart stepped away from the table and walked resolutely to the doors to the living room. He opened one and stepped inside.

Ginger followed him, her head held at a proud, almost defiant angle. Curt followed, his shoulders squared as if ready to ward off any sort of attack. Sabra brought up the rear of the small column, making mental notes of her children's attitudes.

Bart sat down in an easy chair and motioned for the youngsters to sit on the couch. Sabra took an easy chair opposite her husband.

"Now, what seems to be the trouble this morning?" Bart looked from one to the other and then settled on his youngest child. "Ginger, you seem to be the one who started this. Why did you hit Curt?"

"Yeah. That hurt." Curt rubbed his arm.

"She didn't strike you that hard, Curt," Bart

said. "I think you're overreacting a bit."

"I am not."

Ginger turned to him. "You are, too."

"Stop it." Sabra clapped her hands, and the sharp sound made not only the children jump but Bart as well. "What has gotten into you two? You never fight. You might have a difference of opinion once in a while, but I've never seen either of you hit one another. What is it? What's the matter?"

Ginger looked past her mother as if trying to ignore her.

Sabra turned to Curt. "Did you do something to your sister?"

"I didn't. Honest. I don't know what's wrong with her. I think she's going nutso!"

"That's not a nice thing to say about your younger sister, son." Bart glanced at his wife, a troubled look twisting his features.

"She must be nutso. Why else would she hit me?" Curt turned to Ginger and stuck out his tongue.

"Mommy, he stuck his tongue out at me."

"Good heavens!" Sabra leaped to her feet. "Whatever it is that's bothering the two of you, I want it stopped and I want it stopped *now*. Do you understand me? If you won't tell your father and me what it is that's upsetting you, then it can't be very important. If it isn't important, then there's no sense in carrying on with it. Do you understand? Have I made myself completely clear?"

Curt slowly nodded and half-turned to look at Ginger out of the corner of his eye. Ginger, in turn, did the same thing.

"Do the two of you want to talk it out with your father and me around?"

The children shook their two heads.

"It might be better if you did." Bart glanced at Sabra.

"I'm sorry, Curt," Ginger said quietly.

"So am I." Curt stood.

"That's more like it." Bart got out of the chair and walked toward the dining room. Opening it, he went through and the children followed him. Sabra brought up the rear once more and looked around the room. She wanted to rearrange the furniture in the parlor and would probably do it one of these days. She closed the door behind her and took her seat once more. She glanced at Marcy and saw her daughter half-covering a grin.

Sabra frowned. That, too, was uncharacteristic. "Is something funny, Marcy?"

Marcy looked up, her high cheeks blushing to an exquisite pink. "No. What was wrong?"

"It's all taken care of, isn't it, Ginger? Curt?" Sabra looked from one to the other.

Ginger nodded.

Curt nodded and drained his orange juice.

"See?" Sabra made a tiny shrugging motion and picked up her coffee cup.

"Oh, Daddy," Marcy said, turning her attention to her father, "I forgot to give you this note."

She handed Bart a small envelope.

"You're expelled already?" Bart laughed as he slit the envelope open with his table knife. His eyes scanned the single sheet of paper and looked up. "The bus will stop in front next Monday at eight-fifteen. Looks like you kids are losing your private chauffeur. You'll just have to ride in the yellow bus like all the others."

Sabra smiled. "That's good. It would have been an awful drag on you to have to do that every day of the school year."

Bart looked at her. "Or you, my dear. Don't forget I had you get a license so that you could share in the monotonous, dreary and thankless jobs that go hand-in-glove with having a family."

Sabra looked at the children. "Your father is only kidding." She fixed her attention on Bart. "You were kidding, weren't you?"

"Of course. What makes you ask? You should know that after seventeen years of marriage."

Sabra looked away. "It's just that this morning got off to such a bad start. I'm not sure of anything right now. I'm sorry." She felt as if she might burst out in tears any second. She bit her tongue to stop her overly emotional reaction.

Bart stood. "No apologizing. I felt sort of weird, too. Come on, kids. Time to hit the yellow-brick road to school." Curt stood and went to the stairs to get his books from his room.

When Curt stood in his room, he sat down on the edge of the bed. Something was bothering him—but what? He couldn't put a finger on it. There was something he had wanted to do. What? The thought hung on the periphery of his mind, tantalizing him with both its vagueness and nearness. Whatever it was, it had been something naughty, something he had not done before but something that at the time he felt would be a great adventure. What was it? Maybe it was something real bad. He thought for a moment, but nothing would form in his mind.

"Come on, Curt. Do you want to make everyone late?" Bart called out from the foot of the steps.

Curt lurched back to his senses. Grabbing his books, he ran from the room, and then, without knowing why, he ran back to the bed and pulled the covers up over the pillow. That wasn't good enough. He laid his books on the nightstand and carefully pulled the sheets taut. What were those yellowish spots? He shrugged and continued pulling up the sheet and blanket. Once the bedspread was in place, he smiled and grabbed his books once more.

"Come on, Curt!" Marcy called from the first floor.

"I'm coming. I'm coming." He raced down the steps and, after a hurried peck on his mother's cheek, ran through the kitchen and outside.

When they were alone, Sabra turned to Bart. "What do you suppose brought all of that on this morning?"

Bart shook his head. "I don't have a clue."

"Maybe it's the move taking its toll on them."

Bart pursed his lips and ran a hand through his brown hair. "I suppose that could be it. I just hope it doesn't happen again."

"You're not alone there. Coming right back?"

"I'm stopping for gas, but other than that I'll be back directly."

He kissed Sabra on the mouth, and for an instant it seemed as if it might grow into something more than just a good-bye-for-now-I'll-see-you-in-a-few-minutes type kiss.

She tagged along and went out to the back step, waving at her family as Bart backed out of the driveway. When the car had pulled around the bend and was out of sight she went back into the house.

She turned on the hot water for the dishes, knowing she'd have to let them soak or press Bart into service when he returned. She looked at her bandaged finger. Perhaps the hot water would do the wound good. She raised her finger and looked at it more closely in the natural light pouring through the window over the sink.

Her finger, her hand, the window and its frame slowly dissolved, and clouds raced in to fill the void.

"Now, you kids behave in school today," Bart said as he pulled up to the front entrance of the three-story building. "I don't want any fighting, Ginger. No beating up on the bullies. Got it?"

Ginger smiled her pixy smile. "I'll be good, Daddy."

"And you, young man, don't go pinching any-body today or slapping some young hussy across the face. Understand?" Bart smiled.

"I won't, Dad. We gonna work on the yard gym again tonight?"

"Not until we can go ahead and finish it, son. Don't worry, you'll be helping me. Have a good day."

Curt jumped out of the wagon and held the back door for Ginger.

"Got a kiss for Daddy?"

Ginger leaned over the seat and kissed her father on the cheek.

" 'Bye, Daddy."

"You finished your homework, didn't you?"

Ginger hesitated for an instant and stared at her father. Smiling broadly, she said, "Sure. 'Bye."

She followed Curt, and Marcy opened the front passenger door. "See you this afternoon, Daddy."

Bart nodded. He wished she would give him a kiss, but he knew how temperamental teenagers could be about such things. "Have a good day, sweetheart."

Marcy leaned back into the car. Puckering her lips, she kissed Bart on the corner of his mouth.

Startled, Bart enjoyed the brief show of affec-tion and pulled back when she did. "What brought that on?"

The Curse

Marcy smiled, her even white teeth glimmering between her pink lips. "Nothing. I just happen to love my daddy. 'Bye."

"S'long."

She closed the door and was lost in the rush of students who were pouring from the bus that had pulled in behind the station wagon.

Bart shifted into gear and pulled away. After he filled the tank, he'd head for home.

Sabra's hand, held rigidly in front of her face, trembled slightly. Her eyes widened as the clouds closed in about her. Off in the distance she could hear voices yelling and screaming; some even sounded as if they were pleading for something. Maybe the something might be someone's life. She didn't know. The visions were never the same. The intensity of the cries pounded in her ears, and she wished they would stop.

The clouds thickened even more and then just as quickly began receding, scudding to each side as Sabra's line of vision raced through them. She looked out over a lush, green countryside, growing thick with trees and wild shrubs. Rich, thick grass carpeted the earth. Even though she could still hear the voices, she could see no one.

Propelled along the ground by some unseen force, her feet not touching the ground, Sabra watched as trees, rocks and shrubs passed at a dizzying speed. Into valleys, up hills, across rises, she flew, all the while aware that the voices were growing louder.

When she plunged into a valley, she suddenly found herself surrounded by people. For whatever reason, her journey ended as she found herself standing in a throng. She had seen people like this before in her visions, but who were they? Where was she? Certainly these people were not from her own time. They couldn't be. The women and men were dressed in similar ways with long, rough cloth costumes that stretched from neck to foot. Some had cinctures made of rope at their waists, while others drew their cassock-like dress together at the waist with crudely tanned leather belts. Most feet she saw were bare or with sandals. Some wore head dresses that varied in color and shape. One wore what looked to Sabra like the biretta priests used to wear, but she hadn't seen one in years.

Women wailed, while the men seemed to be mouthing angry words. But Sabra could not understand the language they spoke. She listened intently. Perhaps she might recognize an inflection or pronunciation that would identify the peculiar language.

One man, larger than the others, grabbed a woman. Her long, greasy hair swung about as he spun her around to face him. He tried to kiss her but she resisted. Forcefully pulling her dirty hair, he bent her head back, and when she screamed, he stuck his tongue in her mouth.

Sabra shuddered.

The man tore at the neck of the woman's dress, finally succeeding in tearing it to her waist. Her large breasts flopped out, and the brute roared, laughing as he held her up to be ridiculed by the rest of the people. An expression of fright mixed with loathing crossed the woman's face when the man turned his attention back to her.

She shrank back, but he pulled her to him, reaching out to squeeze one of her breasts. She screamed as his fingers sank into the yielding flesh. He threw her on the ground and dropped onto her body before she could move or roll away. Lifting his own cloak-like wrap, he exposed his blood-gorged penis and, spreading the woman's legs until her dress bunched together at her fat waist, thrust himself into her vagina. She screamed, and while he thrust into her, he laughed at the woman's plight and chortled with his own pleasure.

Sabra wanted to yell out for him to stop but found herself fascinated by the cruelty of the rape. The other people milled about, chasing members of the opposite sex with but one purpose in mind. Some were imbibing and held roughly made cups filled with wine, which were emptied as fast as they could be filled.

What was going on? Where was she? Who were these people? Sabra had heard the voices before as she passed over the countryside, but she had never seen them. Other times, when there had been no voices, she happened onto people going about their daily chores. They had been dressed like the people milling about in the orgy she now was witnessing.

She wanted to scream but found her own vocal chords unwilling to cooperate. She tried to cry out but nothing came forth. God, what was she to do? She didn't want to be in this place.

For some reason she couldn't understand, the noise level died away and then an utter silence fell over the valley. A group of men, their heads shaved except for a fringe of hair around the perimeter, approached and entered into the midst of the revelers. From the way the people acted, these men were—of course! They were monks of some kind. Sabra remembered pictures of monks in history books she had studied in school.

One of the holy men stepped away from his fellows and began speaking. Again it was in the language Sabra had not been able to identify. He waved his arms as he spoke, obviously chastising the people for their debauchery. Most of the people dropped their attention to the ground, unable to face the man accusing them of sin.

Sabra silently cheered the monk's efforts. She looked at the pair who had been copulating and found the man kneeling, looking at the monk, an expression of hatred crossing his features. The woman, aware that she was no longer the center of the brute's attention, wriggled backward. When she was clear of him, she leaped to her feet and ran as fast as she could from the crowd, her pendulous breasts bouncing about her front.

When the people fell to their knees, the monk who had been speaking raised his arm, brought it down in front of him and then moved it from one side to the other in the shape of a cross. Satisfied, the monk passed through the seemingly repentant sinners, his entourage following him. When they walked over the hill and the last monk disappeared from sight, the people began talking in muffled whispers. Then the voices grew louder. Someone drained his mug of wine and another began laughing hoarsely.

The rapist suddenly realized his victim was gone and looked about, bewildered. His eyes seemed to fall on someone standing behind Sabra, but she turned to find that no one stood there.

Turning back, she gasped when she saw the bulk moving toward her. But she had never been bothered physically before in her visions. For some reason, she merely was witnessing these things as they unfolded. She wasn't part of them. The man came closer until he stood within two feet of her. He smiled, his foul breath washing over her face as he breathed out. She wanted to run, to scream, to do something to break her own sense of helplessness, but everything she tried failed to work. Her feet seemed rooted to the very ground on which she stood. She opened her mouth to scream, and when nothing came out, the man roared with what sounded like pleasure to Sabra. His gutteral sounds changed to a strange purr, rising in volume every once in a while. Then he coughed and sputtered.

A silence fell over the group, and the man took one final step until his clothed chest rubbed Sabra's breasts. She turned away when his fetid breath gushed over her again. Never in her life had she smelled such a fetid stink from a human mouth. His body had a heavy, sweaty smell that came only from one who never bathed. He opened his mouth and laughed, the laughter turning into the purring noise again. It rose in volume and then roared to a loud pitch. She'd never heard such a sound come from a person.

He opened his mouth and ran a thick, drooling tongue over his cracked lips. Long whiskers that never had been trimmed held droplets of saliva as he eyed her. His strange purring noise continued, and when he closed his mouth, it sounded not unlike a car door being shut.

Sabra shook her head and found herself back in the kitchen. When the purring noise continued unabated, she suddenly realized that it was the sound of the backhoe working on the hill. She leaned forward to look out the window and realized that Bart was home. It had been her husband getting out of the car and slamming the door that she had heard when she thought the man was closing his mouth.

The man! Where was he? She started nervously and looked about but found herself alone. It had been another vision. The worst one she'd ever experienced.

Again, she leaned forward and looked through the window. Bart was coming toward the back door, and she didn't want him to see her like this.

Turning, she ran for the bathroom. She needed a couple of moments to gather her thoughts. If Bart found her right after having experienced a vision, he would know there was something wrong.

Just as he opened the kitchen door, she closed the bathroom door. She was safe. What a ridiculous thought. Safe? From what? Her husband? No. From his concern and worry. He would be overly concerned if he knew she had had another vision and would worry needlessly since she was perfectly all right. She hadn't been harmed. She'd never been harmed by one of the visions.

Sabra closed her eyes for a moment, and the huge brute of a man loomed in her mind's eye. Of course, she'd been in danger. Who was she trying to kid? That man wanted to rape her. If she hadn't for whatever reason been able to return to her kitchen, she'd be back there—wherever that was—being raped right at this second. She shuddered and began trembling. She had to get a hold on her nerves. If Bart were to see her right now, he wouldn't have to ask what was wrong. He'd know.

She jumped when Bart called her.

"I'm in here, Bart. I'll be out in a few minutes."

"No problem," he called through the closed door.

When she said nothing further, he asked, "Are you all right?"

Sabra thought for a moment. How did he know? No, he couldn't. He was just concerned. "I'm fine, Bart. Were the children all right when you dropped them at school?"

"I think so. I got kisses from Marcy and Ginger, and Curt is looking forward to helping me with the yard gym. I'll sure be glad when the bus comes by Monday to pick them up. It's really inconvenient to have to take them back and forth."

Sabra felt better. Her heart, which had been racing, slowed down, and her breath was coming in a more normal fashion. It was strange. She hadn't even been aware of the fact that she was breathing so fast or that her heart had been pounding so hard. "You aren't tired of the kids, are you?" She forced a teasing lilt to her voice.

"Of course not. You know I'd do anything for them."

"I know."

"I'll be in the office. I've got to get to work. Don't stay in there all day."

"I won't," she said and leaned against the wall. She knew she couldn't do that, but the idea seemed appealing. She'd be alone and maybe she could think through this weird thing of the visions. Who was she kidding? Reaching up she played with her crucifix. Everytime she'd had one she had tried but had never come close to an answer. Neither had Rose Allen.

Sabra waited a few minutes and then flushed the toilet. Unlocking the door, she stepped into the deserted hallway and went through the dining room to the kitchen. To get her mind off her problems, she'd go outside and watch the men work for a while.

Ruth Donner tucked her blouse in, accentuating her breasts that usually were hidden among the folds of the same blouse when she stood normally. She looked out at the second graders and smiled. She had a good group and knew they'd accomplish great things before the end of the school year.

"Did everyone finish their work sheets?" she asked, sitting down at her desk.

A show of hands shot up and smiling faces greeted her. "That's fine. Will the first row bring their sheets up and lay them on my desk?"

The first row, nearest the door, stood and paraded to the front of the room, where they stacked their work sheets on the desk. The second row did the same once the first row was seated, and they were followed by the third, fourth and fifth row.

Ginger looked straight ahead when the children in her row, the fifth one, stood and went to the front of the room.

Ruth Donner caught sight of the little blond girl sitting there staring into space. "Ginger?"

No answer.

"Ginger Narman? Are you here today?" Ruth

waited for the child to answer. She was really daydreaming.

Tommy Claymore, the boy sitting across the aisle from Ginger, reached over and touched her on the arm. "Teacher's talking to you, Ginger."

Ginger turned, glaring defiantly at him. With the suddenness of a rattlesnake, her arm struck out, her open palm striking the boy full across the face.

"Ginger!" Ruth shrieked, leaping from her desk chair and running to the back of the room. "Whatever are you doing?"

Ginger glared up at the woman and stuck out her tongue.

"Stop that this instant. Why did you slap Tommy? Do you have your homework?"

Ginger defiantly shook her head and crossed her arms.

"Why haven't you finished your homework? Why did you slap Tommy?" Ruth asked again. This wasn't right. Second graders weren't supposed to act like this. She'd never had a situation remotely close to this before in her nine years of teaching. Suddenly aware that Tommy was crying, she turned her attention to him. The other children sat stunned at their desks or stood fascinated at the front of the room.

Tommy sobbed, his face marked with an ugly red welt where Ginger's hand had slapped him.

"Are you all right, Tommy?"

"She . . . she . . . slapped me, Miss Donner. Why? What'd I do?" He wiped his eyes on his shirt sleeve and reached in his pocket for a handkerchief. He blew his nose and looked to Ruth for an answer.

"I don't know, Tommy." She turned her attention back to Ginger, who still sat erect, her arms folded, staring into space. "Why did you slap Tommy?"

Glaring at the woman, Ginger said, "Because he touched me. He touched me."

"Do you have your homework, Ginger?" Ruth asked, preferring for the moment to ignore the child's reason.

Ginger shook her head.

"And why not?"

"My brother ate it. We don't have a dog."

The other children erupted in laughter, happy to have something to laugh about after the extraordinary event.

"Children! Be quiet and sit down at your desks. Now!" Ruth ordered. "Did you do it?"

"Of course. I slapped him. You saw me do it. Didn't you see him touch me?"

"That's not what I meant. Did you do your homework?"

Ginger shook her head, her blond hair flying about her head. "No. My Mommy said I could go outside and play. So there."

"I think we'd better take a trip to Sister Rita's office, young lady." Ruth motioned for Ginger to stand.

The girl got to her feet, and before Ruth could defend herself, Ginger kicked out at her, catching her in the shin of her left leg. At the same time, the girl lashed out with both fists, striking the teacher on her breasts, as hard as she could.

Sucking in her breath, in an effort not to scream, Ruth stepped back and Ginger streaked past her, running for the door. She opened it and ran into the hall. Seconds later, Ruth caught her, and they climbed the stairs to the principal's office.

Sabra leaned against the trunk of the oak tree that stood some 40 feet from the house. Her drawing pad, resting against her thighs, held her attention as she sketched in charcoal the hill which was a mile or so away.

Her hand continued darting about the sheet, adding a bush here, a tree there, her concentration so fixed she didn't notice her hand turn the almost completed sketch over. She looked up toward the sky, seeing nothing. Still, her hand continued sketching. People dressed in cassock-like costumes populated the paper. She drew them in every conceivable position. One couple, fornicating, dominated the center of the scene. When her hand froze and drew no more, she continued sitting in the same position, legs propped up, head tilted toward the sky.

She felt the clouds swarming about her but couldn't see them. A blinding light washed everything from her sight. For some reason, although she heard nothing, she felt someone was calling her name. The voice was beautiful and mellifluous as it sounded her name. The two syllables flowed sweetly and rang in her ears.

"Sa-bra. Sa-bra."

She lowered her head, an almost beatific smile on her face. Without looking, she sketched in one more detail and then stood. She walked toward the house and entered it.

She crossed the dining room and went upstairs, barely making a sound. She entered the master bedroom and went to the bed. Throwing back the covers to the floor, she lifted the mattress and slid the closed sketch pad in on top of the box spring.

After remaking the bed, she walked back downstairs and went to the kitchen. The only thought that crossed her mind was that she had to prepare their evening meal.

She opened the refrigerator and took out a package of meat.

PART II

*THE TERROR BEGINS
SEPTEMBER 10 TO
SEPTEMBER 16*

Chapter Six

Sister Rita leaned back in her chair and watched Ginger Narman leave her office. The girl was to sit outside the principal's office until she felt she was ready to return to class. In addition, she'd have to apologize to the boy she struck and to Ruth Donner in front of the class.

"What provoked the child, Ruth?" Sister Rita sat forward, anticipating the teacher's answer.

Ruth shrugged. "That's just it. Nothing was done to upset Ginger."

"Tommy Claymore did nothing?"

Ruth shook her head. "Not that I know of. Ginger said, just like she did here, that Tommy touched her arm and then she slapped him."

"She certainly overreacted, didn't she? How are you feeling?"

Ruth's right hand instinctively went to her breasts, but she checked the motion. Her face reddened, and she said, "I believe my pride was hurt more than I was physically. She took me off guard."

Sister Rita fell silent for a moment. Had she been fooled by Ginger's transcript of school records? A straight "A" student usually didn't act the way Ginger had that morning. Something must have happened at home to upset the child and make her lash out. The other two Narman children had excellent records as well. For an instant, the principal wondered if they, too, might misbehave in the way Ginger had. She breathed a silent prayer that such would not be the case.

"When you go back to your classroom and once Ginger returns, don't make too much of her apologizing to Tommy and you in front of the class."

Ruth looked at her, a surprised expression crossing her face. "I don't understand. Won't that encourage her and maybe others to misbehave if she gets off this easily?"

"I'm not saying make light of it. I'm merely suggesting that once you have her do it, get on with the school day. Making anything more out of it will only embarrass Ginger and make her an object of ridicule for the other children. You know children's teasing can be vicious. Heaven forbid it should be the other way around and the children think that Ginger is some sort of hero."

Ruth nodded and stood. She crossed the small room and opened the door. "Should I let the door stand open?"

"If you would, please," Sister Rita said and focused her attention on the papers in front of her.

Ruth stopped for a moment and looked at Ginger, who sat, head down, next to the door of the principal's office. Without a word, she turned and made her way to the stairs and her own classroom.

Ginger looked up when the teacher walked away and stuck her tongue out. She'd get that teacher somehow. That Tommy Claymore, too.

She wondered what Sister Rita was doing. Was she peeking at her, laughing at her while she sat in the hall. What if the other kids—big kids like Marcy—should see her sitting here in the hallway? What would Marcy say? What would Marcy do? She'd tell their parents and Ginger would be in trouble. She had gotten in some hot water at home already that morning when she hit Curt. That wimp couldn't even take a little hit on the arm.

Closing her eyes and putting her head against the wall, she recalled how she'd found the doll and kettle. Last night came into focus and she remembered Curt coming into the girl's room. What had he asked? Something about . . . showing something. That was it. Curt had said, "If you

show me yours, I'll show you mine." At first she
wondered what he had meant, but after a while it
had dawned on her what it was he wanted to do.
A smile curved her lips into a tiny, pink scimi-
tar. That would be fun. She'd have to remind
him that they hadn't shown themselves to each
other.

"But you must be careful."

Ginger looked around the hall. Who had said
that? She peeked around the corner of the open
doorway and found Sister Rita, head bent down,
doing something with papers on her desk. She
hadn't said anything.

*"You can't see me—only hear me. You must
help me. I'll do wonderful things for you if you do."*

"Yeah? Like what?" Ginger said, her voice tiny
and afraid.

"Help me and find out."

"Where are you? I can't see you."

*"I cannot tell you where I am. I have been curs-
ed. Help me, please?"*

"What do I have to do?" Her voice grew louder.

*"Sh, don't talk. I know what it is you want
to say."*

"How can you do that?"

"I just can. Will you help me?"

Ginger leaned back in her chair. Her palms
were wet. What would she have to do to help
whoever was talking to her?

"Strike with iron."

She sat bolt upright. "What?" she asked loudly.

"Ginger?" Sister Rita called from the office. "You are not to speak to anyone until you are excused. Do you understand?"

"Yes, Sister."

What did that mean? Strike with iron?

She waited for an answer, but none came. Whoever had been speaking to her was gone. She was just as happy if the person was gone. She'd only get in more trouble than she already was.

An endless quarter of an hour passed, and she got off her chair. Standing in the doorway, she said, "Sister Rita, may I go back to my classroom now?"

Sister Rita looked up. The child appeared so beautifully innocent, the nun still found it difficult to believe she had done what Ruth Donner had said.

"Are you ready to behave, Ginger?"

"Oh, yes, Sister. I won't be a bad girl anymore. I promise."

"Very well, then. You may return to your room."

Ginger turned and started away, only to retrace her steps, seconds later. "Sister Rita?"

"Yes?"

"Are you going to tell my parents?"

Sister Rita placed her pencil on the desk and got out of her chair. Moving around the desk, she approached Ginger. "I'm not sure. What you did was certainly most unladylike. You struck your teacher and disturbed the other children.

I'll have to wait and see how you behave in the future before I make up my mind."

A look of happiness crossed the blond girl's face as she turned and walked toward the stairs.

Curt followed the other boys from the gymnasium locker room to the baseball diamond outside. Father Richards led the way, carrying a duffel bag with equipment in it. When they reached the playground, the priest opened the bag and dumped gloves, bats and balls onto the ground.

"While we don't have a regular sports program here at Saint Boniface's," he said, "it's still important that you get some exercise and learn how to play different games."

Curt smiled to himself. He had wanted to play a game with Ginger last night but dumb old Marcy had interferred. Maybe they could play tonight. He hoped so. He was curious. They could go back into the trees where no one would see them.

"You, Curt Narman!"

Curt jumped. Who had called him? He looked around and found Father Richards, a broad grin on his face, looking directly at him.

"Today, Curt, we're going to play kitten ball, not daydream and pretend like Calvin and Hobbes do in the comic pages."

Curt felt his face turning red. "Yes, Father."

The fourth, fifth and sixth grade boys were divided into two teams of 11 players each. Curt was designated as right fielder and ran to the outfield when his team was given the home team advantage. Four runs and three outs later, his team came in to bat.

"I'll bat first," Curt said, picking up a bat.

"You'll bat when you're supposed to bat," Joe Gregory, a sixth grader and the captain, snapped.

"Sez you," Curt said and picked up a bat.

"Drop the bat, kid."

"Make me," Curt said, his voice growling out the words.

Joe lowered his head and charged. Curt swung with the bat but missed the boy's head.

"Hey! Hey! Hey!" Father Richards, who had been talking with the opposing team's pitcher and had had his back turned to the team at bat, turned and ran for Curt who was winding up to take another swing with the bat at Joe's head. The priest reached out and grabbed the bat. Curt spun to the ground from the force of his aborted swing.

"What's going on here?" he asked, looking first at Curt and then at the team captain.

"Hey, Father, he's crazy," Joe said, pointing a finger at Curt.

"I am not. I just want to bat first, that's all." Curt glowered at the boy and then stared up at Father Richards.

"Well, I'll tell you one thing, Mr. Curt Narman. We don't use baseball bats to settle our differences here at Saint Boniface's. We use gloves.

Now, if you and Joe feel you have a serious enough difference of opinion, we'll all go inside and help you lace on a pair of boxing gloves and the two of you can settle your dispute that way."

Curt looked at the priest and then at Joe. Joe was at least four inches taller than he and probably outweighed him by at least 10 to 15 pounds. But what difference did that make? He wanted to beat the hell out of that kid. Curt would show him a thing or two. Still, he'd never had a pair of boxing gloves on in his life. What kind of place was this? Priests promoting fights to settle arguments? Well, let it happen. Curt was ready.

"Well?" the priest asked, drawing out the one word question. He looked down at Curt and then shifted his attention to Joe. "Joe here is a champ of sorts, aren't you, Joe?"

The boy nodded and appeared embarrassed by the compliment.

"You see, Curt," Father Richards went on to explain, "Joe has handled several of the bigger boys in school. They wanted to bat first, too, so to speak. Joe went on to join the Golden Gloves team and is really learning the sport. How's it going, Joe?"

Joe flashed a quick smile and then fixed his attention on Curt.

"Are you sure you won't let your team captain select the batting order, Curt?"

"No. I want to bat first."

"Very well. If you win, you bat first. If Joe wins, you bat whenever he tells you. Fair enough?"

Both boys nodded.

While they walked back to the gym, Father Richards put his hand on Curt's shoulder. "Have you boxed much?"

Curt shook his head and continued walking toward the door. "I've never had gloves on in my life." He walked on ahead, faster than the rest, and was the first one to enter the building. The rest of the class followed.

Within minutes, both boys were outfitted with 16-ounce gloves and stood facing each other in the center of the wrestling pad. Four boys had been appointed to act as seconds to the boxers.

"Now, boys," Father Richards said, glancing from one to the other, "I want a fair fight. Break when you clinch if I say 'break.' No hitting below the belt line and no hitting on breaks. Keep your punches up. You'll box for three one-minute rounds. Any questions?"

Both boxers shook their heads. Joe offered to touch gloves as a sign of good sportsmanship but Curt refused, and they returned to their corners.

Curt eyed Joe across the imaginary ring. He could take him. Curt had watched a couple of boxing matches on TV and thought it looked rather easy.

One boy, who had been appointed time-keeper, yelled, "Time," and Joe Gregory danced out to the middle of the ring. Curt watched him for a second and then imitated him. The other boys began cheering and yelling. A chant quickly set up. "Joe! Joe! Joe!"

Curt stayed up on his toes and shuffled back and forth from left to right and right to left, ignoring the partisan cheering. He kept his eyes on Joe's, and when Joe flicked out a left jab, Curt thought it came at him in slow motion. He easily pushed the big glove away and continued his dancing. Joe bore in on him, flicking out another jab, which Curt pushed aside. He threw a wild right at Joe's head that sailed over his opponent's shoulder and careened off the top of his head.

"Oh, you want to play rough, huh?" Joe said and came in at Curt once more.

Curt, instead of backing away, stepped forward and unleashed a right hand that caught Joe flush on the jaw.

Joe went down in a heap, stunned.

The cheering stopped, and a silence fell over the exercise room. Father Richards stood, mouth agape, unable to say or do anything.

"Count!" Curt yelled as loud as he could as if having to awaken the priest.

Startled by the yell, Father Richards moved to start counting over the dazed Joe, who sat up, shaking his head.

Joe slowly got to his feet, and the priest wiped his gloves on his white shirt.

Curt closed in, and the timekeeper yelled "Time."

Curt smiled confidently at Joe who returned to his corner on wobbly legs. Curt turned and went to his corner.

"Geez, you really creamed him," Louie Phillips, one of Curt's seconds, said.

"Yeah, but he's going to get his head knocked off if he keeps leading with his right," Kyle Johnson said.

"Hey," Louie said, "he can take care of himself."

The two seconds continued arguing, ignoring Curt, and when the timekeeper yelled again, Curt was ready for action even though the disagreement over fighting styles continued in the corner. The rest of the class began its chanting and cheering again.

Curt danced out and found Joe still fuzzy from the blow. Without waiting, he moved in. Curt threw a straight left that caught Joe on the nose. He followed up with a right to the body and a left to the jaw.

Joe's knees buckled, and he reached out to grab Curt. He wanted to hang on and clear his head.

Curt sidestepped the lunge and drove a left to the boy's stomach, before catching him on the side of the head with an overhead right as Joe sank to the canvas again.

Father Richards stepped in, blocking Curt's progress. "That's enough, Curt. You've proven you're the better boxer. Stand back. Give him air."

"Hit the sonofabitch!"

The voice echoed in Curt's head, and without thinking or trying to figure out where the voice had come from, he wound up and hit Father Richards as hard as he could in the crotch.

The priest's face drained of color as he doubled over, gasping for air.

Curt stepped around the injured referee and went after Joe again. He fell to his knees and began pounding the prostrate boy.

What had been cheers at seeing a knockout turned to yells of indignation, and several boys went after Curt to stop his unwarranted attack on his downed opponent.

When he was held securely by two boys bigger than himself, Curt slowed his breathing and waited to see what would happen next. Father Richards slowly regained his breath, and his cheeks took on color as they returned to their normal hue.

"Well, young man, I believe it's time you and I went to see Sister Rita."

"What was it like living in Yonkers?"

Marcy looked at Brenda Starling. "It was nice. You know, lots to do all the time. It's not like Cascade."

"Oh, please. There's nothing like Cascade. It is *so* dull around here."

Marcy had met Brenda the first day of school but hadn't talked with her much until right before class that morning. Marcy wasn't real good at making friends in a fast way, but when she did make friends they were usually good, solid relationships.

Carla Mohr and Becky Caston sat with Marcy and Brenda, sipping their Cokes during lunch period.

"So tell me, what do you guys do around here for fun?" Marcy looked from one to the other.

"Like not much. By the time you're a senior, you'll be able to drive your folk's car without too much hassle," Becky said.

"How do you get around?" Marcy asked.

"Like we date older men."

"Older men?" Marcy felt her mouth open and purposely closed it.

"You know. Like seniors who have their licenses."

"You date a senior?"

"Sure," Carla said, "we all do. What the heck. We're fifteen, sixteen years old. They're seventeen or eighteen. Not that big of a difference. But enough to get around and, well, you know . . ." Her voice trailed off.

"Like what Carla's trying to say is, guys that age know a little bit more about women than boys our age."

Again Marcy looked from one to the other. She had never been on a real date in her life. She wondered what it was like. A feeling, foreign to her, crept over her. A feeling of doubt in herself quickly changed to one of distrust in her parent's judgments and opinions.

There she was, the new girl in high school in a small, dinky town, fresh in from Yonkers where she had attended a school of several thousand students, and she was suddenly unsure of herself.

Why hadn't her parents allowed her to date? Obviously these girls dated and were quite worldly and sophisticated about it. And she herself had never had a date.

"Like what are you doing Friday night?" Brenda asked.

Marcy snapped her attention back to the table and the other girls. "Why . . . er, nothing. Why?"

"Herbie is taking me for a ride. Like you want to come along?" Brenda looked intently at Marcy and waited.

She didn't want to be a third party. That would be awful. "Gee, I don't know, Brenda. Is Herbie your boyfriend?"

She nodded. "He's a senior and has his dad's car. Like he's not much to look at but who cares as long as he has wheels."

"I don't want to—you know, be in the way."

"You won't be. I've got my period so we won't be doing nothing real heavy."

Marcy did her best to keep her composure. Brenda and Herbie were having sex? Why, she couldn't be any older than Marcy was herself— 15. She had promised both her mom and herself that she wouldn't get involved with anyone in that way for a long, long time. But it wouldn't hurt as long as Brenda had her period, and she and Herbie would have to behave themselves.

"I don't want to say." She hesitated for a moment. "Like I'd have to ask my parents first."

Brenda shot a quick look at Carla and then nodded. "That's fine. Let me know and we'll pick you up around eight o'clock."

The rest of the afternoon Marcy thought about the fact that Brenda, unlike Marcy herself, was not a virgin. She wondered what it would be like, having a boy's penis inside her.

When the last bell rang, ending the classes for that day, Marcy found herself wet between the legs. It wasn't time for her period. Now what could have caused that?

Sabra stood at the kitchen window and was just about to turn away when their station wagon turned into the driveway. The sound of the backhoe working at the hill filled the afternoon air.

She watched as Bart braked to a halt and the doors opened. She expected her children to bound out of the car and into the house as usual. But Ginger got out of the back seat first, followed by Curt, who appeared to be subdued. Marcy, usually quite ladylike in her decorum, got out of the front seat and ran to the house. She entered first.

"Mom? Mom? Can I go out Friday night with Brenda and some other kids? Please?"

Sabra couldn't remember the last time Marcy acted so excited about something.

"What's going on? A party? A dance? Something at school?"

"Nothing in particular. I asked Daddy and he said to ask you. He's a little grumpy after talking with Sister Rita. Can I?"

"We'll see. Why did your father see Sister Rita?"

"I don't know."

"I'll tell you," Bart said from the entryway door. "Curt, you and Ginger go to your rooms and do your homework this instant. There'll be no TV, no outside, no Nintendo—nothing until after your homework is finished to your mother's and my satisfaction. Understand?"

Curt nodded sullenly and trudged for the dining room and the stairway. Ginger followed him, an equally passive air about her.

Bart looked at Marcy. "You'd better do your homework, too, honey. I've got to talk with your mother."

Marcy looked at him, confused. "All right, Daddy." She turned and left the room.

When they were alone, Bart said, "Let me tell you about the day our two youngest children had."

Sabra couldn't speak. Bart wasn't talking about their children. He couldn't be. They never did things like that. She nervously twisted her crucifix chain. They were normally very good in school. In fact, she recalled Bart saying how impressed Sister Rita had been with the transcripts of their grades from the schools in Yonkers.

She thought back to breakfast. The whole day had started wrong for Ginger and Curt. "I wonder if maybe this whole episode of today's misbehaving can't be put on the move." Sabra looked at Bart in an intense way, searching his face to see if he might have an explanation for the erratic behavior.

Bart shrugged. "I don't know. All I *do* know is that it was mighty embarrassing to find the principal of the school waiting at the front door to talk to me."

"Let's not worry about your embarrassment right now, Bart. I want to know what has gotten into our children." Sabra folded her arms.

"I suppose that the move could be responsible. It is, after all, the first time we've moved since Marcy was a baby." He paused and turned to look out the window. The hill was half-gone. Another day or so and the land would be level for almost 100 yards in that direction.

He turned back to face his wife. "I suppose it could be the move."

"I hope it doesn't happen again."

"It had damn well better not happen again. Maybe one of us should talk with the youngest ones. Maybe we haven't noticed that they're unhappy about the move."

"Actually," Sabra said, leaning back against the kitchen counter, "I'm surprised that it isn't Marcy acting up. After all, she had gone to school with some of the kids in Yonkers for quite a few years. Still, she seems to be the one who's happy. Really, it should be the other way around."

"Do you want to talk with them?" Bart moved through the kitchen toward the dining room door.

"I will if they're still acting grouchy when they finish their homework."

"Sounds good." Bart went to his office.

Sabra stood at the counter for a long minute and then busied herself with preparing supper.

"All right," Sabra said. "Your homework looks as if you've done it correctly. Are you both certain you have nothing more that should be done?"

"Honest, Mommy," Ginger said, smiling.

"How about you, Champ?" Sabra asked, good-naturedly poking her son on the shoulder. They'd had their talk, and she felt that it was just a fluke in their behavioral patterns. She felt confident that something like the episode that day would never happen again.

"I got nothing else in homework," Curt said, ignoring his mother's playfulness. "Can we go outside now?"

"I think that maybe I should look at your homework every night for a while." Sabra stepped back and waited for an answer to the suggestion.

"Why?" Curt asked.

"Well, it's still a new school even though you've gone there a week or so. We're living in a new house in a new community and you guys are just little people. Sometimes it's pretty hard to adjust to things like that."

"I don't care." Curt turned to Ginger who nodded her approval.

"Now, can we go outside?" Curt stared up at his mother, a look of impatience wrinkling his nose.

"Yes, but don't go too far. Supper will be ready before you know it."

The children raced out of the house and headed for the grove. They stopped as they passed the work area where Ginger bent down and picked up a red stone.

"Look at the pretty red rock," she said, holding it up for Curt to see.

He'd never seen anything like that before and wondered what it was. He took it from Ginger and turned it over in his hand.

"What'd you find?" Jim Recton asked, coming up behind them.

"What kind of rock is this?" Curt held it up for him to see.

"It looks like it might be a piece of iron ore."

"Is it worth money, a lot of money?" Curt looked at the rock more closely.

"It could be if you had a lot of it. Say as much as a hundred piles as big as your folk's house."

"Aw, darn it, I thought we had something."

Recton laughed and walked away.

Curt threw up the piece of ore and caught it.

"I want my pretty rock back," Ginger said, tugging on Curt's shirt sleeve.

"Here." He thrust it into her hand and started for the trees.

Ginger followed, throwing the rock up in the air and trying to catch it. She dropped it more than she caught it and was several yards behind her brother when he entered the grove.

When they stood near the kettle and doll, Curt squatted on his haunches. Ginger did the same.

"What's the matter, Curt?"

"I can't figure out why that lid won't come off." He spotted his father's hammer which he had forgotten to take it back to the garage where the other tools were kept. It was a good thing his father hadn't wanted it for anything. He'd best take it back there right now before he forgot it again.

The sound of the landscaping crew leaving filled the air as the truck and two cars started up.

When the noise died away as they left, Marcy called out for the children to come into the house and wash up for supper. Deciding they hadn't heard her, she walked toward the grove, calling them.

Marcy found them several yards inside the grove of trees. "There you are. Supper's ready, and if you two don't want to be on Mom's and Daddy's 'awful kid list,' you'd better get going."

The Curse

She waved her arm, motioning for them to hurry and started back several steps before stopping to wait for them, her arms folded the way her mother folded hers when she was impatient.

"Come on, Ginger," Curt whispered. "Maybe we can come out after supper and take a look at the kettle and try to open it again."

Before they left the grove of trees, Curt walked over to the hammer and picked it up. It would take only a second to drop it off in the garage.

"Look at your hands, Ginger. What did you get all over them?" Marcy pointed at her sister's hands.

Ginger looked at the palms of her hands. The rust-colored smear on her hands matched the piece of ore she held. "Oh, they're so dirty." She threw the rock over her shoulder and didn't turn back when it struck the sealed pot. She followed her brother out of the grove toward the garage.

Marcy hung back for a moment, looking around the grove. It was spooky. She ran to catch up with her brother and sister.

The piece of ore flew off to the side, away from the kettle, and landed in weeds that surrounded the bole of a tree.

A heavy silence fell over the grove and was broken when a high-pitched giggle sounded from the kettle. The laughter grew in volume until it filled the trees. Then, stillness filled the air once more.

Chapter Seven

Bart finished the dishes and turned to Sabra. "When will your finger be healed enough so that I can retire from the head dishwasher position?"

She glanced down at the bandage. It probably could have come off within a day or so of the accident, but she had to follow through with the idea that the cut had been severe enough to make her cry the way she had been doing when Bart found her.

"I think," she began, "I can take the bandage off by tomorrow. It looks quite good and has healed well."

"I'll be glad when you can start carrying your own weight around here, lady." He winked and then smiled. "Want to go for a short walk around our land?"

Sabra nodded. She felt that Bart might want to go out and appraise the work that Jim Recton and his crew had done thus far. Recton had telephoned that morning and told them another job he was working on was ready to have cement poured and that he and his men would have to do that in order to keep that project on schedule. They'd be back working on the hill the following day.

Sabra and Bart walked through the back door and stood for a moment. The trees hadn't started changing yet, but there was a briskness in the air that forewarned autumn would be early and the leaves might start changing any time. Hand in hand, they made their way toward the part of the hill that remained. What had once been a mound some 25 feet high and about 60 feet or so across had been reduced to half that.

"The whole thing would be gone if Recton had had a trackhoe," Bart said.

"What's a trackhoe?"

Bart pointed to the backhoe Recton had been using on the hill. "A trackhoe is bigger than that. It has a bigger bucket and would move a lot more earth faster."

"Won't this do just as well?"

"Of course. It's just that the hill might very easily be gone now if he'd had one."

"You're always in such a hurry."

Bart looked at her and grinned. "Yeah, you're

right. I'm like that even when I'm not involved. The price he quoted was darn reasonable, and I should be glad he's getting as much done as he is."

They continued walking toward the gouged-out hillside and went around it. On the far side of the mound, the land was relatively flat, and once he could see to the end of their property, Bart stopped about 100 yards away. The lot, with the exception of the hill they were removing, was fairly level. It ended almost 70 yards from the road at the base of some hills that were on the next property and stretched along the road for a length of six running acres. The two-story house was situated a little off center, and the lot was bordered on the side opposite the work area by a grove of trees that tended to shelter the house from the onslaught of winter winds.

"Where are you planning on putting the building for the exercise equipment?" Sabra scanned the lot, not quite certain as to her husband's plans.

"Just about on the edge of the hill on this side, away from the house."

"It can't be too soon for me," she said, patting her tummy. "I've got to get back to a regular exercise program. I'm getting fat."

"I'm just happy that we have the room to build our own gym. Considering what we spent in Yonkers for membership in the athletic club, the building will probably pay for itself in a matter of a dozen years."

They walked farther and stopped again.

"The fact that I'm getting fat doesn't seem to bother you."

Bart turned to run an appraising eye over his wife's body. "I don't see any."

"I feel it. I'm going to have to start exercising some in the house just to stay ahead of any weight gain."

"Yeah, you're right. I should, too. But it won't be long."

"How long?"

"Well, if Recton can finish with the hill as quickly as he's started, I would think that the contractor could start as soon as—oh, within two weeks or so."

Bart explained the building was already designed and that the time taken to build it would not be that long. They could be inside within six weeks, exercising to their heart's content.

"There's one other thing," he said. "Next spring I want to have a tennis court installed along here." He pointed to a place that would be next to the gym. "We might have a bubble erected over it so we can all play year round."

Sabra beamed. "That would be fantastic." Tennis was the one sport she loved to participate in. With her exercise program and the tennis she often played, Sabra was in excellent condition. How many times had she been taken for a woman in her late twenties when in reality she would be 43 on her next birthday?

"My birthday," she said suddenly.

Bart looked at her and laughed. "What about your birthday? Worried you won't get a present?"

"No. I was just thinking and it suddenly dawned on me that my birthday is less then three weeks away."

"Well, if you're a good girl, I'll buy you a nice present. Come on. Let's walk over to the grove once. I haven't had a chance to go in there and really look around."

He offered his hand, and they walked toward the house and the trees beyond it.

"You know, I consider myself to be very, very lucky."

Sabra squeezed his hand and said, "Why?"

"Well, deleting yesterday's disasters for Curt and Ginger, I think our kids are pretty special people. They're good-looking, they work hard in school, they obey their parents, and I probably have the sexiest looking wife north of New York City."

Sabra stopped and yanked her hand out of his. "Now, just who in New York could possibly be sexier looking than me?"

Bart turned and frowned and then broke out in a loud laugh. "No one, I guess. I was just trying to be—Hell. For all I know, you really are the sexiest woman around anyplace."

"Just sexy—nothing else? Not charming or gracious? Beautiful? Intelligent? Fun to be with and a darn good sport to boot? What's with you,

Bart Narman? You've got a real winner in me. Appreciate me—or else."

"Or else what?"

She grinned. "Just 'or else.' You figure it out. If you don't and you don't appreciate me for what I really am, then you'll find out the hard way as to what the 'or else' is."

"Come on, you nut," he said and took her hand again.

They continued walking, and Sabra sobered after the lighthearted banter she and Bart had just had. It hadn't always been like that, teasing and making idle threats that meant something to them in a veiled way. Bart knew full well that she meant she would cut him off from sex. Not that it would actually happen. They enjoyed a full sex life that younger couples would envy.

She thought back to when they were first married. Everything had gone smoothly, and after Ginger was born, she had concluded at the time that their lives together would be as good and enriching as any.

But then the dreams started. After they had harassed her for over two years, she had awakened one night, screaming. Bart had bolted upright in bed trying to help her.

"Darling, what's wrong?" he had asked, his arms about her, hugging her, giving her reassurance that all was well.

Sabra stared into the darkness. She knew then that she should have confided in Bart about her dreams. "Turn on the light."

The nightstand light flooded the bedroom, and she closed her eyes. But when she did she saw the things from her nightmare. She forced herself to open them again.

"What is it, Sabra?" Bart turned her to face him.

"Oh, God, Bart. It was terrible. Awful."

"What was terrible? What was awful? Were you dreaming? Tell me."

She had explained how she had dreamt she was surrounded by huge monsters, monsters that looked like dragons and dinosaurs and some she didn't recognize at all. They were roaring at her and attacking her as if they were going to devour her. But the dreams had continued.

Sabra forced a grim smile that Bart didn't notice as they walked past the house and on toward the trees. The ironic aspect of the first dream was that it would prove to be the mildest of any she would experience during the next five or six years.

Then the visions started. She had said nothing to Bart about them, preferring to live with them since they usually happened when she was alone. Ginger had started school, and fortunately for Sabra, she had never had one of the visions when her youngest was at home alone with her mother. Whenever Bart was in his office working, Sabra would usually be working in the house. She always felt anxious about going into work in the office for fear she would experience one of the visions and Bart would witness it. She had no idea as to what happened to her while she was having a vision. Most of the time, she would find herself pretty much in the same position and place as she had been when the hallucination started.

She remembered the one, awful day Bart had asked her to help out in the office. It had been winter and she had just finished making a pot of chili for their evening meal.

For the most part, the visions had continued in the same vein as the dreams, with monsters and beasts attacking her. Never had she come to the point of actually being attacked in her dreams or visions but there had been close calls. That day Bart had asked her to call Whitehead Manufacturing and speak with the traffic manager there. Bart had figured out a new routing that would save them not only time but a considerable amount of money as well.

"Just get Gary on the line, sweetheart," Bart had said. "I'm getting some coffee. You need a refill?"

Sabra nodded.

Bart took her cup, and she dialed the number after finding it on the Rolodex. When Gary said hello, she said, "This is Narman Traffic calling, could you please hold?"

"Sure."

Sabra reached out to press the hold button and froze as the clouds blurred her vision. The roars of monsters began. She held her breath.

Maybe this one wouldn't be as bad as the others. She waited, and the clouds thinned and then disappeared. Huge animals, some breathing fire, milled about, grunting, roaring, screaming. She wanted to throw her hands over her ears to shut out the cacaphony but she couldn't move.

One, a huge beast, its cavernous mouth open, displaying rows of dagger-like teeth, turned suddenly and looked directly at her. His tail swishing back and forth, the monster roared and walked in its lumbering way toward her.

She tried to move but couldn't. She wanted to look away, but she found she could not even move her head. It was as if fear had paralyzed her. She fought to close her eyes as the animal stood over her. Again, he roared mightily and bent down.

For the first time, she felt something—a physical contact with her vision. She could feel and smell the creature's breath as that gigantic mouth closed over her. Why couldn't she run or move at least? She wanted to scream. She had to scream. She finally managed to throw an arm up as if it would deter the monster. The teeth closed on her wrist, and as she felt their needle-like sharpness, the spell was broken.

She screamed, long and loud, as loud as she could. Shaking her arm to free it, the monster tightened its grip.

"Sabra! Sabra, for Chrissakes! What's the matter?"

Bart had grabbed the phone from her, and she

stopped screaming when she realized it was Bart holding her arm.

It had only been Bart's friendship with Gary Townes that kept the account alive. She apologized over and over to Bart, but he had had it with the dreams and the screaming in the middle of the night. He said it appeared to him as if she was starting to do the same sort of insane things during the daylight hours.

When he had suggested counseling, she had resisted. She didn't want to sit in a room with a stranger and tell her innermost thoughts. That was too much like going to confession to a priest. She hadn't done that in a long time.

When Bart threatened divorce if she didn't seek help, she readily agreed. Her love for her family and husband was too much for her unreasonable attitudes so she began counseling with Rose Allan.

"Are you happy?"

Sabra looked around. Who had said that? She found Bart smiling at her, waiting for an answer.

"Of course I'm happy, darling."

"Are you glad we moved here?"

She pursed her lips. "Let's say I'm very happy with the exception of yesterday's little dramas with Ginger and Curt."

They were almost to the grove of trees on the opposite side of the house when Sabra suddenly found herself wanting to turn and run. Something was wrong. The same sensations that she had experienced several days ago suddenly washed over her. The sense of evil she had felt then hammered at her every sense. Whatever was causing her to react like that must be in the trees.

She looked down and found Bart still holding her hand. She drew strength from him. Bart was a strong person and would protect her from this terrible feeling. Still, she must not let him know about her peculiar feelings or the fact that the visions were reoccurring and that suddenly they had changed.

When Bart stepped into the grove, Sabra held back.

"What's the matter?"

"I . . . I don't want to go in there."

"Why not?"

Sabra shook her head. "I don't know. I'm afraid I might feel closed in, if I do."

"You? Claustrophic? You've never been like that. Why now?"

She shrugged. "I don't know."

"Tell you what. Try it. If it bothers you, leave. It's that simple."

She hesitated and coughed. "All right."

She stepped into the grove and followed Bart, all the while holding his hand in her tight grasp. After going only 15 feet, she stopped.

"I . . . I can't, Bart. I can't go on. I've got to get out of here. The whole place is closing in on me. I can hardly breathe." The overwhelming weight of the sense of evil pressed in on her. It wasn't really the trees that bothered her, but she couldn't tell Bart that. If he knew she'd regressed to the point of the visions reoccurring, there was no telling what might take place. He might take the children and leave. She'd fight for them. But what judge would award her custody if she were actually losing her mind?

"If you feel that bad, go back to the house. I'll look around and then come up. Or do you want me to go with you now?"

Sabra shook her hand and waved off Bart's offer. "No. Go do whatever you planned. I'll be all right once I get to the house. I'm sure I will."

"What if the house closes in on you like the trees are?"

She turned and started out of the grove. "I'll be fine. I'll see you at the house."

She hurried out of the grove and went toward the house. The sense of evil lessened until she was barely aware of it by the time she reached the back door.

Once inside, a sense of relief flowed over her, and she fought off the tears she felt building. She didn't want to cry—not now, not with Bart almost ready to come back to the house. If he found her like that he might get suspicious, and then in time she'd have to tell him everything—that she wasn't all right, that the visions were back, that for some reason they'd changed. Without Rose Allan close by, what would she do? To whom could she turn?

Suddenly, the feeling of evil began growing

again, just as it had when she had approached the trees. She felt as if her body were being invaded by it. Every pore, every drop of blood, every muscle exuded evil. She could barely tolerate the sensations. What was wrong? Why was this happening? What if Bart came in and found her like this?

She looked at her hands. They shook, and she trembled throughout her body. She wanted to cry, to weep as hard as she had that day in the yard, but she had to fight the instinct. That would be an instantaneous giveaway as far as Bart was concerned. She had no cut finger to blame tears on this time.

As the evil continued growing, she wanted to scream at the top of her lungs. She drew in a breath. She had to scream. It would help. It *had* to help.

She opened her mouth and the door swung in.

Bart stood in the doorway. "Hey, look what I found." He held up the earth-stained kettle and smiled.

Chapter Eight

Bart held the kettle up to the height of his shoulder and smiled broadly.

Sabra's head swam. The room spun dizzily before she fought back for control of her senses and equilibrium. She had to recoup. She had to! Whatever was affecting her was winning, and she wouldn't hear of that happening. At least she wanted to be able to put up some sort of resistance, even if she were to be completely overwhelmed by—by whatever this thing was.

The room righted itself, and she fixed her undivided attention on her husband, who still stood in the doorway of the kitchen. When she saw the dirty old kettle he was holding, she drew in a deep breath. Was the kettle causing her to reel? It had to be. He had to get that thing out of the house immediately.

"Get that dirty thing out of my house, Bart. Now! Get it out *now!*"

Bart stared at her, a puzzled expression crossing his features. "What's wrong with it? A little soap and water and you'll have a unique planter or whatever you want to use it for."

Sabra backed away, slowly, deliberately. She didn't want to startle Bart or alert him to something being out of the ordinary where she was concerned. "Please, Bart, take it outside. I don't want it in the house. It—it's so filthy. Please?"

Bart looked at the pot as if seeing it for the first time. "Yeah, you're right. It is dirty. I'm sorry, Sabra. I'll take it outside. But I want to clean it up for you. All right?" He turned to leave the kitchen.

"Where'd you find it, Bart?"

He stopped in the entryway and turned back to face her. "In the grove." He laughed. "At first I thought I'd found the pot of gold at the end of a rainbow but there wasn't any rainbow."

"Is—is there anything in it?" Sabra asked, her voice barely audible, fearful of any answer at that point.

Bart shrugged. "I don't know. I can't get the lid off." Again, he turned to leave.

This time Sabra let him go. The sooner that thing was out of her house the better she'd feel. The awful feeling of fear and evil still permeated the kitchen but it seemed to lessen when Bart left the entryway.

Had she pulled it off? Had her husband noticed how upset she was when he first entered the kitchen? She wasn't sure. She wouldn't be certain until he returned without the kettle. Would he notice anything about her? For some reason she felt as if her appearance had changed somehow. If she were right about that, he would say something almost immediately. She hoped he wouldn't. She didn't want to lie to him about anything. But as much as she didn't want to do that, she didn't want to have him know that her problems were still with them and that they seemed to be growing in magnitude.

As her breathing slowed down, she felt as if she might be returning to normal. Why had he brought that filthy thing into the house? She paused and thought for a moment. That was the second time she had referred to the kettle as filthy. It was just as good if she did use that word. Bart would think she meant the physical condition of the pot, while in reality she meant that the thing was filthy with evil.

She couldn't understand it. How could a pot be evil? And if that really were the situation, then why was she feeling that wickedness herself? It was so real that she felt that she could reach out and touch that element of vile blackness where the kettle was concerned.

Sabra leaned against the wall. Was she going insane? People—normal people, that is—didn't sense evil in that way, did they? Why was she so positive that the kettle was something that would bring harm to—? Who would be harmed by that pot? It was nothing more than a cooking utensil. At least that was what it appeared to be.

The screen door opened and slammed shut before Bart entered the kitchen. He smiled sheepishly. "I'm sorry, honey. Really, I am. I got excited when I saw it lying there next to a tree. At first I thought it might really be worth something, you know, a treasure of some sort. I'm sure now that it's nothing like that. I'm sorry about bringing it into the house. I didn't for an instant think about dirtying the floor or anything."

"It's all right," Sabra managed to say. She wished he'd stop carrying on about the damned thing.

"Are you all right?"

"I'm fine."

"No more claustrophia?"

"No. I'm fine, really." Why did he have to keep asking her? She felt upset and nervous enough as it was. He wasn't helping matters any, but she couldn't ask him to stop for fear of arousing his own suspicions. "What are you going to do with that old thing?"

"Well, first thing I want to do is clean it up. I think there might be some sort of design or something on it. At least it appears there's indentations all over the thing."

"Indentations?"

"It looks like there are, but there's dirt in them. If the thing was buried for any length of time, dirt would fill up the design and make it appear smooth. That's the way it looks now for the most part. Some of the indentations have been cleaned out by someone. Who knows? Maybe the dirt just fell out."

Sabra frowned. "You said you found it next to a tree but that it looks like it was buried."

Bart nodded.

"Who dug it up? Who cleaned some of the indentations?"

Bart shrugged. "For all I know, the kids did. It's not important as to where it came from or who put it where I found it. What's important is to get it cleaned up and see what the design is. You may want it for a planter, like I said."

Sabra pursed her lips. She had to give Bart that argument. It would make a nice planter—there was no doubt about that—but did she want it in the house or even close to the house? If it was the kettle that emanated that feeling of evil, she wanted no part of it. It could be dumped in Lake Champlain for all she cared.

"Aren't you going to work anymore today?"

Bart shook his head. "I've got one telephone call coming in and that's it—other than going to school to pick up the children. Of course, you could volunteer for that duty. Interested?"

Sabra could go into town for the children and maybe leave a little early and stop by the shop that sold art supplies, not that she needed anything. But it would be a perfect way to get away from the house and that terrible feeling that seemed to hang over their new home like a pall. She nodded. "I'll volunteer, sir." She saluted her husband and grinned foolishly. Was she overdoing it?

"Hey, that's great. What have you got that I can use to clean up the pot?"

Sabra went to the sink counter and opened a lower cabinet where she stored household chemicals and cleaning appliances. She handed him a bottle of liquid cleaner and a brush. "Here, clean to your heart's content." She looked up at the kitchen clock and saw it was almost two o'clock. "If you don't mind, I'm going to go now. I want to stop at a couple of shops first."

Bart stepped into the entryway and turned back to face her. "Have fun."

When the screen door slammed shut, Sabra went to the dining room and got her purse. She had to get away from the house even if it was only for a few minutes or an hour.

In seconds she was in the station wagon with the engine roaring to life as soon as she turned the key. She backed around and drove out of the yard, waving to Bart who was unreeling the garden hose.

With each passing second, as the house fell further and further behind her, she felt the awful feeling leaving and her own sense of welfare returning.

Bart watched Sabra back around and wave as she drove from the yard. "Bye," he called but she didn't hear him.

After connecting the garden hose to the faucet at the side of the house, he returned to the kettle that lay near the back step where he had put it after taking it from the house. Playing the jet of water over the kettle, the pot quickly turned from the light brown earth tone to one of muddy blackness as the dirt washed off it. Satisfied for the moment, he turned off the nozzle and bent down to take the lid off. He grunted and pulled at the lid handle when it didn't respond to his first efforts.

He gave up after several futile minutes of trying to remove the lid. He'd worry about opening it later. When something in the ground next to the back step caught his attention, he bent down to look at it. At first it looked like a scroll of some sort, but it was made of metal. Playing the stream of water on it, he washed some of the dirt away. Gradually, the top of an old iron boot cleaner appeared. He laughed. Maybe they should search out all of their land and see what other antique treasures they might find.

Antiques. That wasn't a bad idea. He'd take the kettle into one of the antique dealers and

have someone look at it. Maybe it had some
value of which Bart and Sabra weren't aware.
Maybe the darned thing was loaded with gold
or something else of value, like diamonds or
jewels. He grinned to himself. He felt like a
kid.

Aiming the nozzle of the hose at the kettle
he pressed the handle and the stream of water
washed over it once more. Nothing happened.
He had removed everything he could with the
hose. The next step was to scrub it down with the
liquid soap. He poured some of the soap directly
from the bottle onto the side of the kettle and
picked up the brush. Vigorous strokes quickly
brought a white foamy lather over the kettle.
He brushed more, hoping the job would not be
a long drawn-out one.

When he felt he had scrubbed all the dirt off
and was down to the bare metal of the pot, he
picked up the hose and washed off the soap.
A wet blackness covered the side of the pot
where he had scrubbed. Indentations had been
stripped of the earth that had been pressed in
and held there for—how long? He wondered
how long the kettle had been buried if indeed
it had been. Suddenly romantic about his find,
Bart decided it had been buried for many years.
For all he knew, some early settler could have
buried it.

He lay the hose and brush aside and studied
the indentations. They didn't appear to be a
design but seemed to be letters of some sort.

He peered more closely. The letters, if that was what they were, appeared squared off for the most part. It certainly wasn't English. He was positive of that.

Standing up, he stretched. He had to get back to exercising. His legs had cramped, crouching down like that. He picked up the kettle. Once he had it completely cleaned, Sabra would have no objections to the pot being a planter in the house.

The water on the cleaned pot slowly evaporated, showing a dull blackness. With the lid off and leaning against the pot, a bunch of yellow mums would appear striking set against the utter blackness of the pot itself.

Bart turned to look at the grove of trees. Were there any other finds to be had out there? Other artifacts? Maybe over the weekend he'd take the time to look.

The ringing of the telephone cut through the quiet, and at first, Bart didn't react. His telephone call! He dropped the kettle to the ground where it clanged dully against the boot scrape. Bart hurried into the house to answer the telephone.

The kettle rolled in a semicircular path and stopped. The lid eased off and fell to the ground. The rush of icy air pouring out enveloped the house and yard.

Inside, Bart picked up the telephone and shivered for a moment as a chill washed over him. "Hello?" He shuddered and wondered if he might be catching a cold from having gotten his hands and feet wet while working on the kettle.

"Bart? Al Giles, here. I'm returning your call."

Outside the kettle lay still and a heavy silence fell over the yard. Birds suddenly flew away, and the buzz of any insects that might have been heard before faded into nothingness.

Then the hoarse chuckle wound its way over the house and yard.

When Bart came back out, he was delighted to find the lid off the kettle and set to scrubbing the remaining dirt from the sides.

Shortly after three o'clock, Sabra and the children pulled into the yard.

Marcy raced ahead to get started on her homework while Curt followed on her heels. Ginger walked toward the house but stopped, staring at the back step where Bart sat, wiping off the kettle.

"Daddy! You got my pot."

Bart looked up, and Sabra stopped at the kitchen entryway door.

"Your pot, sweetheart?" Bart stood up and walked over to his daughter.

"I found it."

"Where? Back in the trees?"

Ginger shook her head. "Over by the side of the garage. Curt and me took it to the trees."

Bart felt foolish. The kettle hadn't been buried after all. He recalled his boyish wishes for gold or jewels and smothered an outright laugh for fear Ginger might think he was laughing at her.

"Did you clean it for me, Daddy?"

"I'm not sure if that's a good toy for you, Ginger," Sabra said, walking up behind her daughter.

"Why not, Mommy?"

Sabra shrugged. "Well, it's very dirty and—"

"I beg your pardon, ma'am," Bart said, purposely drawling out the words. "If'n you look real close like, you'll see that a super, spectacular job has rendered the 'dirty, filthy thing,' as you so graciously referred to it, into a planter pot of the finest quality."

Sabra suddenly noticed she no longer felt the pure essence of evil any longer. She looked around Bart toward the kettle. It was lovely. Stepping off the riser, she squatted, to look more closely at it. "What is the design on it?"

"That's the strange part, Sabra. It looks like words or at least letters from some old alphabet."

"What?"

"Look for yourself." He picked up the kettle. "See?" He ran a finger over the rows of small, intricately formed letter-like indentations.

"For heaven's sake, what do you make of it?"

Bart shrugged. "Nothing. Absolutely nothing. I've been thinking while I was working on it that maybe one of the antique dealers in Cascade would know what it is. They deal in old stuff all the time. Want to go along?"

"When?"

"Now."

Ginger pulled at her father's arm. "Daddy, are you going to sell my pot?"

"I don't know, sweetheart. It might be worth a lot of money and—"

"Do I get to keep the money? I found it. It's mine."

Bart looked at Sabra and smiled. He dropped into a crouch and looked at his daughter who returned his scrutiny with a serious look of her own.

Bart cleared his throat. "Tell you what, Ginger. If it's worth more than five dollars, you get the money and we'll open a bank account for you. How's that?"

"I thought maybe some candy and toys, Daddy."

Sabra laughed. "Let's wait and see how much money Daddy can get for it first."

"Oh, all right." Ginger started for the back door.

"Don't forget to do your homework right away, Ginger," Sabra said. "I'll be up before dinner to check over what you've done."

"Okay, Mommy."

"And tell Curt the same thing I just told you."

"Yes, Mommy." The door slammed as if punctuating her sentence and ending her part of the conversation.

"I assume there was nothing inside," Sabra said when they were alone. She knew there was nothing in it. She could see that it was empty. There couldn't have been before either. What could have been inside that made her feel like she had? Whatever had made her feel the presence of evil had to have been something else. It couldn't have been the kettle. She felt fine now.

"That's the strange thing. The lid was on so tight I couldn't begin to budge it. I scrubbed one spot on the kettle and saw the writings or whatever those marks are, and I was just about ready to start another section of it when the phone rang. I dropped the darned thing, and when I came back out, the lid was lying next to it. It probably landed just right and the lid popped off."

Sabra said nothing. She had made too much out of the kettle's presence in the house. For all she knew, the sense of evil or whatever it was she had experienced was nothing more than part of her visions and nightmares.

"So do you want to go along into town?"

"No. I'm making that chicken and pineapple dish you like so much. I've got to be there every minute. If you're going, be back no later than five."

Bart picked up the kettle and placed the lid on it before depositing it in the rear of the Taurus wagon.

Sabra waved when he pulled out of the yard and then entered the house.

*   *   *

The bell attached to the door rang when Bart entered the antique shop. He had passed a couple of others when he remembered this shop had a sign in front that said "Appraisals." That meant the owner felt confident in his or her knowledge that they knew the antique business. The last thing he wanted was making a round of all the antique shops in the area to get nothing but differing opinions.

His eyes adjusted to the dark interior of the shop, and when he could see well, he made his way toward the back.

"Yes. May I help you?" a woman's voice said from the shadows off to his right.

Bart jumped and turned in that direction. "Hello. Yes, you may."

"What is it you're looking for?" she asked, stepping into the dim light.

Bart stared at the woman. Her shoulder-length red hair contrasted sharply with the white blouse she wore. Skin-tight jeans outlined her hips, and he wondered how she might have gotten into them that morning.

"I'm not really looking for anything in particular," he said, finally pulling his attention away from her. "I was wondering if you could tell me if this kettle is worth anything." He held the pot up.

She stepped nearer, her perfume engulfing him. He didn't recognize it as one Sabra had ever worn. He wondered what the name of it might be. It would be a pleasant addition to those his wife used.

"May I see it?" she asked. "I'm Veloy Delmonica. I own the shop and make the appraisals."

Bart handed the kettle to her and thought that she displayed an unusual strength when her arm didn't react to the sudden weight.

She set it on the counter and turned on another overhead light. Her perusal didn't take long, and she looked up. "Kettles like this normally are quite plentiful, and dealers will take whatever they can get for them. The demand is not too high for such pieces."

Bart nodded. He understood that antique dealers liked to dicker over prices and products, but there was something in her voice that told him this kettle was somehow different from the run-of-the-mill type to which she just had referred.

"Is it worth anything?" he asked.

"As a kettle? Only if you intend to cook over an open hearth. Of course the handle is gone but that could be easily replaced if cooking is your intent." She smiled showing even white teeth. "I don't think it is. Am I right?"

Bart grinned and nodded. He fought again to divert his attention from her. Milk-white skin intensified her red hair, and when he chanced a look, he could see she was braless.

"As a piece with intrinsic value, I don't think it qualifies either. The reason I say that is the market is flooded at times with identical pots such as yours."

"Are you trying to build me up for something?" Bart asked. "Or to let me down?"

She looked up at him, startled by the question. "No, indeed. I was just about to say that the writing on your kettle is what makes it unique. What language is it?"

Bart shrugged. "I have no idea."

She slowly nodded, barely moving her head when she did. "Neither do I. It looks strangely familiar, but because of the shadows caused by the indentations, I can't quite make it out. Has anyone else seen this?"

Bart shook his head. "We just bought a home outside of town, and we're having some landscaping work done. The men may have unearthed this. My youngest daughter discovered the kettle lying next to the garage. I found it today and cleaned it up. That's all I know about it. You're the first one to see it other than my family."

"I'd like to suggest something. Why don't you take it to Professor Jerome Pendergard. He's a retired college professor who taught, among other things, ancient history."

Bart frowned. He knew that name, but from where? Of course, Sister Rita had mentioned him. "Where would I find him?"

"He lives here in Cascade. He was born here and came back when he retired. I've consulted him before on a couple of items. He's most charming. I'll give you his address."

While she jotted down the address, Bart said, "Can I just drop in on him unannounced?"

"He'll welcome the call, I assure you. He's widowed and lonely." She handed the note to Bart.

Picking up the kettle, he said, "Thank you."

"I'm sorry I couldn't be of more help." She stepped around from behind the counter and walked with him toward the front door. "If that is writing and he can help you translate it, stop back and tell me what it says. I'm curious."

"I'll do that. Do I owe you anything?"

"Of course not. I didn't do anything."

"Well, thank you again." Bart opened the door to the accompaniment of the bell and left.

He looked at the address which was on Main Street. There weren't that many streets in Cascade that he couldn't have found any one of them just by looking. Minutes later, he parked the Taurus and got out in front of a brick Italianate mansion. When he retrieved the kettle from the back, he walked up to the front porch and, after checking once more the address the woman had given him, rang the old doorbell.

It clanged loudly, echoing through the old mansion. Minutes later, he heard someone walking toward the front door. When it swung open, a gray-haired man in his early eighties confronted Bart.

"Professor Jerome Pendergard?"

"Yes. Ah, do I know you?"

"No, we've never met. I'm Bart Narman. Miss Veloy Delmonica suggested I call on you to show you this kettle."

"I see. Come in, come in." He threw open the door and stepped aside. "I thought that perhaps you might have been one of my students over the years that had stopped by to see me. That happens more frequently than I ever thought it would. Come, let's go into the library."

Bart followed him and marveled at the glassed-in shelves lining the four walls of the library. One window broke up the walls of books, and other than several overstuffed easy chairs and a desk, nothing else was in the room. A huge dictionary sat on a stand off to the side of the desk.

"Now what's this about a kettle, you say?" Professor Pendergard looked over the edge of his wire-framed glasses at Bart.

Bart quickly told him how he had come by the kettle, and when he finished, Pendergard asked to see it. Bart placed it on the desk as the professor sat down.

After several minutes passed, he looked up. "Can you leave it here with me? It certainly is writing, and I would like to take a try at translating it. It'll give me something new to do. But I would need time."

Bart thought about Ginger's attachment to the kettle. If something were to happen to it, he could always tell his daughter that he had sold it for more than five dollars and started a bank account for her. But that would be lying. He'd cross that bridge when he got to it.

"Of course you can keep it for a while. Would you like to call me when you're finished with it?"

"That would be fine, Mr. Narman." Pendergard stood and came around to Bart's side of the desk.

"Call me Bart, Professor. Everyone does."

"Call me Jerry. My real name is Jerome but most people around here call me Jerry."

Bart liked the man. There was something both dynamic and dignified about him. He offered the octogenarian his hand.

Pendergard took it in a firm grasp and shook it vigorously. "Very well, Bart. I'll give you a call when I'm finished."

"Any idea as to how long it might take, Jerry?"

Pendergard frowned. "It might take a day and it might take me the rest of my life." His eyes suddenly twinkled when he smiled. "Of course a day might be the rest of my life." He laughed. "I would say that if the language is what I think it is, I might have trouble translating and would need assistance from another man here in town who could help. I would say within a week or ten days at the outside I would have your translation."

Bart offered him one of his old business cards with his new telephone number written in. "Here you go, Jerry. Give me a call. If I'm not home, my wife Sabra will be."

Bart opened the heavy front door and left, an air of expectation weighing heavily upon him.

Chapter Nine

Ruth Donner surveyed her class of second graders. "Children, I want you to take out your arithmetic workbooks and open to page nine."

A flurry of activity followed, while the eight year olds fumbled through their desks, pulling out the tablet-sized workbooks. One by one they opened them to the designated page and looked up at their teacher, waiting.

"I would like to have you work on page nine and page ten. I'm scheduled to go to a meeting at Sister Rita's office and while I'm gone I want . . ." she hesitated. Who would make a good monitor? She skimmed over the roomful of little heads and settled on a blond-haired girl. It might be risky but she wanted to be able to show Ginger Narman that she held no grudge against the child for having struck her. She cleared her throat. "While I'm gone, I want Ginger Narman to come up to the front and be the monitor. Ginger bring your workbook. You can sit at my desk."

Ginger stood, picking up her workbook, and walked to the front of the room. A smile played at the corners of her mouth. She was used to this sort of thing. In her school back in Yonkers, she'd been given responsible duties that other children had not been entrusted with and she'd done well with them. She'd never been a monitor before because there had always been a teacher's helper, some mother or older adult who had volunteered to help out in the overcrowded school.

After situating herself at the desk, Ginger looked up at Ruth.

The teacher handed her a notepad and said, "If anyone talks or misbehaves while I'm gone, I want you to write their name down on this pad. Do you understand?"

Ginger nodded.

Tommy Claymore, the boy Ginger had slapped, raised his hand.

"Yes, Tommy?" Ruth asked.

"Who's going to watch Ginger?"

The others in the room snickered, but Ruth held her hand up for silence. "That wasn't kind, Tommy. Ginger will make a fine monitor."

She turned and went to the door. "I'll be back

in about twenty minutes." Opening the door, she pushed it against the outside wall. With the door left open, it was less likely the children would make any sort of noise for fear of being heard by other teachers who weren't involved in the meeting.

Walking up the steps to the third floor where Sister Rita's office was located, Ruth wondered what the meeting was about. The list of people who were to attend had been at the head of the principal's memo she'd found in her box in the teachers' lounge that morning. Father Richards, Sister Nancy Armstrong, one of the more worldly nuns at Saint Boniface, Corinne Casey, the fourth grade teacher, Sister Rita and herself were to be in attendance. Ruth liked Sister Rita. She might be more traditional in her values but the other three nuns assigned to the school were too modern for Ruth.

When she entered the office she found she was the last one to arrive.

"Sit down, Ruth," Sister Rita said, gesturing toward the only empty chair in the room.

"The reason I've called you all together is a matter of prevention rather than an immediate problem. At least, let me say that maybe we're preventing a problem from happening if we all work together." Sister Rita scanned the faces of the four people in the room. They had no idea as to what she was talking about. Perhaps that was good. Maybe she was overreacting and there was no cause for alarm, yet—

"When Father Richards told me about the impromptu boxing match the other day in his gym class for the fourth, fifth and sixth graders, I began to wonder and then worry some."

"What do we have to do with a boxing match?" Corinne Casey asked, smoothing her skirt over her thighs. Reaching up she nervously patted her hair.

Sister Rita quickly related the incident as Father Richards had told her. At the time he had mentioned the fight more in passing than as a report of disciplinary action. When she finished, she waited to see if there would be any reaction.

Ruth Donner cleared her throat. "I assume that this Curt Narman is a brother to Ginger Narman?"

Sister Rita nodded. "Why don't you tell the others what happened in your class, Ruth?"

Ruth told of Ginger slapping Tommy Claymore and how the girl had kicked her in the shins and struck out at her breasts.

"Curt is a regular little gentleman in my room," Corinne said almost defensively. "He's very well-behaved."

Sister Nancy, the home room teacher for the tenth grade, sat up, fluffing the front of her blouse. "I have Marcy Narman in class and she's an excellent student. I like her a whole lot as a person, too. She's quite personable."

"I don't doubt that she is, Sister," Sister Rita said. "I'm sure that the little problem Ruth had with Ginger and the fight that Father Richards so kindly refereed, was brought on by the tension involved in the Narman family moving to Cascade, attending a new school and meeting new people. It's not uncommon for children to revolt at being moved. However, the manner in which the two younger Narmans behaved gave me cause for worry, and I felt that if we were all forewarned we could be forearmed."

"Just because a boy wants to show off for the benefit of his new friends and a fistfight is avoided by having them settle their differences in the ring should be looked on as normal behavior. It's certainly no potential problem, Sister," Father Richards said. He was sorry he had brought Curt to the principal's office.

Sister Rita fixed her full attention on the priest. "I wish you'd get rid of the boxing gloves, Father. Really. It's a savage and barbaric sport at best. How you could allow two ten year olds to swing at each other with all their might is beyond me."

Father Richards smothered his smile. "Ah, Sister, one of them was twelve years old."

"That's even worse. The fight was not fair. I'm surprised that Curt wasn't seriously injured."

"Curt had nothing to worry about, Sister. He won. It was Joe Gregory who took the licking." His voice sounded smug, even proud.

Sister Rita stared at him. "Are you enjoying yourself, Father?"

"How do you mean, Sister?"

"You seem to think it's all right that these two

youngsters tried to beat each other's brains out. And to chortle because the younger of the two won is—"

"I wasn't chortling, Sister. It's just that Curt had never had boxing gloves on before in his life, or so he said, and he made Joe, who has had boxing lessons, look bad."

"I don't care who won, Father. I don't care who gave whom a boxing lesson."

"I couldn't help but think of David and Goliath, Sister. You know, from the bible."

"Will you get rid of the equipment, Father?" Sister Rita asked, ignoring the priest's try at religious humor.

Father Richards frowned. "Sister, if I may . . . The gloves weigh sixteen ounces each and are to these little guys as big as pillows. They really couldn't have hurt themselves."

"I thought you said the Gregory boy was knocked out. Was he?"

Father Richards paused and bit his lower lip. "Yes. That's true. Well, almost true. Joe was dazed. In the excitement, I never once thought about the fact that Curt had knocked him down and almost out with those gloves. Can I ask you to reconsider, Sister, or at least shelve the order for now? Let's discuss this more fully sometime in the future. Can we?"

Sister Rita toyed with a pencil for several seconds. "Very well, Father. The subject of boxing was not the purpose of the meeting. I'll bring it up at the next full faculty meeting. Now, do any of you have anything else to report where the Narman children are concerned?"

No one offered any further information until Sister Nancy said, "I know I've seen Marcy's transcript. Are the other two as impressive?"

Sister Rita nodded. "Yes. They're very fine children. I'm certain there's nothing to be overly concerned about at this time. All I'm proposing is that all of us watch them." She paused for a moment, then smiled ironically. "For all we know, they've been fighting and disruptive in class before and got away with it. After all, Saint Boniface is a small school in a small town. The Narman children went to huge schools by comparison and were probably nothing more than a number to the administration there."

Ruth Donner motioned to be heard.

"Yes, Ruth?" Sister Rita said.

"If they were like that before in the schools they came from, how could they have gotten such high marks in all of their subjects? Certainly children who are naughty don't usually score that well in tests and day-to-day class work and activity."

"That's true, Ruth, and that very thought crossed my mind. That's why I'm more prone to put the blame on the family's move here rather than on a behavioral problem. All I want to do is have all of us be a little extra alert. If there's nothing wrong, our concern will have been in vain. However, if the children are developing some sort of antisocial behavior, we may be able to nip it in the bud. Any questions?"

Those present shook their heads and stood to leave.

Ruth hurried down the steps, and when she entered her classroom, she found it quiet and orderly. Ginger looked up and smiled at her.

"Thank you, Ginger. You may return to your desk."

Ginger stood and made her way down the aisle. Allison English stuck her foot out in the aisle, but Ginger saw it and made a face at the girl when she stepped around it.

Once Ginger was seated, she stared at the back of Allison's head. She'd get her for that. But when she did, she'd be careful and none of the teachers would know.

Marcy fluffed her hair and then pirouetted in front of the mirror on the dresser. She felt nervous, excited, almost queasy in her stomach, yet confident when she turned her back to the mirror. When she faced it, she felt dizzy again. Was she pretty enough to go out with Brenda and the others? She'd never gone out at night alone. In Yonkers, she had not gone to the basketball games during her freshman year. When she reached her sophomore year, she had thought she would get to go to the home games but didn't. When the move came up and she learned they were moving to Cascade, a little town, she didn't know what to expect as far as any kind of social life was concerned.

But here she was, ready to go out joyriding on Friday night. She looked in the mirror and thought she looked all right after all. She resembled her mother in many ways, and when she pouted out her lower lip just a bit, she thought their mouths at least were identical. While her mother's eyes were icy blue, practically white/blue, her own were a deep blue that bordered on purple.

She stood sideways and tucked in her blouse. Her breasts stood out, away from her body, in a proud sort of way. After adjusting her bra strap, she made one more turn in front of the mirror.

"You look nice," Ginger said from the doorway.

"Thank you," Marcy said.

"Why are you all dressed up?"

"I'm going out tonight."

"Oh, yeah? Does Mommy know?"

"Of course, she knows, silly. I couldn't go out without asking Mom and Daddy's permission. You know that."

Ginger didn't answer and jumped on her bed. "Where you going?"

"Oh, just out with some friends."

"Who are your friends? I'll bet you're going with a boy. You are, aren't you?"

"I am not. And stop saying that. Do you want me to get in trouble with Mom and Daddy? They'll think I lied to them."

"What are your friends' names?"

Marcy sat on the edge of her bed. "Oh, there's

Carla and Brenda and Becky."

Ginger folded her arms as if she weren't satisfied with the answers. "So, where are you *really* going tonight?"

"I told you—out."

"I don't believe you."

"I'm going out to get away from you and your questions, Ginger." Marcy grinned and stood. Crossing the room, she left her sister sitting on her bed, a grumpy look on her face.

Marcy ran down the steps and found her parents in the living room. Bart held the local weekly newspaper and barely looked up when his oldest child entered the room.

Sabra eyed her daughter and motioned for her to stand still. When she made a circle with one finger, Marcy slowly turned around. "You look very nice, Marcy."

"Are you sure? You're not just saying that, are you, Mom?"

Sabra smiled. "No, I'm not just saying that." She and Bart had agreed that it would be soon enough if Marcy began occasional dating when she was in her sophomore year. There was no sense in pushing her toward a social life when she was still in grade school, not that that wasn't the norm in Yonkers and other places she'd heard about. Sure, boys and girls would go steady from the time they were in first or second grade, but it never amounted to anything. The way things had changed for school children during the last ten years, just about the length of time Marcy had been going, had made Sabra and Bart have a serious talk.

Sabra had heard of children eleven and twelve years of age having sex. In many instances, the girls were more aggressive than the boys, and she vowed her daughters would not act like that. She covertly looked at Marcy again. Marcy was beautiful but naive about her looks, considering the way she had come in asking her mother if she looked all right. Anyone hearing her ask that would have concluded that Marcy was soliciting compliments. She was beautiful and wasn't aware of it. Sabra rather liked that idea. It would keep her daughter a teenager that much longer. She had the rest of her life to be a woman.

"What time are they picking you up?" Bart asked, laying the newspaper aside.

"Around seven-thirty."

"I want you to remember that you have to be home by ten this evening," Sabra said.

"I know. I won't be late."

When she was alone, Ginger frowned deeply, her lovely face transposing itself into a mask of hatred. Slipping off the bed, she tiptoed down the hall, not making a sound. When she stood at the top of the stairs, she could see the door at the bottom was open and could hear the voices of her parents and sister talking in the living room. Where was Curt?

Then she remembered he said he was going

outside for a while after supper. She was alone upstairs.

Turning, she went to her parents room and turned on the nightlight next to her father's side of the bed. She found the telephone book and opened it to the section on Cascade. Running down the list of people whose names began with "E," she stopped when she came to the Englishes. There were three. Which one was Allison English's house?

She'd have to be careful. She lifted the receiver from its cradle and heard the dial tone. It seemed awfully loud. She dialed the number as fast as she could and waited while the phone rang. A grumpy voice answered.

"Hello," the man said gruffly.

"Is . . . is Allison there?"

"You got the wrong goddamned number." The man banged the receiver down.

Ginger jumped and looked around the room. Had anyone heard him say that? She waited, and then it dawned on her that no one other than she could hear what was on the telephone.

She dialed the next number and waited. The phone rang ten times before she hung up. What if that were Allison's house? She'd have to call another time if the next person told her there wasn't anyone named Allison living there.

She dialed the last English in the book. When the phone rang, Ginger held her breath when she heard the voices from downstairs suddenly grow louder. She didn't move. When the voices died away, she knew her parents and sister were going into the kitchen.

Just then, the phone was answered.

"Hello?"

"Is Allison there?" she asked softly.

"Just a minute," the woman said. "Allison! Telephone!"

Ginger smiled to herself and waited.

"Hello?" Allison said.

Ginger opened her mouth to speak, then stopped. A coldness swept over her and she felt full, as if she'd eaten too much supper.

"Listen, bitch," the gutteral voice coming from her mouth said, "try tripping me again and I'll kill you. I'll slit your belly open and yank your goddamn guts out. Understand?"

Heavy silence poured from the earpiece and then sobs. "Mo—Mommy. Come here!"

Ginger deftly placed the phone back on the cradle and stood. After she turned the light out, she left her parents' bedroom and went downstairs to the kitchen.

"Bye, Marcy. Have fun," Sabra said from the entryway. Bart waved and turned back into the room.

"Well, young lady, what have you been up to?"

"Nothing, Daddy. I was up in our room. I had to brush my hair after Marcy left."

Bart laughed and picked up his youngest child. "I suppose you'll be wanting to go out next? Am I right?"

"I want to watch TV. Can I, Daddy?"

"Well, I suppose that's possible, isn't it, Mommy?"

Ginger giggled. "You called Mommy, 'Mommy.' She's not your Mommy. She's mine."

"Well, you'd better take care of her or I'll say she's mine and then you won't have a mommy."

The three of them walked into the living room after Bart called for Curt to come in.

"I like your blouse, Marcy," Brenda said.

"Thank you. I got it for my last birthday."

"Where do you two want to go?" Herbie asked from behind the wheel of his father's Oldsmobile.

"Just drive around for a while. If we get close to the Snack Shack, stop and we'll get a Coke or something." Brenda turned her attention back to Marcy.

They chatted about school and the boys who were in their class and how immature they were. Marcy laughed, enjoying herself and taking part in the boy-bashing that Brenda seemed to enjoy. Marcy noted that Herbie seemed to be tuned into his own little world and wasn't paying them much attention.

After 40 minutes of driving up and down Main Street and making passes along the dark residential streets that paralleled it, Herbie suddenly slammed on the brakes.

"What's wrong?" Brenda asked turning away from Marcy.

"We're here."

"We're where?"

"At Pop's."

Marcy looked past Herbie and through the driver's window. They had pulled into a parking lot and she could see the neon sign flashing: Pop's Snack Shack.

"Oh. Let's get out, Marcy."

"Hey, hang back, Brenda." Herbie grabbed her shoulder. "I got a question I gotta ask you."

She turned to face him. "What?"

"How long is she gonna be with us. I'm horny."

"Honest to God, Herbie. You haven't got brain cell one in your head. I told you I'm on the rag. We can't do anything tonight. Marcy's going to stay with us for the whole time. Got it?"

Brenda slid out of the car and closed the door. She found Marcy standing next to the car, a hurt look on her face.

"Hey, Marcy, don't pay no mind to Herbie. He's being a real dickhead tonight. Come on in. I'll introduce you to Pop. She's a real nice lady."

Marcy stopped walking. "What did you say?"

Brenda thought for a moment and then laughed. "Oh, you mean about Pop? Pop is a woman. She bought Pop's Snack Shack from the guy who owned it before. His nickname was Pop. As the new owner, she couldn't afford a new sign and kept the old one. So she became Pop."

By nine o'clock The Snack Shack was filled with teenagers. The jukebox blared, and when

173

three young men, dressed in black leather jackets entered, no one paid them any mind.

Marcy saw them and pointed to them. "Who're they?"

Brenda turned to look. "Oh, them? They ride bikes. Run around with a bunch of real jerks. They've all dropped out of high school and work at nothing jobs during the day. But at night, they're the kings of the highways. Or so they think."

"Do you know any of them?" Marcy asked, staring across the crowd at the three bikers standing near the door.

She couldn't take her eyes from them. One was especially handsome, and she found that his looks appealed to her.

"Do I know any of them? I went to school with some of those jerkoffs." Brenda turned in her seat again. "Yeah, I know them. They should be juniors or seniors but they're bike riders. That one is a real dream, though, isn't he?"

"Which one?" Marcy asked without thinking. Of course she knew the one Brenda meant.

"The tallest one. Chains Lindstrom. Want to know what his real name is?"

Marcy nodded, her eagerness not too well hidden.

"LaVern. LaVern Lindstrom. Isn't that a hoot? LaVern, the motorcycle tough. If I was him, I'd want to be called Chains, too. He's like Herbie."

Marcy tore her eyes from the youth and stared at Brenda. In Marcy's eyes, Herbie wasn't that much to look at. He was underweight, had pimples and his hair was combed straight back. "How do you mean, Brenda?"

Brenda studied Marcy's face for a moment. "Oh, Christ! I know what you're thinking. Not in looks. Christ, no. Herbie's real yucky when it comes to looks. No. I don't think he begins to compare with Chains in looks. They both think with their dicks. Got it?"

Marcy tried to look worldly and nodded, attempting an all-knowing, all-wise expression.

"Oh, my God!" Marcy whispered.

"What's the matter?"

"He's coming this way. Oh, God, he's coming over here."

"Don't bet on it. He probably sees a chick he can lay without any trouble."

Seconds later, Chains stood next to their table. He looked down at Marcy. "Well, you're a decent addition to the scenery around this dump. Wanna go for a ride on my Harley?"

Marcy started to shake her head but stopped. She looked at Brenda and then up at Chains. He was so damned handsome. She felt like squealing—squealing like she'd seen girls on TV do whenever Mick Jagger sang.

Suddenly, she felt chilled. She felt as if she were about to shiver. Then she relaxed and felt fine, warm and tingly all over.

"It's sort of warm in here," she said, smiling up at the biker. "Where would you take me?"

"C'mon. I'll give you the ride of your life."

Marcy stood and looked down at Brenda whose mouth hung open. "Wait here. I'll be back in a while."

Brenda nodded, still too shocked to speak.

Chains turned and led the way toward the door. Marcy followed him, knowing all eyes in the restaurant were on her.

Chapter Ten

Marcy, her arms around Chain's chest, hugged him in a tight embrace. She lay her head against his back, enjoying the exhilerating ride through the dark countryside. She had no idea as to where they were or where they were going, and she didn't care.

The wind whipped her hair about, tangling it into a wild disarray.

The sound of the Harley Davidson Sportster filled the night, drowning out the sound of Marcy's quickening pulse.

"You like?" Chains called back over his shoulder.

"I love it." Marcy was amazed at the way her voice sounded. She seldom raised it above normal talking level and here she was, yelling at the top of her voice to answer a question while she and a boy she had not even been formally introduced to blasted along a pitch-black highway.

"Chains" eased back on the throttle and slowed down. Seconds later he turned off the road and skimmed along a smooth blacktop drive. He revved the engine and turned it off. The ensuing quiet of the night pressed in on them, screaming for more sound to fill the void.

Marcy slowly, reluctantly released her hold on Chains and got off the bike. He followed and unzipped his jacket.

"Where are we?" she asked.

"At a rest stop. We gotta rest." He laughed and took off his jacket.

With the bike's headlight out, Marcy had difficult seeing at first. Slowly, the forms of trees took shape, and she could see off to the left the road some 40 or so yards away. There was no traffic.

"C'mere," Chains said, grabbing her by the shoulders.

When he pulled her roughly toward him, Marcy felt an initial fear but it disappeared in the next breath. A fullness in her abdomen momentarily swept over her, then disappeared.

The touch of Chain's hands sent a shock of electricity through her body and she responded. Their lips locked, and she felt his tongue poking into her mouth. Opening wider, she welcomed the wiggling, exploring thing as it swept between her teeth and onto her own tongue.

She clutched Chains in a tight embrace, rubbing her breasts against his hard body. When his tongue slipped out of her mouth, her own went in pursuit of his, worming its way onto his tongue, below it, alongside of it, into the area between the teeth and cheek. She wished her tongue were longer so she could explore his throat.

After several minutes, Chains pushed her away. "Hey, take it easy. Give a guy a chance to breathe."

Marcy smiled. She had enjoyed the kiss but she wanted more. She wanted whatever this kid could give her.

"Where the hell did you learn to kiss like that?" he asked, pulling out a cigarette. He offered one to Marcy but she shook her head.

"If you like the way I kiss so goddamned much, what the hell are you lighting up for?"

The flare of the match lit up Chain's face for an instant. He drew on the cigarette, its glow brightening then fading. He blew the smoke away and grabbed her by the arms again. "Get that goddamned blouse off, kid."

As Marcy obediently began unbuttoning the shirt, Chains stepped back, a shocked look on his face. He reached up to pull off his own greasy T-shirt.

Marcy undid her bra, slipped out of it and stepped closer to the biker. He took her by the arms again and she pressed her naked breasts against his thin chest. She detected the difference in body temperature—his cool, hers burning hot. A chilly breeze washed over them, and she shivered.

Their tongues fought a slippery battle for rights to the other's mouth when Marcy pushed back.

Chains glared at her in the dark. "What the fuck's the matter?"

"What time is it? I gotta be home by ten."

"What time is it? I gotta be home by ten," Chains mimicked. "Whatta you mean you gotta be home by ten?"

"Just what I said, Chains." She slipped into her bra and fastened it before the youth could say anything. She put on her blouse and buttoned it. "Come on. Get going. If I'm late there'll be hell to pay and I won't get to go out for months, maybe years."

"Come on. We gotta do it. I gotta hard-on that won't quit. We can't go." His voice whining for release sounded peculiar in the dark.

Marcy smiled to herself. The big, motorcycle tough was begging her. That was good. She had a power that could bring men to their knees and she liked the idea.

"Look, Sport, if you don't have me back in town so I can be home no later than ten o'clock, you're going to find yourself in one big pile of trouble and that rhymes with bubble and I'll pop yours if you don't get that goddamned, fucking shirt and jacket on—now!" Marcy swallowed.

Had she actually said that?

"Don't threaten me, bitch!" Chains slowly pulled on his shirt and then put on his leather jacket. "You don't scare me none."

"Yeah? How 'bout if I told you I was only fifteen?"

Chains didn't answer right away. "You ain't no fuckin' fifteen. Nobody fifteen got a body like yours, and they sure as hell can't kiss like you. Next thing you'll tell me you're a fuckin' virgin."

"Virgins don't fuck, Chains. Come on. Let's get going. You won't go to jail and I won't be grounded for the rest of my life. And who knows? Maybe we can get together and finish this little episode one day or night. Game?"

Chains threw a leg over the bike and started it. "C'mon."

Marcy hiked up her skirt and got on behind him, putting her arms around him once more. He pulled the Sportster onto the highway and roared away. Once they were cutting through the night again, he slipped a hand around behind him and found Marcy's leg. He ran his fingers up as far as he could but stopped when he realized he couldn't reach her crotch.

Several minutes later, they roared by something that looked familiar to Marcy. She turned her head and looked more closely. In the dark she wasn't sure but she thought they had just passed her house. Had they come out this way? What if her parents saw her riding on the back of a bike like this?

Her head swam for a moment. She had to be reasonable. How or why would her parents have looked out at the precise moment they had ridden past? That was silly. There was no way either of them would have or could have known it was she who was on the bike, even if they had looked.

Chains allowed the bike to idle back and they kept to the speed limit going through Cascade's business district. Most of the shops were closed, and with the exceptions of a few bars and the convenience store, nothing else was open.

Marcy caught sight of a clock in the window of a service station and saw she had eighteen minutes to get home. Brenda and Herbie had to be at Pop's. If they weren't, Marcy really would be in for it. She wanted to go home with the people she had left with earlier in the evening. She didn't know why. It just made sense that her parents would expect her to return with the same people who had picked her up.

When they pulled into the parking lot, she breathed a sigh of relief when she saw Brenda standing in the middle of the lot. Herbie was leaning against his father's car, his arms folded.

Chains braked to a halt, and Marcy jumped off the back.

"Hey? How's 'bout a g'night kiss?" he asked.

"Here? In the middle of the lot? Besides, we've never been introduced properly." Marcy tossed her wind-whipped hair and walked away.

"Gee-zus Christ!" Chains moaned. "Fuckin'

women! Who can understan' 'em?" He kicked down the stand and leaned the bike over. Walking into the restaurant, he slammed the door behind him.

"Are you all right?" Brenda asked.

Marcy nodded. "Of course I am. Why? Were you worried or something?"

"Good God, girl! You just don't go riding off with one of those bastards like that. I'm surprised he didn't rape you or something."

"Oh, he's all right. Just unsure of his manhood and wants to prove something, I think." Marcy nodded toward Herbie. "What's wrong with your boyfriend?"

"He's pissed 'cause he can't get laid tonight."

Marcy felt dizzy for a second and reached out for Brenda.

"Hey, you okay?"

"Yeah," Marcy said, not quite sure what was wrong. "I guess I'm just getting my legs back. I should be getting home, Brenda. Can you and Herbie take me?"

"I'll see." Brenda walked over to the gangly youth and talked to him. He turned away, but when she dropped her hand to his crotch, he turned back to face her. A second later, he smiled and reached in his pocket for the keys.

"All set," Brenda said, coming back. Herbie walked around the car and got in.

"What'd you say?" Marcy asked.

"I told him I'd give him a nice surprise if he

got you home before ten. We've got about six minutes."

Marcy wondered for a split second what Brenda had promised Herbie, but the thought of being late and that they had less than six minutes to get home pushed her curiosity aside. She slipped into the front seat beside Brenda, and Herbie started the car.

"Good thing we can drive through town and be at your house in about four or five minutes," Herbie said.

"Don't speed. A couple of minutes late won't make it the end of the world for me," Marcy said and rolled down the window.

By the digital clock on the dashboard, it was 10:01 when Herbie turned into the driveway at the Narman house. "Sorry," he said. "You're a minute late."

"Thanks, guys." Marcy opened the door and jumped out. "See you in school Monday."

"Or in church," Brenda said as Herbie began backing out.

Marcy heard Herbie say, "Now, Brenda." She stopped to wave and saw Brenda slipping down, out of sight. Had she dropped something?

Lightly running up the steps, she opened the door and walked into the kitchen entryway. "I'm home," she called out.

"And with one minute to spare," Bart said entering the kitchen. Sabra walked behind him.

Marcy mentally frowned and then concluded that either Herbie's clock was a few minutes fast or the Narman clocks were a few minutes slow. It made no difference as long as she was in on time according to her parents.

"Did you have fun, honey?" Sabra asked.

"Yeah, I did. But I'm hungry."

"Didn't you have something to eat when you were out?" Bart asked.

Marcy shook her head. "I almost did but we got talking and one thing led to another, and before I knew it, it was time to come home." She went to the refrigerator and took out a bowl of pasta.

"Well, I'm going to bed. Tomorrow I've got to go into town and buy a yard tractor." Bart crossed the room, bussed his oldest daughter on the cheek and did the same to his wife. "I'll be sound asleep when you come up."

"Night, Daddy."

"Night, sweetheart."

Sabra took her daughter's hand. "So who did you meet tonight? Want to tell me all about it?"

Marcy studied her mother. Something seemed to be bothering her. "Mom, did I do something wrong?" Did her mother know about the motorcycle ride? How could she possibly know?

Sabra stared at ther daughter. "Of course not, darling. Why do you ask?"

"You act like there's something's wrong. As if—"

"It's that noticeable?"

"What?"

They walked into the dining room and sat down at the table. "I took a telephone call tonight from a Mrs. English. She claimed Ginger called her daughter, Allison, this evening and threatened her daughter in a most disgusting way."

"What?" Marcy's eyes widened, forgetting her snack. Ginger? Ginger would never do anything like that. "What happened, Mom? Tell me."

Sabra told Marcy of the conversation and what had been said to the English's daughter.

"Did the girl say that Ginger said who she was?"

"No. Apparently Allison—that's the English girl—tried to trip Ginger in school today. Whoever called Allison said that if she tried tripping her again, that the person who called said they'd kill Allison."

"Good heavens," Marcy said. "Did you ask Ginger about it?"

Sabra nodded. "Your father and I feel that someone called the Englishes and made the threat and are setting Ginger up for the blame. Allison even said it didn't sound like Ginger. It sounded, she said, more like a man, maybe an old man."

"What are you going to do about it?"

"What can we do? We have no idea as to who made the call or from where or, for that matter, why."

186

The Curse

They talked for a few minutes more before Sabra suggested they go to bed. After putting the uneaten pasta away and turning out the downstairs lights, they walked to the second floor. Marcy gave Sabra a peck on the cheek and went to her room.

She tiptoed in and turned on her nightstand light.

"Ma—Marcy?" Ginger sat up in bed, rubbing her eyes.

Marcy went to her little sister's bed and sat down, taking her in her arms. "Why aren't you asleep?"

"You woke me up. Did Mommy tell you what happened?"

Marcy nodded. "I don't believe you did it. You didn't, did you?"

Ginger shook her head, her tousled hair bouncing form side to side. "I didn't. I didn't call Allison. I want her to be my friend. Her mother said I said awful things to Allison. I didn't." Ginger sobbed and pushed her head against Marcy's chest.

"Of course you didn't. You would never do such things." Marcy smoothed her sister's hair and kissed her on the forehead. "Go to sleep. Tomorrow none of this will seem important. Tomorrow's Saturday. What do you want to do?"

Ginger shrugged. "I don't know."

"Well, you think of something and I'll play with you for a while. Okay?"

Ginger nodded. "What did you do tonight? Did you have fun?"

Marcy tucked Ginger in and began undressing. "Oh, we went riding for a while and then we went to Pop's Snack Shack and sat around and talked. We—" Marcy turned back and saw Ginger sleeping. She slipped into her pajamas and pulled back the covers on her own bed. After she was in, she reached over and turned out the light.

She lay on her back, staring into the darkness. The night had been fun, but the darkness in her room bothered her for some reason. Why? It seemed to remind her of something. It never had bothered her before in the past. She yawned. She should have brushed her hair. It was full of tangles for some reason. Wait! That wasn't right. Why should her hair be tangled? It had been blown about wildly, hadn't it? And she had been chilled above the waist for some reason, hadn't she?

Marcy sat up. Why was she thinking things like that? None of it made sense to her.

She had forgotten to do something. What? She had a peculiar taste in her mouth. Of course. She had forgotten to brush her teeth.

Slipping out of bed, she went to the bathroom and quickly brushed and flossed her teeth. Her tongue hurt a bit as well. What was that from? It ached in a way. When she finished she turned out the light and went back to bed.

In seconds, she was asleep.

The Curse

*   *   *

Outside, the wind picked up as the sky clouded over. A zephyr whined around the house picking up in intensity until it sounded not unlike a moaning laugh. The laughter rose, then fell into a gutteral growl that snarled viciously.

As quickly as the wind had built, it died down and a stillness lay over the Narman house. Overhead, the clouds dissipated and split into two groups, both wending their way toward the eastern horizon.

Minutes later, the three Holstein heifers that were pastured some 600 yards away next to the Narman property began to bellow, and soon all the animals cried out in fright and terror. One by one, the animals abruptly stopped crying out. Only the sound of night insects could be heard. A crushing silence filled the countryside until a soft, hoarse chuckling sounded.

Then the insects stopped.

Chapter
Eleven

Bart trudged around the kitchen, searching for the coffee. He had not paid much attention to where Sabra and the children had put things, so he searched for ten minutes before finding the Folger's. He usually felt angry with himself for not sleeping later on Saturday morning, but for some reason he didn't want to waste time in bed. As the coffee brewed, the aroma filled the kitchen and he smiled.

He went to the back door and stepped out onto the step. There was something in the air, not something physical or tangible but an atmosphere of excitement. He wondered what he was sensing. Was something about to happen? Was something wrong?

Bart was about to go inside again when he heard a car slowing down. He glanced over his shoulder and saw a Chevrolet, a star emblazoned on its front door, about to turn into their driveway.

Glad that he had slipped into a pair of slacks, Bart pulled his robe around his waist and stepped down to wait for the law officer to come to a stop behind his Taurus wagon.

A uniformed man stepped out of the car and strode over to Bart. "G'morning. I'm Sheriff Pat Haselton. You're—?" The sheriff held his hand out to Bart.

Bart thrust his own out and grasped the tall man's hand. Despite his own height, Bart found himself looking up at Haselton's square-cut face. "Bart Narman. You're out and about pretty early, Sheriff. What can I do for you?"

"Answer a few questions for one thing."

"Questions? About what? Or should I say who?"

"It's a 'what.' You live here alone?"

Bart shook his head. "No sir. My wife, Sabra, and our three children live here, too. What's up, Sheriff? What's going on?"

"Did you hear anything unusual last night?"

Bart pursed his lips. What did the sheriff mean by unusual? He thought back to last night. He had gone to bed first, after Marcy arrived home. Sabra and she must have stayed up for a while talking. He didn't hear Sabra even come into the bedroom. Taking a defensive step backward, Bart looked at the sheriff and then slowly shook his head. "I don't recall hearing anything, Sheriff. What was it I should have heard?"

"Before I tell you that, I'd like to speak with the rest of your family, if I could. It may be that one of them heard something."

Bart jumped when Sabra spoke from the back door. "I didn't hear anything out of the ordinary."

Haselton tipped his hat. "G'morning, ma'am. Sorry to disturb you people so early. Are your children up yet?"

Sabra shook her head. "No, they're not. It's Saturday morning and they're sleeping late, the way they always do."

"Ah, Sheriff," Bart said, "just what is it we should have heard?"

"You know the Gundrys down the road?"

Bart shook his head and turned to find Sabra stepping out onto the backstep. She, too, was shaking her head. "We just moved in a little over a week ago, Sheriff. I'm afraid we haven't met our neighbors yet. In fact, we haven't driven anyplace other than into town. Where do the Gundrys live?"

The sheriff motioned toward the direction from which he had come, away from Cascade. "They have a farm about a mile in that direction. George called me this morning right after sunup. He went out to his pasture to check on three prize Holstein heifers he had bought a few days ago and found them dead."

"Dead?" Bart studied the sheriff. "Surely you don't think I or we had—"

"Of course not. Remember I asked if you had heard anything unusual. I'm trying to figure out just what happened."

"What *did* happen, Sheriff?" Sabra asked.

"Their heads are gone and all three are half-eaten."

"What?" Sabra shot a look at Bart and then concentrated on the sheriff. "How could that be?"

"I tell you I've never seen anything so weird before in my life. There's not a drop of blood around, but the heads are gone—as if they never existed. A lot of meat was taken, too. And there aren't any footprints around. There's no sign of any kind of predator. Nothing."

"What kind of predators are in this area?" Bart had not thought of anything like that when they bought their home. Were there wild animals roaming around that could kill cattle?

"There's nothing that big that could kill a young cow like that. No sir. Other than a pack of dogs that's gone wild, there's nothing that could kill a cow."

"What did the cows look like, Sheriff?" Sabra asked.

"All three heads were taken off clean as a whistle."

Bart stared at him. "What do you mean by 'clean as a whistle'?"

Sabra pulled her robe around her more tightly and shuddered from the early morning coolness.

"Well, they don't look like they were chopped off, you know what I mean? Cut off in one slice. They almost look—now don't think I'm given to wild ideas, 'cause I'm not—but they look like the heads might have been taken off with a chain saw or like they were bitten off. There's ragged edges around the neck stumps but not a drop of blood anywhere."

"What do you think happened, Sheriff?" Bart stepped nearer the lawman.

Haselton shrugged. "I remember talk back when I was a teenager about cattle being slain all over the country. There was never any blood at those scenes either. That was what made them so strange."

"Did they ever find out who or what was responsible for those slayings?"

"If I remember right, they never did find out."

"Well, I didn't hear anything. Did you, Sabra?"

Sabra shook her head and absently fiddled with her crucifix. She had gone right to sleep once she got in bed after talking with Marcy. "I hope you find out who or what did this, Sheriff. I don't want to lose any sleep over some maniac running around loose. For all we know, he or she might go after a person next time."

Haselton stared at Sabra as if seeing her for the first time since she had stepped out. "I certainly hope this is the end of it. If it's not solved and there aren't anymore such killings, everything will settle down in no time." He tipped his hat to Sabra again and turned to retrace his steps to his car. When he opened the driver's door, he looked at the Narmans and said, "If you or your children hear or see anything that looks like it might be connected to this case, give me a call. Understand?"

Bart nodded and waved at him. Sabra turned back to enter the house. Once inside she poured them each a cup of coffee and they went into the dining room.

"What do you make of that?" she asked after sipping her coffee.

Bart shrugged and set his mug on the table after sampling it. "Darned if I know. First, that Mrs. English calls and upsets last night and makes Ginger cry—and now this. What's next?"

Sabra smiled and picked up her mug. "I don't think they're related in any way, Bart. We certainly don't have anything to do with those cattle or the fact that they're dead."

Bart took a long drink of coffee and got up to go to the kitchen. "And we don't need any problems like that. I hope Mrs. English and her overly imaginative daughter go away and that the sheriff solves his little mystery right away." He picked up Sabra's cup and went to the kitchen.

A short time later, Marcy and Ginger came downstairs, and when their parents asked if they had heard anything during the night, they both said they hadn't. When Curt got up, he gave the same answer.

The weekend passed without further incident, and on Monday morning the children were picked up by the school bus. Bart went to his office earlier than he usually did, and Sabra finished cleaning the downstairs by ten o'clock.

She entered Bart's office and found him looking at a map. "You don't need me for anything right now, do you?"

He looked up. "Why?"

"I thought I would go into town and look around for a chair for the living room. Also I want to talk about having curtains and drapes made with a woman whose drapery shop I saw on Main Street."

"Will you be home for lunch?"

"I might be a little bit later. You fix yourself something. That way I won't feel pressured to get back here at a certain time."

Bart refocused his attention on the map and said, "Have fun."

She turned, walked past the dining room table and picked up her purse. Seconds later, she was backing out of the driveway.

Jim Recton and his crew were hard at work, knocking down the remaining hillside. Sabra smiled to herself. Maybe she should have jogged into Cascade and done her shopping. After all, she wasn't going to bring anything home with her this time. If she found a chair—an antique chair was what she wanted—she could very easily have the chair recovered in an appropriate color before having it delivered. If the woman who made drapes and curtains had the time to work for Sabra, measurements first would have to be made before anything could get started.

Sabra smiled as she drove. It was fun decorating her new home. It wasn't the fanciest house around, but she had felt an affinity to it from the instant she had first laid eyes on it. When she finished with it and the yard was completely landscaped with a small gym, the property would be worth more than the price they had paid for it.

She felt content—not satisfied but content. She doubted if she'd ever feel totally satisfied, but she had learned shortly after leaving the convent that one could be content yet still dissatisfied with any given situation.

The convent. It was strange but she seldom thought of those three years. They had been pleasant enough, working and praying, but there had been a sense of unrest, of being ill-at-ease without being able to pinpoint the cause.

Sabra had thought she had a vocation all through grade school and during her four years of high school as well. She seldom dated. When other girls told her what they did on dates, she found herself being both bored and confused by the varying accounts. Why hadn't she wanted to be with boys?

She had found herself being alone more and more of the time. She had no close friends, and her parents, both set in their ways, never seemed to have time for her. She read a lot and her grades were always good in school. Of course, that gave her parents no reason to chastise her for not working hard. As a result, Sabra had been a lonely child and spent most of the time by herself without ever having found a close friendship with anyone, including her parents.

After announcing her intentions to join the Convent of Perpetual Adoration, her parents had acted as if they were relieved. At the time, Sabra had wondered if their relief was because she would no longer be around to be a concern to them. In the first year at the convent, during which she studied nothing but religion and the lives of the saints, she had baffled her sister advisor the day she walked into the office and asked for a conference. During the meeting Sabra had told the nun that she felt she was special in some way. The older nun had glared at her, accused her of being pompous and self-centered, and advised the young postulant to beg for God's forgiveness. She should be humble. No one was special. Only God could determine who was special and who was not.

Sabra had gone away from the meeting more confused than ever. She suppressed the idea that in some way she was supposed to be special. Still the feeling persisted.

The Curse

Sabra slowed for the business district's 20 miles per hour speed limit and frowned. She had always used the word special, but was that the correct word? Now that she thought about it, special wasn't the correct word. What was the word she should have used? Particular? Distinctive? Peculiar? A smile crossed her lips when she thought of her dreams, nightmares and visions and of being helped by a psychologist. She was certainly peculiar in that regard but that was now, and peculiar wasn't the word to describe how she felt when she was in her early twenties. Whatever the word should have been, the feelings she experienced ultimately convinced her that she did not belong in the convent, and before voicing her final vows, she left the order.

Both her parents had died while she was studying to become a nun, but the strictness of the order prevented her from attending the funerals. One of the first things she did upon leaving the convent was to go to the cemetery and visit the graves of her parents.

She remembered the hollow feeling she experienced when she saw the marker, big enough for all three members of the family. Her name had been etched into the granite along with her date of birth. She had stared for a long time at the space where her date of death would go one day. Her parents had never told her that she was to be buried there. Her skin had crawled at the thought of being dead. She had so much to do with her life now that she was out of the convent. She had no idea as to what her goals might be or what they should be. On occasion, the notion that she was somehow different would enter her mind but, recalling the words of her sister advisor, it was quickly smothered and pushed to the farthest recesses of her mind.

Sabra pulled up in front of the drapery shop and got out. While visiting the seamstress, Janet Manter, she lost herself in the world of window treatments, drapes and curtains. After selecting a pattern in lace that would look good in the living room, she chose others for the dining room and master bedroom. Bart's office would be draped as would the children's bedrooms. Two hours after entering, Sabra left and, noting that it was only 12:20 P.M., decided she had more than enough time to search through some of the antique shops. Bart could fend for himself in the kitchen, finding something for lunch. Sabra wasn't hungry, and any food cravings were satisfied by thoughts of her home being almost finished once Janet came to the house for measurements.

She stood on the sidewalk and glanced about. There were so many shops. Which one should she visit first? The sign for Delmonica's Antiques caught her attention and she crossed the street. She recalled Bart telling her about the stunning redhead who ran the shop where Bart had taken that old kettle. She pursed her lips. She hadn't thought about the kettle since Bart had left it with some retired professor to examine. She wondered about the iron pot and what the writing on the sides meant.

When she pushed open the door, the bell clanged. A musty odor hung over the interior of the shop heralding the age of the contents. Dark forms of furniture loomed out of the shadows, and she found herself gazing at a counter filled with antique jewelry.

"May I help you?"

Sabra jumped at the sound of the woman's voice and turned to find Veloy Delmonica standing a few feet behind her. The woman reached up and pulled a chain, flooding the immediate area with light from an unfrosted 200 watt bulb. Sabra looked up, blinked her eyes at the brightly glowing arc and quickly turned away.

"Yes. I'm looking for a chair. An occasional chair. Do you have anything that might fit that description?"

Veloy smiled and perused her customer, running an appraising eye down Sabra's body and back up again. "Well, I'm not sure if we have what could be called an occasional chair in the store, but we can certainly look. You want something in the Victorian era, I would assume?"

Sabra nodded slowly. If she saw the right piece she'd know it, but she wasn't into the proper terminology of period furniture.

Veloy led her toward the back of the shop and stopped to turn on another light. The furniture that had appeared as lumpy shadows when

Sabra first entered the store took on shape and form with the light glaring from overhead. One chair in particular caught her attention and held it. Dark cherry wood curved gracefully upward from the front of the seat and had intricate roses carved into the legs and at the top of the back. What had been a white-on-white patterned fabric had turned ghostly gray over the years.

"How much is that one?" Sabra asked.

"That's one of a pair. That is the lady's chair, and there's a man's chair that goes with it. They make a lovely setting with a small table between them."

After seeing the second chair, Sabra dickered with the price, and when Veloy lowered her original asking price by 25 percent, Sabra and the owner went to the front of the store to finalize the deal. Veloy would arrange to have it taken to the town's only upholstery shop where Sabra would go once she decided on colors.

"Are you from around here?" Veloy asked while Sabra wrote out a check.

She told the dealer how they had just moved to Cascade and where they lived. When she mentioned Bart's bringing the kettle in for an appraisal, Veloy relaxed and said she remembered. Had they found out what the writing was and what it meant? They chatted for a few more minutes, and when Sabra turned to leave, Veloy said, "You must know about the cattle mystery then. The Gundrys' place is next to your house."

"Yes, we heard," Sabra said, pausing at the door. She turned back to face Veloy. "The sheriff asked if we had heard anything."

Veloy's eyes widened. "Did you? Did you hear anything?"

Sabra shook her head. "No. I almost wish we had."

"You do? Why?" Veloy's full lips stayed parted, displaying her even white teeth.

"Well, the sheriff didn't seem to have anything to go on. If we'd heard something, he'd at least have that much information to work with."

Veloy nodded. "I see what you mean. From what I've heard the sheriff hasn't a clue as to what happened."

They visited for another few minutes before Sabra excused herself. She wanted to get home. She suddenly felt panicky. For what reason, she had no idea. When she sat behind the wheel of the car, she turned over the engine and backed out of the parking place. At the next intersection, she turned right, planning to go around the block and then head for home. When she drove slowly down the quiet back street, she slowed even more when she saw the church off to her left, snuggled against the hillside.

Pulling over, she got out and crossed the street. The little Gothic-style church seemed to beckon to her. Without debating if she should or should not go in, Sabra walked up the concrete steps and pushed on the door. It swung inward on silent hinges.

The smell of furniture polish and stale incense filled her nostrils. A holy quietude held the interior of the church in a gentle, fragile grasp. The decor was simple enough with small framed pictures of the stations of the cross on either long wall. The altar sat back in an alcove-type sacristy. Two statues of angels, each holding a staff with electric lights, knelt on either side of the small altar. She walked along the nave toward the front of the church and stopped short when she saw the paintings on either side of the sacristy. Indians danced around the figures of two men bound to a stake. Fire leaped up around the feet and legs of the two white men, one of whom was dressed in a long, flowing cassock.

Sabra tore her attention from the gruesome depiction and turned to the opposite side of the church. Balancing the first large painting was one of what appeared to be the Roman Colosseum. People tied to stakes were about to be devoured by lions.

She was shocked at the pictures and wondered why Bart or the children hadn't said anything about them after having attended Mass here for two Sundays in a row.

Stunned by the paintings, she sat down in one of the pews and let her mind wander. Her thoughts went back to those memories she had had in the car while driving into town, and her attention slowly moved toward the altar and the figure of the crucified Christ hanging on the cross. She reached for her own crucifix and gently massaged it.

"Why?" she asked quietly. "Why can't I bring myself to attend Mass like my family does?"

The face of Christ seemed to look at her. It was a sad face of Jesus hanging on the cross, dying for all of mankind's sins.

Sabra stared at the face. "Why can't I come to church and pray like my family?" She coughed. She was talking too loudly. Turning in her seat, she found she was alone but resolved not to speak above a whisper if she were going to continue praying.

"I want to come here. You know that, Jesus. I pray the only way I can when I'm at home alone. But I want to come here. Why won't you let me? Are you the one preventing me from coming to Mass? Help me get rid of these visions. They're not natural, and they can't be good. Help me, Jesus. Help me. Please?"

Sabra closed her eyes for a moment and opened them, stifling the scream she felt building in her throat. The flames in the first picture were dancing about and the Indians were moving around their captives, prodding them with lance tips and arrows. The men writhed from the awful pain of the fire but they uttered not a sound. Off in the distance, Sabra could hear the cries and whoops of the Indians as they tortured the men.

Forcing herself to look at the other painting, Sabra half-turned and found the people being devoured by the lions. Huge chunks of flesh were torn from the Christians by the beasts while the people in the gallery seats cheered. Then, as if by magic, the people in both paintings changed and appeared to be the same people she had seen in her visions.

Sabra had to get out of the church as soon as possible. She was going mad. There was no other explanation. She had had no business going into the church in the first place.

She ran down the aisle toward the double doors and threw them open. Without stopping, she ran down the steps toward the station wagon.

When she sat behind the wheel, she was hyperventilating, trying to regain control of her body. Was she actually going mad? Rose Allan had said no. The visions and dreams were not indications that she was losing her mind. But if that were true, then what was going on? Why was she seeing such horrible sights?

She reached down, her hand trembling, and turned the key. The engine roared to life, and she pulled away from the curb. As if seeing it for the first time, she read the sign in front of the church. Church of the Holy Martyrs. She laughed ironically to herself. That explained the horrible paintings.

But it certainly didn't explain her problems. Unless she found out what the matter was with her, she would wind up going stark raving mad.

Chapter Twelve

"Come on," Curt yelled, motioning with his arm toward Nick Tumzer. "What're you waiting for?" He burped, and the uneasy, full feeling he had had for the last few minutes passed.

Nick stood still, unmoving, staring at Curt. He slowly shook his head. Curt retraced his steps toward the reluctant boy. "What's the matter with you?"

"I don't want to. We're not supposed to go off the school grounds during noon hour."

"You're chicken."

"Am not."

"Are, too. You're a fraidy cat."

"I don't want to get in trouble."

Curt stared at him. He wanted to lure Nick off the school grounds and get even with him for lipping off to Curt that morning before classes started. There was no way he would let him get away with that. He smiled at the boy, doing his level best to win his confidence. He felt certain the boy didn't think anything of what he had said to Curt that morning, but Curt wasn't about to let it pass and go unpunished.

Curt smiled again and threw an arm around Nick's shoulder. "How are you going to get into trouble?"

"By going up on the hill with you."

"If I don't get in trouble, how will you get in trouble?"

Nick shrugged his shoulders. "You ever go up there before during noon hour?"

Curt stepped away and said, "Sure. Lots of times."

"And you've never got caught?"

"Not once. They don't check stuff like that."

Nick shook his head, dismayed that Curt had never once been apprehended for going up on the hillside behind school to mess around. "Why is it against the rules then?"

"Because, you dummy, the nuns and the teachers have rules like that to make the parents think they're watching us all the time. They don't care at all what we do during the noon lunch break. C'mon."

Curt took off running for the hill, and after a moment's hesitation, Nick started running in a halfhearted way and then broke into a full run. The two boys started up the steep slope and were quickly swallowed up by the trees and wild shrubs growing on the hillside. They pulled themselves up, grabbing sapling trunks and bushes.

Ginger hurried through the hallway toward her room. She had finished eating and wanted to get a hanky from her desk. Her lunch had tasted good, but suddenly she felt as if she were bloated and thought she might be sick. The sensation passed as she entered her classroom.

After retrieving her handkerchief from her desk, she blew and wiped her nose. She bent down to stuff it back into her desk when something caught her attention. Straightening up, she looked at Mrs. Donner's desk. There, right in the middle of it, stood the teacher's purse.

Ginger slowly walked to the front of the room and stared at the purse for a long moment. Then, quite deliberately, she took it from the desk and opened it. A coin purse drew her attention from the other things inside and she opened it. There was a lot of money inside—a small roll of bills and a lot of change. Emptying the contents of the purse on the desk, she took the change purse and walked down the aisle toward her seat. She stopped three desks away from where she sat and opened it. After dropping the small red pocketbook in, she closed the lid.

Then, skipping from the room, she returned to the playground.

"What are we going to do up here?" Nick asked, stopping to catch his breath when they both stood on a level spot.

"I don't know about you but I'm going to teach you a lesson, smart ass." Curt grabbed Nick by the arm and threw him to the ground.

"What . . . what did I do?"

"You know what you did."

"No, I don't. What'd I do?" Nick's voice rose several pitches, a sense of terror and fear beginning to sweep through him.

"You know what you did, smart ass. You interrupted me when I was talking to Shirley Schrayder. I wanted to meet her up here this noon and fool around. But no. Smart ass here had to open his mouth and start talking about homework. Didn't you, smart ass?"

"Let me up. I'm sorry, Curt. Really I am. I don't want to mess with you."

Curt smiled to himself. It was all right having a reputation as a tough guy. Ever since he'd pounded Joe Gregory in the gym, the fourth, fifth and even most of the sixth grade boys went out of their way to be nice to him.

"Sorry's not good enough. I wanted to play around with Shirley, but you screwed it up, asshole." Curt picked up a fallen tree branch as big as his arm and raised it over his head.

Nick cowered on the ground, raising his arm to fend off the branch in the event Curt carried through the threatening gesture. "Don't. Don't hit me with that, Curt."

"Shut your face," Curt growled and brought the branch down across Nick's arm.

"Yeoww! Stop it. That hurt. Leave me alone." Nick crab-walked backward away from Curt.

"No way, asshole." The branch swung through the air again and caught Nick across the face, ripping open his cheek and smashing into his left eye. Blood sprayed over Nick's shirt.

Nick's cries and sobs were the only sounds in the trees, mixing with the muted but happy voices of the children at play below.

Curt brought the branch around in a full circle again and whacked Nick across the face one more time, breaking his nose. Blood spurted from the nostrils, mixing with the blood pouring from the cheek wound.

Throwing the branch aside, Curt reached down and picked up Nick by the arm, helping him to a standing position. "Now, listen, shitface. You're going to tell Mrs. Casey that you fell down the hill when you came up here alone this noon. Got it?"

"But—but I—I didn't. That would be lying."

"Take your choice, stupid. Tell her that or I'll get you good if you tell her the truth."

"O-okay, Curt. Just don't hurt me anymore. Please?"

"You know, Nick, you prick, I think you may tell her what happened and not tell her that you fell down the hill. Tell you what. I don't want to make you lie. So I'll help you out there."

Without waiting for any sort of reaction, Curt pushed Nick backward. The boy's feet went out from under him and he crashed down the hillside, head first, through the shrubs and bushes.

Curt stood with his hands on his knees, watching the boy fall. When he landed and finally got to his feet, Curt smiled evilly and walked along the hill for a short distance; then he started down. When he reached the playground where his classmates were involved in a game of kitten ball with the fifth and sixth graders, he walked up to the nearest fourth grader and said, "When do I bat?"

The boy looked at Curt and smiled. "You're up next, Curt. Think we'll win?"

Curt shrugged. "I wouldn't be surprised."

Ruth Donner stared at the contents of her purse, strewn over her desk. She picked up a key ring that had fallen to the floor as well as a packet of Kleenex. She glanced up to find her second graders staring at her. She wanted to cry. She wanted to scream. Things like this weren't supposed to happen in the second grade. What sort of little monster would do this?"

Then the absence of the coin purse caught her attention. Where was it? She fumbled through her purse but it wasn't there. She stepped back and looked under the desk. Not there either.

She coughed to clear her throat. "Do any of

you know anything about this?" She gestured toward the open purse.

A uniform shaking of heads gave the room the sudden appearance of waves of water.

"I believe someone took my coin purse that had some money in it. Did anyone see anything? Speak up now before I have to go to the principal's office to report this.

No one spoke.

"Very well, then. Take out your arithmetic workbook."

A flurry of activity followed, and as the lids of the desks were closed one by one, the plopping of the coin purse when it struck the floor sounded like a cannon shot.

A little boy turned and looked on the floor. He started wagging his forefinger at Allison English, who's mouth hung open, her eyes wide, while she stared at the coin purse that had fallen from her desk when she took out her workbook.

"Allison. Come with me." Ruth Donner said and started for the door. "The rest of you start working on page eight. Ginger Narman will act as room monitor until I return."

Sabra swished the dishwater over the last pot. She was tired—physically tired and mentally tired. She was tired of trying to fool her husband into believing that everything was fine. It wasn't. She was tired of having visions or hallucinations or whatever they were. She was tired of not being normal.

She looked up and through the window over the sink. Was that true? Was she not normal? Did other women her age have the same sort of nightmares and delusions? She shook her head. She didn't know. And if she did know, of what possible use could she put it?

A movement and then a noise caught her attention. What was that? She leaned forward and peered to either side of the window. Then she saw Bart. He was riding on the new John Deere yard tractor he had bought Saturday afternoon. The grass was long and needed cutting, and since he was caught up on his work and because she had said she would listen for the phone and the fax machine, he had said he'd cut the lawn that afternoon. She hoped and prayed that no such calls came through. She wasn't sure of herself at that moment, and that was terrible. She should be the most assured person in the world. She had a husband who loved her and three beautiful children who were models of decorum. They had no financial problems, and the house they had just purchased would transform itself, under her guidance, into a comfortable home.

What, then, could be wrong? Sabra felt she might be losing her mind. The incident in the church the day before slammed back into her memory. Could she blame what she thought she saw onto her past problems, or had she actually seen the Indians burning two white men alive and lions devouring Christians in the Roman

Colosseum? Was it any wonder she had had the experience? When she thought about the savagery of the paintings, she wondered why anyone would even want to attend Mass in that place. Had Bart seen them? If he had, why hadn't he commented on them? She wondered the same about her children. They had gone to Mass there as well as Bart, but no one had said a word about the two oils that graced either side of the sacristy.

She emptied the sink and looked up. Had she seen them, or had she merely imagined she saw them?

"Stop it!" she cried out and jumped at the sound of her own voice. She had to stop thinking such things. She *wasn't* losing her mind. She *wasn't* going insane. She was *all right*. Goddamn it! *She was all right.*

Sabra hung up the dish towel and stopped short. Something was wrong. Something was missing. But what? At once, she realized that the new tractor had stopped and that she heard voices approaching the back door. Someone was there. But who? Who could be visiting them on a Tuesday afternoon?

She stepped back when the door opened and Bart walked in followed by Father Paul Wisdom.

"Look who's here, Sabra," Bart said, gesturing behind him at the priest.

Sabra didn't know if she should say hello or wait until Bart introduced them. She decided on the latter approach.

"Honey, this is Father Paul Wisdom. He's pastor of Holy Martyr's Church. Father, this is my wife, Sabra."

Wisdom held out his hand and she slowly took it in her grasp. "How do you do, Father?"

"Well, I'm fine now that we've finally met. I missed you when I stopped out here a week ago Friday."

Sabra had to put on an act when she saw the puzzled look cross Bart's face. She pursed her lips and frowned. She was about to lie—and to a priest—but she couldn't take the risk of arousing Bart's suspicions. Reaching up, she twisted the cross hanging around her neck.

"A week ago Friday?" She looked at Bart, then back to the priest. "It must have been in the afternoon."

The priest nodded. "Yes, it was around 2:30 or so, if I remember correctly."

Sabra looked at Bart again, as if for help, but turned away before he could speak. "You must have gone for the children at school, Bart. I think I went for a walk on the other side of the hill. Was there some special reason you had come by, Father?"

"I was in the neighborhood and thought I'd stop by and meet you. I had met Bart at school the previous day, so I wanted to welcome you to the parish as well."

"That was very thoughtful of you, Father," Sabra said. "Won't you come in?" She motioned in the direction of the dining room and walked toward it. Wisdom followed, and Bart brought up the rear.

Sabra stopped in the dining room and turned to the priest. "Could I get you a cup of coffee, Father? Or tea perhaps?"

"Coffee would be fine, Mrs. Narman. Do you have decaf?"

"As a matter of fact I do. And, Father, please call me Sabra."

"Very well, Sabra."

Bart guided the priest by the arm toward the living room. "We can go in here and wait for Sabra to join us, Father."

The two men were seated when Sabra entered a few minutes later, carrying a tray with three cups and saucers along with sugar and cream. They got to their feet and waited until she had placed the tray on the coffee table.

"Please, sit down," she said, picking up a cup and saucer and handing it to the priest.

When Bart had his, Sabra took the remaining cup, went to the opposite side of the room and sat down in an easy chair.

Father Wisdom smiled after sampling his cup and said, "I haven't seen you in church, Sabra. Have you been ill?"

Sabra felt her face turn red. Was he always so forthright? She placed her coffee on the table next to her. "Not really, Father. I'll come—sometime."

Wisdom fixed his full attention on her. "When?"

Sabra didn't feel embarrassed anymore, but she did suddenly sense that she could get into an argument with this man. And it would be an argument for which she had no words. She couldn't put into words why she didn't want to go to church. "Don't—don't push me, Father."

Wisdom blushed. "I'm sorry. Here I've just met you and I'm starting to push you around. Forgive me?"

Sabra studied him for a moment and concluded the priest was actually sorry for what he had said. He looked not unlike a contrite little boy who had said the wrong thing.

Sabra smiled, hoping the tension she felt would quickly break. "I *will* come though. I like your church. I stopped by yesterday afternoon and made a visit, sort of." She laughed but stopped when she decided it sounded almost phony.

Wisdom smiled. "How does one make a visit—sort of?"

Sabra felt foolish and turned away when she saw a quizzical look on her husband's face. "Well, I haven't gone to Mass in quite some time." She held up one hand. "Don't ask me why, Father, because I have no idea why I haven't gone. I feel close to God, probably closer than most people who are very religious, and I keep his commandments and laws. But for some reason, I simply cannot bring myself to go to Mass on Sundays."

The priest set his cup and saucer on the tray.

"I find that interesting. Go on."

"I had no idea as to where Holy Martyrs was located and was simply going around the block to return home after doing some shopping yesterday. When I saw the church, I had an almost overwhelming urge to see the inside. I went in and—well, to be honestly frank—I couldn't bring myself to pray once I saw those paintings." She felt Bart's gaze, as if it were a tangible thing, touching her, asking her why she hadn't said anything before.

Father Wisdom glanced at Bart and then returned his attention to Sabra. "What paintings?"

Sabra mentally froze. She couldn't go on and tell them what happened. Nor could she describe the paintings. What could she say? From the way Father Wisdom had said, "What paintings?", she knew there were no such things in that church. If she persisted, Bart would have to be told everything that had happened with the visions reoccurring and that might be more than she could handle. It would be best if she tried to bluff her way through the situation.

"The-ah-stations of the cross. They're paintings, aren't they? I didn't go close enough to look."

Wisdom laughed in an embarrassed way. "I don't care much for them either to be honest about it. I wish we had the money to have plaques put there instead. But Holy Martyrs is a poor parish."

"What's wrong with the stations of the cross the way they are?" Bart asked, looking from Sabra to the priest and then back to his wife.

Sabra nodded to the priest. She wanted to hear what he would say first; then she could echo and embroider on his opinion as to the reason why she didn't like them.

"First, they're very faded, and secondly, the artist, whoever the poor untalented person was, did not do a very good job in proportioning the figures. I'm sure they were well-received when first presented and the artist's intentions the very best in the world. But sometimes it's better to leave something alone than it is to push it to the hilt, if you know what I mean."

Sabra nodded, ignoring the confused look on Bart's face. "I majored in art in college, Father, and I agree wholeheartedly with your appraisal. They are in a word—awful."

Bart shook his head. "I'll have to look at these monstrosities next Sunday. I confess that I haven't looked at them that close."

They chatted for a while longer, and when the priest left, Sabra felt relieved that the meeting was over. He hadn't pushed her further than her agreeing to attend Mass in the future, and Bart had seemed affable enough not to have noticed that she almost tipped her hand about the awful paintings she thought she had seen in the church. Actually, she should have known better than to believe a church of any denomination would have such bloody images on the wall to compete with the sufferings of Jesus Christ.

She felt a strange affinity for Father Wisdom and waved as he drove away from their home. She liked what he had said when he stood by his car and looked back at them. "When you're ready to come to church, Sabra, it and I will be there, waiting." He wasn't going to push her anymore. For that she was thankful. But the underlying thing that bothered her the most was his attitude. To her, it seemed that Father Paul Wisdom understood why she wasn't able to attend Mass.

When the children arrived home from school, Sabra was busy in the kitchen. "How was your day?" she asked, turning to greet her offspring.

"Great," Curt said. "I had a lot of fun today."

"Doing what?"

"The usual. You know. We played kitten ball during noon hour, and I hit a home run. Also the work in school was easy today. No problems."

"That's good, son. How about you, Ginger? What did you do today?"

"Everything I was supposed to do." She gave her mother a hug around the waist. "We're learning to play volleyball in gym class." Her face clouded and she turned away.

Sabra caught the sudden shift in mood and reached out for her youngest child. "What's the matter, Ginger? What's wrong?"

Ginger turned back to her mother. "Allison

English got into trouble at school today."

"What happened? You didn't laugh at her, did you?"

"No, Mom. I wouldn't do that. It wouldn't be right. And it wouldn't be nice either, would it?"

Sabra shook her head. "No, it wouldn't. Do you want to tell me what happened?"

Ginger hesitated for a moment and looked at Curt who stood in the dining room doorway, waiting to hear what she was going to say. She turned and saw Marcy watching her, as well. "I guess she stole some money out of Mrs. Donner's purse or something."

"That's a shame," Sabra said. "Don't any of you children ever do anything like that, do you hear me? If you need money for something, you come to your father or me. Understand?"

"Yes, Mom," Curt said and turned to leave.

"Do your homework, Curt."

"I will," he called back from the dining room.

"How about you two? Do you have lots of homework to do?"

"I got some worksheets to do," Ginger said. "They won't take me long."

"I have to have a short story written for English class by Friday. Can you imagine? That Sister Mercy."

"What's wrong?" Sabra asked after Ginger left the room.

"That's not much time, you know."

"Well, you have tonight and Wednesday and

Thursday nights to work on it. How long does it have to be?"

"At least over a thousand words."

"You can do it. I went to school with a boy who's a writer today. William Essex. He used to groan about writing assignments just like you are now, Marcy. Now he's an author. Maybe you'll wind up the same way."

"Sure, Mom, right away. There's a dance Friday night at school. Can I go?"

"What kind of dance?"

"It's a fifties sock hop."

Sabra smiled. She remembered dances like that. She hadn't gone to many, just one or two, but they had been fun. She wanted Marcy to have more fun while going to school than she had had. In some ways, she could blame her parents for that, but in others it was her fault as well. She frowned. It was almost the same situation that she faced when she thought about her inability to go to church. There was no rational reason as to why she couldn't. There had been no reason she could think of then or now that would have kept her from going to the social functions at the school she attended.

"It's not a date affair, is it, Marcy?"

"No. It's a mixer. They have them every other Friday. The B.Y.O. puts them on."

"B.Y.O?"

"Boniface Youth Organization. Can I go, Mom? Please?"

"If it's all right with your father. He'll have to

take you and pick you up."

"Maybe I can get a ride with Brenda and her boyfriend."

"We'll see. Your father still might want to take you and pick you up."

After dinner, Marcy went to her room to begin her short story. At first, her thoughts ricocheted from one subject to another. She doodled on her paper, drawing stick figures and girls' faces. After sketching a dog, she drew an oval, then another linking it to the first, then a third, linking it through the second. After several minutes passed, she stopped drawing and looked at the paper. "Looks like a chain," she said softly.

An hour after Ginger had been tucked into bed, Marcy still had not come up with a solid idea for her assignment. The paper she had doodled on lay off to one side of her desk and she picked it up. The chain held her attention. What was so different about a chain? Not *a* chain but chains. Why did the word "chains" suddenly seem so important?

She crumbled up the paper and threw it in the wastebasket. Staring at the top sheet on her tablet, she moved her pencil to the paper. She wrote one word across the top: *Fire.*

No one in the small town of Jonesville thought for an instant that there would be a fire in their town that clear September night.

The stars twinkled overhead in the cloudless

skies as the tiny town of Cascade settled in for another night.

There was a block where shops lined the street, but the buildings were old and mostly made of wood. A fire in that section of town would wipe out the entire city block. And when the fire started it didn't start in one place only, but the buildings all seemed to burst into flames at once.

A car drove along the main street, its driver heading for home. The roar of motorcycles suddenly split the quiet night as they sped in the opposite direction, passing the motorist and heading toward the highway south of Cascade. After they passed some of the antique shops, a deep silence fell over the business district.

Mary Smith turned over in her bed and suddenly woke up when she heard the sound of fire engines screaming through the night and the voices of many people yelling and shouting outside her home.

Marcy looked at the first page. It didn't read too badly. Perhaps she was onto a good story line. She yawned and counted the words. She had over 100 words already. If she got started earlier tomorrow night, she could maybe finish it and then take Thursday night to work on it and copy it for class the next day. She turned out her desk lamp and went to the bathroom.

The silence that hung over the business district grew deeper and more dense until it engulfed the entire town. When the wood

buildings erupted in flames, the conflagra-
tion happened all at once, and within one
second the entire block was a roaring infer-
no.

Chapter Thirteen

Sabra and Bart got out of the wagon and walked through the crowd toward the smoking ruins of what once had been a city block in Cascade. Bart had gotten up, dressed and driven into town when they had heard the sirens around 11:30 the previous night. Fire departments from Scyhuler Falls and Peasleeville had come to help the Cascade department around 12:30 in the morning, and the fire had been successfully contained within the one block.

Bart had told Sabra what had happened when he returned home a little after 3:00 o'clock. She had sat up, watching the writhing glow on the rim of the hills separating their home from the town. Her first thoughts had been that the fire might jump the hills and threaten if not destroy their home.

After the children left for school on the bus, Bart and Sabra drove into town to see how bad the damage actually was. From the comments they heard as they walked toward the scene of the fire, the whole block was in ruins but nothing else had been burned.

Veloy Delmonica walked toward them, not seeing anything of the people around her.

"Miss Delmonica?" Sabra said, trying to get the woman's attention. Sabra's only interest in the woman's shop at the moment was the two chairs she had bought and paid for, and she wanted to know if they had been sent to the upholsterer or if they had burned in the fire.

Veloy continued walking, not hearing anything.

"Let her go," Bart said. "We can find out later about the chairs. If they're protected by her insurance, we'll get some if not all of our money back. If they aren't . . ." His voice died away as if to say, that's the breaks of the game. He'd have to check with his own insurance man. Perhaps they would be covered by their own policy if the shop had no insurance.

"There's the sheriff," Sabra said, pointing toward Sheriff Pat Haselton.

The tall, lanky man leaned against the wall of Kathy's Kitchen, a small delicatessen, staring at the smoking ruins. People stood around, some talking, most just looking at the blackened city block that lay in ashes.

Sabra and Bart walked over. Perhaps the lawman could tell them what had happened.

"Good morning, Sheriff," Bart said, trying not to sound too cheerful.

Haselton turned and nodded. "Morning." Without another word he turned his attention back to the remains of the fire.

"Did you find out how it started, Sheriff?" Bart asked.

"No, it's too soon. I've got to keep everyone out of there until the state boys show up. They'll want to investigate for arson and so on. I won't know a thing for several days, probably weeks if things are normal."

Sabra thought how ironic it was that he should use the word normal. The first time they had met, he was asking questions about cattle that had been mysteriously slaughtered and partially devoured without leaving a trace of blood or a clue as to who or what might have been responsible. Now, he was investigating a fire that had wiped out an entire city block. Things definitely were not normal around Cascade at the present time.

"It'll keep you busy for a while, right?" Bart asked.

Haselton kicked at a pebble on the sidewalk. "I sure don't need anything else to keep me busy. I'm busy enough as it is."

"What did you find out about the dead cattle?" Bart asked.

Haselton turned and stared at him for a long moment. "Oh, sure, I know who you are now. You folks live next to the Gundrys, right?"

Bart and Sabra nodded.

"That hasn't progressed much at all. I haven't been able to find anybody who might have seen or heard anything that night. The ground's been gone over with a fine tooth comb and there's just nothing to go on. It's the damnedest thing I've ever seen. Now, this."

"Nothing here either?" Bart asked.

Haselton shook his head. "One woman. That's all I've got so far as witnesses go. One woman. And she's not much help either. She lives by herself over the drugstore in the next block. Claims she couldn't sleep last night and got up to get a glass of milk. She looked out and saw nothing, nobody, nothing out of the ordinary. Then, all at one time, the whole block just sort of erupted in flames according to her."

Bart glanced at Sabra, then redirected his attention to the sheriff. "You mean that somebody planted something, some device to start fires in the different buildings all at the same time?"

The lawman shrugged. "I'm not saying anything. I sure as hell don't want to be the one to start rumors around here. No sir. Without any corroborating eyewitness or evidence, I'm not believing anything." He chuckled and turned away.

"Sheriff?" Bart asked, glancing at Sabra. "What's so funny?"

"Oh, nothing. I just thought of what the woman said. Something about the devil starting the fire or some fool thing like that."

"The devil?" Bart waited for him to explain.

"She said she saw the figure of the devil dancing in the flames once the fire got going. A giant figure. I shouldn't laugh, but I've been so damned busy it just seems sort of funny to me. I guess that's what happens when you live alone. You start seeing things and hearing things and all that sort of thing."

Sabra frowned and found her right hand at her throat, twisting the crucifix on the chain. For some reason she didn't seem to think the idea was funny in the least.

"I shouldn't be telling you folks this stuff, you know. It's official business. Still, I can't take my only eyewitness in a serious way when she starts wanting to blame the devil for the fire."

Bart chuckled. "Maybe the devil ate your cattle, too, Sheriff."

Haselton looked at Bart, a serious expression on his face. Then, realizing Bart was merely carrying on with the sheriff's own joke, he started laughing. "I never thought of that." He yawned and stretched. "I hope my deputy gets back here soon. I've been going for over twenty-six hours straight without a wink of sleep. Everything's going to start striking me funny if I don't get some shut-eye soon."

"Well, take care, Sheriff. If you think we can help with anything, feel free to call on us." Bart took Sabra's arm and steered her away from the burnt-out block.

Haselton took off his trooper's hat and scratched his head, watching the couple walk away. Nobody had ever offered to help him before, and the surprise showed on his face.

Sister Nancy Armstrong slammed on the brakes of the Chevette and slid to a stop outside the rectory of Holy Martyrs Church. Leaping from the car, she ran to the front entrance and rang the bell, pounding with her other free hand on the door. Something was wrong. Father Wisdom had called in saying that he wouldn't be able to teach religion class that morning. For some reason, Sister Nancy had thought he had been crying when she took the call. Before she could finish asking, "What's wrong, Father? You sound as if you're crying," he had hung up. Concerned, she had decided to leave school for a few minutes and drive to Holy Martyrs.

She pounded with both fists but still there was no answer. Frustrated, she stepped back and, hands on her hips, pondered her quandry. Something was wrong. Of that much, she was absolutely certain. She glanced at the stone church and saw the fluttering paper on the front door. What was that? Abandoning her post at the front door, she ran to the church to investigate the paper.

Panting, she held the sheet of paper still. Scrawled in large letters were the words: NO MASS THIS MORNING. COME BACK TOMORROW. FR. WISDOM.

Sister Nancy pursed her lips. Of course he could cancel Mass anytime he wanted to or had to for that matter, but the way he had sounded on the phone echoed through her mind. She had to find him. Something was definitely wrong. She was positive now that she had seen the note on the front door of the church. Why had he canceled Mass?

She reached out and tentatively tried opening the door, half-expecting to find it locked. When it swung outward, she entered.

A heavy stench, not the usual furniture polish mixed with stale incense, hung in the air as she walked forward slowly. Then she saw Father Wisdom sitting in the corner in the last pew.

"Father?" She started toward him.

He turned to look at her, and she could tell he definitely had been crying.

"Father, what is it? What's the matter? I told Sister Rita how you sounded on the phone and she agreed I should come over and see what was wrong. What *is* wrong?"

Father Wisdom stood and made a sweeping gesture with his arm at the church and sat down heavily once more. He dropped his head, covering his face with both hands.

For the first time, Sister Nancy realized what the smell was, and a shocked, horrified look crossed her face. Someone had defecated in the church. When she tore her eyes from the priest and looked around the church, her eyes widened and her mouth dropped open. Various shades of brown feces had been smeared on the walls. Huge handprints were dabbed everywhere, and oaths and curses were written in letters several feet high. The walls were covered with blasphemous words to the ceiling line. *"God is dead!"* *"The King is here."* *"Fuck and be happy."* *"Screw Jesus."* *"Hate!"*

"Who-who did this, Father?"

"I have no idea," he said. "When I came to church this morning for Mass, I went to the sacristy entrance as I always do. As soon as I entered, I smelled the stench."

"Why haven't you opened some of the windows?" she asked, crossing to the nearest one.

"I tried but—" He stopped when he saw her reach up.

Nancy stopped. The handles on the window lock were covered with feces. "Get me something and I'll wipe it off."

"It won't do any good, Sister. I tried. I wiped one off but the latches still wouldn't open. I tried others but the same thing happened. The windows are apparently to remain closed."

"What are you going to do?" She looked at the back wall. It, too, was covered.

"I have a call in to the bishop, but he won't be available until sometime this afternoon. I believe he'll simply tell me to have the walls cleaned and try to cover the incident as best we can."

"Who could have done this?" Sister Nancy asked again.

Ignoring her question, the priest said, "Come up here, Sister, and see the rest of the desecration." He started for the front of the church and she followed.

When they stood 15 feet from the front, he pointed to the angels.

She gasped. The angels were standing and holding their light fixtures when they should have been kneeling. The hard penises protruding from the front of each angel grabbed her attention and she stared. "How—? Who—? How could anyone—?" She turned to the priest.

"I know what you're thinking. The statues should be kneeling. If it weren't for the filth involved, one could almost say a miracle had taken place. But . . ." Again, he let his voice die away. He knew the statues, cast in plaster, could not be altered in any way without breaking.

"This is unbelievable."

"There's more," Wisdom said and walked to the wall where the stations of the cross hung along the walls. "Granted, I never liked these pictures because of the sloppy art work, but the fact that they represent our Lord's suffering and crucifixion should override any feelings about they way they are presented. Look." He pointed to the white comic-like balloons coming from the mouths of the figures in the paintings.

Sister Nancy stepped closer to read what had been written in the balloon coming from Veronica's mouth as she held the cloth with which she had wiped the face of Jesus. *"I'll need a good detergent to get this clean."*

She had a difficult time keeping a straight face and didn't turn to the priest.

"I know you're trying to keep from laughing, Sister Nancy," he said kindly. "They're all funny—sacriligiously funny. Look at the next one."

She did as he directed and saw Jesus struggling with the cross. The balloon coming from his mouth carried the words: *"I hate fucking parades!"* She continued along the wall and found the one where Jesus hung from the cross. *"This is a helluva way to start the weekend"* was written in the balloon.

"It's terrible, Father, but not the end of the world."

"You don't find this upsetting?" he asked, his hands shaking.

"Don't be uptight about this, Father. You can't let this get you down."

"I'll be sitting here, guarding all of this until it's time to call the bishop. During that time I will ask myself the same questions over and over. Who could have done this? And why would someone do it? I'll ask them and not have any sort of answer. I have no idea as to what the bishop will have to say about it. And you tell me not to be uptight? I swear, Sister, I don't pretend to understand some of you younger religious people. I just don't."

"You should be more like Father Duane, Father. He'd roll with this like you wouldn't believe. He wouldn't let it get him down. Now that the shock has worn off, I can tell you this much, Father. Whoever did this is a frustrated person who obviously doesn't like churches or religion or Jesus or God or maybe even you for that matter."

"I don't believe that for an instant. Look at the statues. How does a frustrated person take statues that are cast in plaster and change them from kneeling positions to standing positions and not break them? How are penises attached to look as if they were cast there initially without leaving some sort of evidence? Where would a frustrated person who doesn't like me or the Church or God find enough human waste to smear on the walls like that?" His voice rose as his thoughts finally cleared and he addressed the offenses head-on.

Sister Nancy smiled. "Perhaps a coven of devil worshippers passed through town last night. Maybe whoever started the fire last night did this, too. Maybe we have Satanists living right here in Cascade. I don't know." She shrugged.

"I don't believe you're right, Sister. I think it came from the devil himself."

"Oh, get real, Father." Her voice carried an edge of sarcasm. "There is enough real evil in the world without creating some mythical scapegoat to take the blame everytime something happens that is difficult to explain. Does Satan even exist?"

Father Wisdom turned to her and found her frowning deeply, her square face taking on an exaggerated look of anger. "How can you call yourself a religious person? You're no better than the person or thing responsible for this."

She said nothing and turned to walk away, stomping down the center aisle.

"You ask, Sister, if Satan even exists. I say the answer is 'Yes!' He exists, and he exists right here in Cascade, New York. I fear that this is just the beginning of something that will bring about a change in you and those who think like you."

Sister Nancy slammed the door of the church and went to the car. Of course she didn't think like Father Wisdom. She didn't even think like Sister Rita. She and Father Duane, along with the other young nuns at St. Boniface, were more kindred spirits when it came to matters of religion. She and the other sisters, with the exception of Sister Rita, thought more liberally and open-mindedly than did Father Wisdom. He was of the old school, and she and hers were of the newer, more free church.

She recalled the priest's words that echoed through the small church as she had walked out. "He exists, and he exists right here in Cascade, New York." Perhaps they'd be getting a new pastor at Holy Martyrs. To her, it sounded as if Father Wisdom was losing his mind to some degree.

Sabra opened the oven door and checked the pot roast she was making for dinner. Within the hour, the children would arrive home, and she wanted to be finished with everything that she had started that day. Going into town with Bart that morning had set her back by an hour, and she had worked hard to make up for the lost time.

She closed the oven door and stood up. Just then, the telephone rang and she picked it up.

"Hello?"

"Is this the Narman residence?"

"Yes, it is. This is Mrs. Narman." Sabra tried but couldn't place the elderly man's voice.

"Is your husband there. Is Bart there?"

"Yes, he is. Please, hold on. I'll call him."

She placed the phone on the counter and went to Bart's office. "Call for you on the other line," she said, referring to the house phone as opposed to his business telephone.

He punched a button and picked up the receiver. "Hello. This is Bart Narman."

"Mr. Narman? This is Jerry Pendergard."

PART III

THE VOYAGE OF BRENDAN SEPTEMBER 16 TO SEPTEMBER 27

Chapter Fourteen

When Bart entered the kitchen, Sabra turned and faced him. "Who was on the phone?"

"Professor Jerry Pendergard."

"Who?"

"You remember. I took the kettle to him on Veloy Delmonica's suggestion. She seemed to think he would be able to tell us about it."

Sabra looked at him and waited. "Well?" What was Bart trying to do? Be dramatic? Why couldn't he just come out and tell her what the man had said?

"He believes he knows where the kettle came from and who owned it at one time."

Again, when he didn't continue, she waited for a moment and then said, "Go on. Who owned it?

Where did it come from?"

Bart sat down on the kitchen stool and looked at his wife. "He didn't say. Rather, he wouldn't say. He wants us to come to his home Friday evening. He'll tell us then."

"He sounds like you. Build it up for the drama involved. Why does he want both of us to come Friday? I'm a little curious but not that interested."

Bart shrugged. "Darned if I know. All he said was, 'I'll have an interesting story to tell you when you and your wife come here. It's unbelievable and will upset a lot of history.'"

"What does that mean?" Sabra turned to look at her husband again but this time made the effort to truly study him. She found a look of confusion on his face, one with which she wasn't all that familiar. Usually Bart had an air of self-confidence about him, but right at that moment he looked very unsure of himself. "Bart, what is it?"

He looked up at her. "Nothing, really. I guess it was just the way Jerry said that he knew what the kettle was about. He sounded so damned mysterious."

"Maybe that's good. We'll have something to anticipate for Friday evening. That way, when he tells us, we can be disappointed then, instead of now. It would be terrible if we were shocked to find out the kettle or pot or whatever it is worth a lot of money. This way we can expect anything, right?" She smiled broadly, hoping her lighthearted approach would make him smile.

He got off the stool and walked over to her, smiling. "Yeah, maybe it is good." He took her in his arms and kissed her, his tongue caressing the entrance of her mouth.

She enjoyed the kiss, realizing it had been some time since they'd had sex. Maybe this evening, if all went well, they could show each other how much they actually did love one another.

A short time later the school bus stopped at their driveway and the children trooped into the yard and then the house.

"Marcy, do you have much homework?" Sabra asked when her oldest child came into the kitchen last.

"Not really. I have to work on my short story but that's about it. We had time during school to do our other assignments. Why?"

"I'd like to change the bedclothes before supper. I should have done it earlier but the day has been out of synch since the fire last night. Was anything said about it in school?"

Marcy stopped at the dining room door and turned. "Just the usual stuff. I want to change first. Can I?"

"Sure. I'll start in our room. Come in there when you're ready."

"Okay, Mom."

Marcy left the kitchen, and Sabra followed her up the steps. She went to the linen closet and took out fresh sheets for her and Bart's king-size bed. After turning down the bed, she pulled the top sheet off and then loosened the bottom sheet from the top of the mattress. Peeling it off, she tugged to pull it free at the bottom but it wouldn't budge. Believing it might be caught on a mattress button, she lifted the thick pad and gasped.

"My sketch book," she muttered, picking up the large tablet. "Now, who put that here? No wonder I haven't been able to find it." She looked up. That wasn't quite right. She hadn't even thought of it for the past week or so. Out of sight, out of mind? Was that it? Well, she had been busy. But now, she could start sketching all over again.

She lifted the cover and studied the first drawing. It was of the hill as she remembered it before Recton and his gang started cutting into it. It wasn't bad and could serve as a model if she wanted to work on a watercolor of it for old time's sake. It would be nice to have a representation of it hanging someplace in the house. She turned the page.

The second sketch was of their property to the east of their home. It, too, wasn't bad. She smiled and turned the page.

Her smile froze. She tried to turn over the page but couldn't. When had she drawn that picture? Men and women dancing about. One couple lying together, fornicating in the very center, held her attention. The man's penis was greatly exaggerated. Then, down in the lower right hand corner, she saw it. The kettle. The pot that Bart had cleaned up and taken to the professor. When had she done this?

She was almost afraid to turn the page to see if there were any other sketches in the tablet. Slowly lifting the page, as if she might find something she didn't want to know about, she suddenly flipped it over and sucked in her breath. The colorless face staring back at her was not human. It was ugly. Thick jowels and fat lips, drool spilling over them, held her attention for a full minute. She didn't draw that. She couldn't have. She wouldn't have done such a thing. Her line of vision rose to the broad nose with but one nostril and then to the feline eyes that glared hatefully at her. They appeared rheumy and filled with tears.

Sabra stared. Who had done this? She had to destroy it. If Bart or the children found it, they would wonder about her. They might even think she needed Rose Allan again. She tore out the offending picture and held it up. Where could she put it so no one could find it? She'd destroy it when she had the chance.

She took one more look at the picture and gasped. It was coloring itself. The mauve-like complexion came first, and what appeared to be open, weeping pustules formed. The eyes took on a yellowish cast, and the thickened lips turned blood red.

Off in the distance, she heard footsteps approaching the master bedroom. She had to do something. But wha—?

The picture burst into a flash of flame and was gone. No smoke. No smell of burning paper. Just gone.

Quickly turning her attention to the tablet, she looked at the picture of the people and stared wide-eyed as it slowly disappeared from the paper. The second page slowly flipped over and she could see the sketch of their property to the east.

"What have you got there, Mom?" Marcy asked, entering the bedroom.

Sabra jumped at the sound of her daughter's voice. She had to be calm, despite her trip-hammering heart.

"What? Oh, my sketch book."

"May I see it? I didn't know you had started already."

"You can look after we finish changing the bedclothes," Sabra said, forcing herself to sound natural. What had happened to the two pictures? She couldn't recall having done them. And how did the one turn into a colored drawing? And what *was* that awful thing? She shuddered to herself and stepped around to the back of the bed.

Thirty minutes later, when they finished, Sabra went downstairs to check on supper, and Marcy went to her room to work on her short story.

"You haven't mentioned the kettle all evening, Bart. Have you lost interest?" Sabra unhooked her bra and slipped out of it.

Bart looked up, his right leg crossed over the left while he pulled off his sock. "I thought about it once or twice but that didn't do much good. I still wonder why Jerry was so mysterious."

Sabra stepped out of her panties and reached for her dressing gown. Pulling the sash tightly around her waist, she stepped over to the mirror and began brushing her hair. "It sort of reminds me of Christmas. You know. What am I getting? What's in that big package under the tree with my name on it? Will I be getting what I really want?"

"He sure was vague in what he said."

Bart continued talking, but Sabra's thoughts flashed back to the sketch pad she had found under the mattress. When had she put it there? Why would she have hidden it like that? Because of the awful drawings inside? And what had happened to them? The ugly one had disappeared in a flash of fire and didn't leave a trace—no smoke, no smell, no ashes, nothing. How had that happened?

She suddenly felt pressure on her breasts and realized that Bart had come up behind her and was embracing her from the back, caressing her front. She snuggled into his embrace and forgot about the sketches. They were gone, and she was undoubtedly better off without them.

He nibbled on her ear and then kissed it, open-mouthed. Icicles of pleasure shot down her spine when he jammed his tongue into her ear. She turned in his embrace and threw her arms around his neck. She lifted her head and, her blond hair falling back from her face and over her shoulders, offered her mouth to him.

Bart covered it with his, and they swayed back and forth at the dressing table. His hand found her breasts again, and she tingled from excitement as he played with her nipples, teasing them, pinching them. She gasped when he squeezed too hard, and Bart lessened the pressure he had exerted. Sabra dropped her hand, groping for his swollen penis. She squeezed and he moaned.

With one motion, he scooped her into his arms and carried her to the bed and put her down. Untying the sash, he opened her gown and smiled.

Her breasts rose and fell, their nipples standing erect in total arousal. Sabra's groin burned, anticipating her husband's touch, the thrust of his penis. She watched his well-muscled body move effortlessly as he lay down next to her.

Bart hovered over her for a moment. "You are genuinely beautiful, Sabra. Your body is a work of art. And I love . . ." He smiled, a suggestion of what was to come, and straddled her. Leaning down he kissed her full on the mouth, jamming his tongue into her mouth. She lightly chewed on it and then sent her own on an exploratory mission. She could feel the length and hardness of Bart's erection pressing against her stomach. She wanted him and wanted him now but was willing to wait as long as her anticipation continued growing.

He ran his tongue from the corner of her mouth across her cheek and to her ear. He jabbed the opening, breathing hard into it.

The shocks of pleasure that ran down Sabra's body electrically quivered, sending out pulsating waves of lust that she hadn't known for a long time.

Bart continued his tongue exploration, dragging the wet, slippery organ across her throat, pausing to nibble there before trailing down toward her breasts. He chewed on the nipples, and Sabra thrust her hips upward, offering herself to him. Refusing to acknowledge her offer, he jammed his tongue into her navel.

Sabra moaned, unable to control herself. She wanted him, desperately wanted him, wanted his penis inside her body.

When he stopped, Sabra opened her eyes just enough to see what it was he was doing. He was positioning himself to enter her, but her attention was riveted on his swollen penis. It seemed bigger to her for some reason. It looked almost exaggerated. She had seen something like that someplace. Where? The sketch! The one that had disappeared. The fornicating couple centered in the picture—the man's penis had seemed too big. She looked at Bart's penis again. It *was* bigger. She'd never seen it so large. It appeared to be much thicker and—

Bart rammed it into her and she gasped. There

was no doubt about it. The thought of the picture evaporated. The wonder at the size of her husband's penis disappeared, and she wallowed in the pleasure that she felt threatening to tear her lower body apart. He moved it in slowly until he could move it no farther. Then slowly withdrew it.

Sabra moaned again. It had never felt so good.

He slipped back in, faster this time, and quickly withdrew it. Then in again, faster yet, and back out.

The next minute's sensations were exquisite until Bart began moving so fast that Sabra felt the lubrication was gone and the friction was beginning to hurt her. She writhed as her own orgasm built to a climax, and when it exploded all she heard was the strange, gutteral breathing of her husband as he continued thrusting his gigantic penis into her body. When would he climax? She wanted it to be soon. She hurt, but if he finished within the next few seconds, the pain she was experiencing would be nothing compared to the pleasure she had felt.

But Bart continued pumping, faster and faster.

She opened her mouth to ask him to hurry, to tell him that she hurt, but he clamped his mouth over hers, forcing her words back with his tongue. As fast as his hips thrust, his tongue matched the rhythm, and Sabra suddenly felt as if she were being raped.

She wiggled, trying to dislodge Bart, but his

penis seemed locked within her. Throwing her head back and forth, attempting to rid herself of Bart's tongue, she found she was helpless. He held fast.

Sabra opened her eyes and almost choked.

It wasn't Bart!

She stared into the rheumy eyes and wanted to scream but couldn't, not with his tongue in her mouth. Closing her eyes, she clamped her teeth onto the tongue and the slippery, worm-like organ withdrew.

She opened her eyes again and saw Bart, his muscular arms holding her lower body up against his while he finished pumping his seed into her. It *was* Bart, not that awful, ugly thing she had seen in her sketch book! She breathed a sigh of relief. What had made her think of that monstrous drawing at that very moment? True, she had just seen it late that afternoon, but it hardly seemed complimentary to Bart to equate him him such an awful visage.

When he finished, he leaned down and kissed her navel. Lying down next to her, he smiled. "We'll have to do that more often. Moving cuts into our love life too deeply. Agree?"

Sabra wanted to ask him if his tongue hurt but was afraid. He might want to know why she had bitten him. When he slipped his arm under her neck, she snuggled up to him.

"Did you bite my tongue, darling?" he asked.

"Why?" She had to bide time until she knew how to answer. Of course there was no one else there who could have bitten him, but for the time being it would be better to play dumb and then, if she had to, pass it off as unbridled passion.

"It's a little sore. Maybe you sucked too hard."

"The passion of the moment," she said lightly but frowned, knowing he couldn't see her face. She had bitten him hard, very hard in her attempt to get him to pull his tongue from her mouth. And all he could say was that it was a little sore? Maybe she hadn't bitten him as hard as she thought.

Bart's steady breathing was the only sound in the room other than her own. She moved her head and looked up. He was dozing. She snuggled back into his embrace once more and felt safe.

Then she frowned again. Why had she, for that millisecond of time, felt that Bart was raping her? Mentally shaking her head as if to dislodge the troubling thoughts, she closed her own eyes and, despite the lights being on, drifted off to sleep.

By Friday, both Sabra and Bart were almost indifferent concerning the mystery of the kettle, and although they would find out that night, they had resigned themselves to the fact that they wouldn't know anything until Jerry Pendergard was ready to tell them.

After dinner, Marcy hurried to get ready for the sock hop, and Curt and Ginger watched television. At 7:30, Marcy was ready, and Sabra called the two younger children.

"Come on, you two. You're not staying home alone."

"Why can't we?" Curt asked.

"You're not old enough," Sabra said. "Come on."

"When will I be old enough?"

"I'll have to decide that," she said and smiled broadly. Curt wanted to be treated like a teen-ager but still had at least three years to go before she would trust him in the house alone. He was level-headed for a ten-year-old boy but there were certain things that he didn't know yet, and until he did she'd have to treat him like the child he was. She wasn't about to push her offspring into being adults ahead of their time. They'd have the rest of their lives to be grown-up, once they reached some degree of maturity. They'd never be able to return to their childhoods.

Bart backed the station wagon out of the driveway and headed for town. When they reached the school, cars were already parked in the lot and several motorcycles leaned on their kickstands off to one side.

"We'll be back here to pick you up at 10:45," Bart said. "Where will you be?"

"I'll be right here at the front entrance of the school," Marcy said.

"Marcy. Over here," Brenda called.

Marcy turned and waved to her friend. "I'll see you then." She turned and ran toward Brenda and her boyfriend, who leaned against the wall of the school.

"Have fun, honey," Sabra called before Marcy was out of earshot.

Bart pulled the car out of the school driveway and onto the street. The next stop would be at the Pendergard mansion. "I wonder what he's going to tell us," he said, turning to glance at his wife.

Sabra shrugged. "I have no idea." She half-turned in her seat and looked at Curt and Ginger. "Are you two going to be all right while we're inside?"

"We'll be fine," Curt said.

"How long will you be in there?" Ginger asked.

Sabra looked at Bart who shook his head. "I don't know," she said. "It shouldn't be too long. How much can there be for him to tell us about Ginger's kettle?"

"Is that where my kettle is?" the girl asked excitedly.

She hadn't thought of it or mentioned it since Bart had taken it away. "He's been studying it."

"Is it valuable?" Curt asked.

"Will I get a lot of money from him?" Ginger asked.

"Just hold your questions. Your daddy and I don't have any answers yet. That's why we're going to visit with Professor Pendergard. You two be good kids out here in the car, and we'll try to get finished as soon as we can. All right?"

"Okay, Mom," the children chorused.

Moments later, Bart parked the Taurus in the Pendergard driveway and got out. Sabra followed him, and they walked up to the door. She glanced up at the imposing mansion and its tower.

"He didn't say why he wanted me, did he?" she asked when they started up the steps of the porch.

"No. He just said to make certain I bring you along." He reached out and pressed the doorbell.

They heard nothing, but in seconds the door swung open and Jerry Pendergard greeted them.

"Good evening. Come in, come in. I'm so happy to see you. This evening I think will prove to be a momentous occasion."

Sabra entered first, followed by Bart who introduced her to Jerry. They found themselves in a paneled entryway with an open staircase to the second floor. Sabra pictured in her mind the house and the front entrance and knew that the tower extended above this part of the house.

"Let's go into the library," Jerry said, leading them toward a door off to his left.

Sabra marveled at the beauty of the house and felt breathless when she saw the walls of the library, lined with bookshelves on all four sides. One window and one door were the only breaks in the walls. A library table was centered in the room, and five leather-covered chairs were positioned next to reading lamps, all of which were lighted. A desk sat off-center in the room, and its lamp was also on. An ornate light fixture was not illuminated.

Jerry gestured for them to sit down.

"Your home is beautiful, Professor," Sabra said.

"Thank you, but please call me Jerry. Everyone does. My professor days are over. Please be seated."

Once Sabra sat down, Bart and Jerry followed suit.

"Well, now, I suppose you're both wondering what it is I've learned about your kettle. Am I right?"

Both Sabra and Bart nodded.

"In way of preparing you for what I'm about to tell you, I must ask if you have paid much attention over the last few years to the books and programs concerning Christopher Columbus?"

Bart shot a quick look at Sabra and nodded. "We've seen some specials, and I recorded the seven-hour miniseries on PBS last year. Why do you ask?"

"I assume then that you're acquainted with the idea that Columbus was not the first to consider the earth round or that it could be circumnavigated?"

"I guess so," Bart said and caught Sabra nodding as well.

"The Greek mathematician Pythagoras declared the earth round as early as the sixth century B.C. Aristotle wrote of rumors of lands to the west of Europe, and Eratosthenes calculated the circumference of the earth and was amazingly accurate—centuries before Christ."

Sabra frowned, wondering where Jerry might be trying to lead them.

"What I'm trying to establish here is that Columbus had access to the idea that the earth was round. It was not his concept, nor was the idea of circumnavigating the globe. There was a Greek geographer, Strabo, who wrote of attempts to sail around the world as early as seven B.C. Pliny the Elder wrote that oceans surrounded the entire earth, adding that the distance from east to west was that from India to Spain. The Romans had ports in India and more than likely explored the South China Sea."

Bart looked at the old man as if to say, "So?"

"The point I'm making, Bart, Sabra, is that long before Marco Polo, there were many people who were aware of the fact that the earth was round. Columbus had access to their writings and charts and maps. He then made his own and, well, as they say, the rest is history."

Sabra and Bart laughed quietly when Jerry chuckled at his little joke.

"Now, we come to the reason for you two coming here. Have either of you heard of Saint Brendan?"

Bart looked at Sabra who mirrored his own quizzical expression. Both shook their heads.

"Then you've never heard of the *Navagatio Sancti Brendani* either, I assume. Saint Brendan is a Celtic saint who lived in the sixth century of our Lord. There are many legends surrounding his character, but several have such authenticity that it is almost impossible to ignore them."

"Legends?" Bart said.

"According to the *Navagatio Sancti Brendani* or *The Voyage of Saint Brendan*, he, along with a group of monks, sailed across the Atlantic in a leather-covered boat and allegedly landed on the North American continent in the sixth century.

"What?" Sabra and Bart asked together.

"Yes. He kept an account, and the voyage was written about later."

"But how can you be sure that he actually did this?" Bart asked, leaning forward in his seat.

"Granted that there is much, much poetic license in *Navagatio Sancti Brendani*, and there is also the fact that it was written some two hundred years after Brendan's death, both of which are neither here nor there. You see, the work is one of the few truly ancient accounts that exist in Ireland today. In fact, there are fewer than a dozen manuscripts dating from before one thousand A.D., and there is very little extant material written in old Irish. Therefore the author of *The Voyage* must be looked on as having written something that was considered important. Surely he used Brendan's writings as a basis. However, the saint's own words have long since disappeared. The author of *The Voyage* took poetic liberties, or perhaps it was Brendan himself in his own writings who did so, when things were described such as crystal columns that were to be found west of what is believed to have been Greenland. Mountains that smoked and translucent waters wherein fish could be seen in deep water had to have been seen by someone, someplace. I—"

"Excuse me, Jerry," Bart said. "Crystal columns west of Greenland?"

"Icebergs, Bart, icebergs. The smoking mountains could have been a volcano on an island in the Arctic. Certainly the waters off Bermuda and the Bahamas are clear enough to see fish in them. There was fog described at the journey's end that could have been the persistent fog banks off Newfoundland, and a grand and glorious river was written of that could only be the St. Lawrence."

"What does all of this have to do with the kettle?" Bart asked, glancing at Sabra who nodded in a way that said she wondered the same thing.

"Be patient. I'll get to it, but I must lay the groundwork first. You see, I've held with this belief for many years when I taught ancient history. In a way Saint Brendan seemed to be the link between ancient history and modern history. At least he worked as a link for me. I won't go into all the details that strengthen this belief, but one more thing that seems to bear out the history is the fact that Columbus wrote in his log aboard the Santa Maria in 1492 that 'therein lay the Earthly Paradise.' This is the same wording as is found in the *Navagatio Sancti Brendani*.

"Some people believe that Brendan made one

voyage while there is a school that believes he made two. I held to the first theory for years, but now I believe that he made two such voyages."

"How can you be so sure, Jerry?"

"Because of your kettle, Bart."

A dense silence filled the room while the professor's words sank in. Then Bart said, "Our kettle?"

"The writing on the kettle is Latin and tells, at least I believe it's going to tell, a most intriguing story when it is finally translated. You see—"

"I thought you had it translated already," Bart said.

Jerry shook his head. "I'm afraid I've taken some liberty with your property. I've given it to someone who can translate it completely and accurately. He's right here in town, so don't be concerned that the kettle will be lost. If you can't trust Father Wisdom, then . . ." His voice died away as he shrugged.

"That part's all right. We know Father Wisdom. But how do you know so much about the kettle if it isn't translated yet?"

"I did a little of the translation when I concluded that it was indeed Latin. At first, when I saw Brendan's name on the kettle. I knew the writing wasn't Celtic or Old Irish. It makes sense that it could be in Latin if Brendan, a monk at the time, had anything to do with it. At any rate, I saw his name first and almost died of heart failure. Imagine. There I was, holding proof in my own hand that this sainted monk had indeed done what the legends purported he had."

"But what makes you think that he made two voyages?" Sabra asked.

"I'm not completely positive but I believe the kettle will tell us that he did make two such trips. We'll know when Father Wisdom finishes his translation."

"How could they have made it across the ocean in a—what did you call it? A leather-covered boat?" Bart rubbed his hands together, a dubious expression still on his face.

"Actually they were called *curraghs*. The Irish copied the coracle or skin-boat from the Britons and improved it into an efficient and more than seaworthy vessel. They stretched greased hides over a wooden frame. The largest such *curraghs* could hold up to a dozen or more people. They used both oar and sail for propulsion, and there's evidence that such vessels were in use as early as the fifth century A.D. if not before."

"And you're hanging this whole thing on the fact that the voyage is mentioned in the book you told us about?" Bart asked.

"It's also written about in *Vita Sancti Brendani* or *The Life of Saint Brendan*. Both are well-preserved and written by different people. They had to have had access to a common source of knowledge someplace."

"What do you think will be on the kettle, Jerry?" Bart asked.

The octogenarian shook his head. "I have no

idea. I think it might prove that Brendan made two such voyages, but beyond that I have no idea. There were a few words that I managed to make out, but none of it made sense."

"Such as?" Bart stood, walked over to one of the bookcases and examined the titles.

Jerry picked up a piece of paper from the desk. Holding it in the halo of light from the desk lamp, he read: "With iron. Is not. But in. Land. Of Brendan. God. Allow. Set loose. Again. And there's one strange word, *Flar*, but I have no idea as to what it would mean. It seems to be used as a noun. As a result, it may be the name of something or someone."

"Do you have any idea as to when Father Wisdom will be finished? I'm really curious now, too," Bart said. "How about you, Sabra?"

Sabra nodded, reaching up for her crucifix. "I think its extremely intriguing. What will this do to all of the celebrations for next month's five hundredth anniversary of Columbus's discovery?"

"Let's not call it a discovery but a confirmation of the facts available at the time," Jerry said, a twinkle in his eye. "As to the celebrations, let them go on. After all, they'll be commemorating a historical fact, without which none of us would be where we are today. If the translation of the words on the kettle bear out that Brendan was here as early as the sixth century, then he is the one who discovered America. Of course, the Indians who originated from the people who crossed the Bering Straits when it was a land bridge might want the title. What difference does it make as to who was first? The Vikings have a claim. Now Saint Brendan has a solid claim. The aborigines have a claim, but Columbus's exploits are the best recorded."

Sabra stood. "Will you let us know when Father Wisdom finishes?"

"Of course."

Sabra couldn't help sharing the thrill of something as significant as Jerry Pendergard's discovery. Or was it her daughter's discovery? After all, Ginger had found the kettle. Again, did it matter? The very fact that the kettle could be over thirteen hundred or fourteen hundred years old was staggering.

She glanced at the clock above the mantle. It was almost nine o'clock. They'd best get going before Curt and Ginger fell asleep in the car.

They chatted for a few more minutes and then excused themselves. Jerry walked them to the front door.

"I'll let you know as soon as I hear from Father Wisdom," he said as they walked down the front steps.

Once in the car, Sabra tried to explain to the children about the kettle and its historical importance. But they were too tired to comprehend what their parents were saying.

Bart drove while Sabra talked, and when she fell silent there wasn't a sound, other than that of the motor in the wagon.

Chapter
Fifteen

"All right! All right!" the disc jockey's voice boomed over the finishing bars of the Amoebae's latest hit record. "That was *Don't Slash Your Gash* by the Amoebae. You kids havin' fun or what?"

An enthusiastic "Ye-a-a-ah" filled the gymnasium, and the students of Saint Boniface High School clapped their approval in addition.

"Well, okay, okay, I think we're all operating on the same wave length here tonight, kids. Right now, I'm gonna take a little break and you kids do the same. Rest up, 'cause I'm gonna have some of the hottest-hippest-hypiest-and-hooray-for-Grandma-apple-pie-and-the-American-flag records you've ever heard. Now, take ten!"

The Curse

"Thanks for the dance, Marcy. You dance real nice," Toby Whiteman said, trying to sound adult and doing everything in his power to keep from looking directly into Marcy's deep blue eyes.

"You dance good, too, Toby," Marcy said, smiling.

"Could I have the next one?" He reached out and took her hand.

Marcy felt some dampness when they held hands but wasn't certain if it was she or Toby who was most excited. "Maybe. I have to talk to Brenda about something right now. See you 'round." Marcy withdrew her hand from his and turned to walk over to Brenda.

She felt good. She hadn't found it embarrassing to dance with any of the boys, and she certainly liked the last one. Toby was handsome in an almost fragile way, which seemed to contradict his husky build. She hoped he'd ask her again later on, before the dance was over.

"Hey, Marcy," Brenda called from near the refreshment stand.

Marcy walked over and dropped two quarters on the counter. One of the parents who had volunteered to work the soft drinks bar returned in seconds with her order of Pepsi.

"Well, what do you think?"

After slaking her thirst, Marcy looked at her friend and said, "About what?"

"About Toby Whiteman. Hasn't he got the cutest buns?"

Trying to sound sophisticated, Marcy said, "I didn't notice."

"Sure, you didn't notice. His dick is all right, too."

Marcy stared at Brenda. Other than her occasional use of gutter language, Marcy liked Brenda. "How do you know? I thought you went with Herbie full time."

"I do. I do. This was back in seventh grade. I made it look like an accident when I brushed up against him, but I copped a real good feel. It was nicer then than Herbie's is today."

Marcy thought it was terrible that Brenda would have sex with someone she didn't really like as much as she let on, just to have a car to ride in whenever she wanted.

A commotion coming from the direction of the main gym doors caused both girls to look in that direction. A few minutes later, when Herbie walked up to them, Brenda said, "What was going on?"

"Oh, that stupid Chains tried to get in."

"Why wouldn't Father Richards let him in?" Marcy asked.

"He's not a student anymore. Dropped out a year ago." Herbie reached in his pants pocket and withdrew a dollar bill. "Give me a Coke," he said, his voice almost demanding rather than asking.

"Non-students aren't allowed?" Marcy asked.

"Especially him. He really caused trouble here when he attended. Now all he wants to do is sleep all day and ride his bike all night. He's doing grass and other junk along in there some-place." Herbie slipped his arm around Brenda's shoulder.

"Want to go to the rest room, Brenda?" Marcy asked.

"I just was before you came over. I'll wait here."

"Okay," Marcy said. Making her way through the small crowd, she approached the entrance, smiled at Father Richards but said nothing.

When she was in the hallway alone, she looked at the door to the girl's rest room. She really didn't have a need to go in there. Tipping the Pepsi can, she drained it, threw it into a trash receptacle and walked toward the front door. She felt light-headed and her stomach began churning. What was wrong with her? She shook her head and pushed open the doors. The fresh night air washed over her and she could smell rain. Looking up, she saw nothing and assumed the sky was overcast.

"Hey! You! Where you going?"

Marcy turned and saw Chains sitting sideways on his motorcycle. He was alone. She smiled, the memory of their ride through the darkened countryside replaying in her mind. She pictured him in her mind with his shirt off and felt a surge of desire flood through her body. Without speaking to him, she walked down the steps and turned to her right, away from where he sat.

"Hey, where you going?"

She didn't answer. If he didn't have brains enough to want to follow her, then he could go to hell. She smiled when she heard his boots thumping on the brick walkway.

"Not talking to me?"

"I'll talk to you. Is that all you want to do?"

"Christ, no. I want to screw the crap out of you."

They turned the corner of the building and continued walking. In seconds they were in the pitch-black playground that lay between the school and the steep hillside in back.

Marcy stopped and faced Chains. "You really want a fifteen-year-old virgin?"

"Yeah. I want you but I still don't believe you're only fifteen."

Off in the distance, the rumble of thunder rolled through the still night air.

"If we're going to do it," Chains said, "we'd better get on with it or you'll get your pretty little ass all wet." He grabbed her and kissed her roughly on the mouth.

Marcy pushed his tongue from her mouth and forced her own into his. She tore at the black shirt he wore, and when the buttons ripped off, he began fumbling with her blouse.

She shoved him back. "Don't. You don't need that off to fuck my cunt." She could feel him staring at her in the darkness. Her eyes had adjusted enough to make out his features. His face held a disbelieving, flabbergasted expression.

The Curse

Marcy reached out and undid the wide belt buckle that surrounded his waist. He stood there, entranced by the touch of her hands. She pulled his pants down and then tugged on the shorts. When he stood there, naked from the waist down, she balanced herself with a hand on his jacketed shoulders and removed her panties.

"See. You gotta be efficient. Come on." She pulled on his hand and Chains hopped along after her, tethered by his pants around his ankles. When they were next to the grass bordering the blacktopped playground, she sat down and gasped at the coldness of the ground.

Chains plopped down next to her and pushed her back on the grass. He covered her mouth with his for an instant and then raised himself up to get on top of her.

Marcy spread her legs and smiled knowingly when he jammed his penis against her hymen.

"Sonofabitch," he muttered. "You really are a fucking virgin."

"And will be for the rest of my life unless you fuck me, stupid."

Chains rammed at her again and broke through the third time. He moaned and let the full length of his penis slide into Marcy.

Marcy gritted her teeth at the sudden pain but then realized that as sharp as it was it had been just as brief and was gone. She ground her hips against Chain's legs and pelvis. It wasn't going good enough for her. She wanted more. Looking up, she found he had a peculiar half-smile on his thin face. The sonofabitch was interested only in his own gratification.

Well, she also wanted gratification, and she was going to get it.

Marcy reached up and grabbing Chains by the shoulders, wrestled him to the ground and rolled over on top of him. Sitting up, she felt him sink even farther inside her vagina and she began riding him as fast as she could. Strange little whimpering sounds came from Chains, and she closed her eyes, concentrating on her own satisfaction.

Her senses reeled and, deafened by her own sexual needs and demands, she failed to hear the loud clap of thunder directly overhead. Grinding her hips back and forth she felt Chains explode within her. Gravity took over, and the wet, gooey stickiness flowed from her body around his penis to settle in his pubic hair.

She continued pumping unabated, demanding satisfaction from the biker. After a few moments, she felt him withering and dying inside her. He couldn't do that. He must not do that. She hadn't reached her own climax yet.

"Stop. Stop for Chrissake's," Chains groaned after a few minutes. He tried to dislodge Marcy from her dominant position but failed. "Come on, you whore. You're hurting me now. I can't stand it. Let me up."

Marcy backhanded Chains across the face. "Shut up, you premature ejaculating pussy-wimp!" Marcy growled out the words and continued grinding her hips on the biker's withered penis.

"Come on, stop it. I can't stand it," he whimpered. "You're hurting me, for God's sake. Oh, Christ! Let me up. Please?"

When the first drops of rain struck Marcy on the face, she stopped pumping. Standing up, she went over to where she dropped her panties and slipped into them. She turned around and looked at Chains. He still lay on the grass, rolled over on one side, moaning, his legs together.

She laughed. "That'll take care of you for a while, lover boy." Turning she walked back toward the school. When it began raining harder, she ran and, entering the front door, brushed her hair back from her forehead.

Marcy shook her head. Why had she gone outside in the first place? Hurrying up the steps to the first floor, she went directly to the girl's rest room. Her clothes were barely wet, and her hair was only a bit disheveled. After fixing it, she went back to the gym. Maybe Toby Whiteman would ask her to dance again.

Sabra looked up from her book and checked the time. "It's ten-thirty, Bart. You'd best get going."

A loud clap of thunder seemed to punctuate her sentence, and Bart stood up. He stretched and said, "Want to ride along?"

She shook her head. "I don't want to leave Ginger and Curt alone, even if they are sound asleep."

"Right."

The wind whipped around the corner of the house, whining like some lost banshee. "When did it start raining?" he asked. "I must have dozed off."

"I think it just started now. You'd better take an umbrella along. There's no sense in getting wet."

She got up, walked with him to the closet and took out an umbrella, one large enough for two.

"See you in a few minutes," Bart said and stepped outside. Opting not to open the umbrella since it wasn't raining that hard yet, he ran to the car and got in. In seconds, he was out of their yard and driving the short distance into town. He loved living in Cascade. If Marcy were attending her first dance in Yonkers, he would have had to have left almost an hour before it was time to pick her up. He hated the idea of school buses that took kids so far from their homes. Living in Cascade was ideal. Here, he could leave five or ten minutes ahead of time and be any place he wanted with a few minutes to spare.

The rain quickly grew into a torrent of water washing over the Taurus and, despite the windshield wipers going at full speed, he found it almost impossible to see where he was going.

The Curse

He felt as if he were the only person out on the streets. Not a single other car was moving. Well, he had his duty. He'd promised Marcy he'd pick her up at 10:45 and it was almost that now. He turned and drove down the street toward the school.

The street was as black as the inside of the kettle Jerry Pendergard had examined for them. He and Sabra had talked some about their meeting with the octogenarian when they arrived home after the two younger children were in bed. But the conversation had died out quickly since they had no information other than that which Jerry had given them.

Bart was naturally curious as to the meaning of the inscription, but he felt it would only be so much dry rhetoric that someone such as Jerry Pendergard would find exciting. Beyond his own curiosity being satisfied, he felt the small cauldron would hold little in the way of interest for Sabra or himself.

He turned into the driveway of the school and was thankful no one else had yet arrived. He parked in front of the door and turned off the motor. Just then, the sodden figure of a young man dressed in a leather coat came around the corner of the building. He walked with his legs held tightly together and slowly made his way, despite the onslaught of rain, toward a parked motorcycle.

Bart watched him and smiled grimly. That was the one disadvantage of riding a motorcycle.

If it suddenly rained, there was no protection.

The biker revved the motor and roared away from the school.

Bart wondered if the young man was a student at Saint Boniface's. Glancing at the digital clock, he leaned back. Marcy should be out in a few minutes.

Marcy smiled at Toby and said, "Thanks again for the dance, Toby."

"That's all right. Can I call you sometime? Maybe we can talk about homework or something."

"That would be nice." Marcy turned to Brenda who stood nearby and caught a glimpse of the wall clock. "I've got to go. My Dad is picking me up at quarter to. Call me, Toby."

"All right, I will," Toby said, smiling broadly.

"I've got to go, Brenda. My Dad's probably outside waiting for me right now."

"Okay, Marcy. I'll see you in school Monday. Take care."

"Will do," Marcy said over her shoulder and walked toward the wall where jackets and sweaters had been hung up for the evening. She found hers and smiled at Father Richards when she walked out of the gym.

Rain fell in thick sheets and she put her sweater over her head for whatever protection it would give her.

"Hey, Marcy. Wait."

She spun around and saw her father standing near the door with a large umbrella. "Oh, hi, Daddy. I'm glad you brought that. I'm afraid I'd have gotten soaked to the skin if I would've had to run to the car. I really had fun tonight."

"Come on, sweetheart. You can tell me all about the dance in the car."

He opened the door and thrust the umbrella outside, opening it in the same movement. Hugging his oldest daughter to him with his free arm they quickly made their way to the wagon.

On the way home Bart asked, "So, how was the dance?"

"It was a lot of fun. I met the nicest boy—Toby Whiteman."

"Should I be jealous?"

Marcy laughed and snuggled closer to her father, as much for warmth as security. "You don't have to worry yet, Daddy. I'll still be your girl for a few years, I think."

Thunder crashed after lightning broke through the blackness of the night. Sabra stood up and put aside her book. She walked to the big window that overlooked the side yard. Flashes of lightning brightened the night for a few scant seconds before plunging the countryside into raven blackness once more. The wind howled around the house, and she felt as if every spirit in the world were outside crying to be taken into her home. She smiled. She used to think about that when she was a girl. Her parents were too unimaginative to think of a storm as anything other than a storm. On the other hand she would imagine all sorts of things from ghosts to monsters attacking their little home.

She moved to the smaller windows on the other wall and looked out. The grove of trees whipped back and forth under the wet fingers of the wind. Gigantic lightning bolts lit up the blackness of the sky and held for a second or two as a connection was made between clouds and earth. The storm continued building, and she couldn't recall ever experiencing one so violent.

Suddenly, she blanched and her hand flew to her crucifix. The lightning half-outlined something that looked too real to her. It certainly wasn't the product of her imagination. She *had* seen something. But what? What had she seen?

The lightning flashed again, and Sabra held her breath when she saw what looked like a dinosaur beyond the trees. After the lightning abated and the outside was dark once more, she felt she could still see the image of the monster. No matter where she looked she could see it.

When thunder smashed overhead again, she whirled back to the window and stifled the scream she felt building. Not only a dinosaur was there but what appeared to be a dragon, its huge mouth open, belched a tongue of fire, its ugly, evil eyes fixed on the house, on the window, on her.

Transfixed, she wanted desperately to stop looking. All she had to do was pull down the shade, but she couldn't move. Her right hand remained at her throat, her thumb and forefinger grasping the silver crucifix, while her left hand and arm hung uselessly at her side. She wanted to turn away, to run, to hide someplace. Where could she go that that monster wouldn't find her? She tried closing her eyes, shutting out the awful blackness. But just as she did, an explosion of thunder tore her eyes wide open, and the lightning flashes outlined the monsters and the horrible face she'd seen in her sketch pad. The creature stared at her for the longest instant, drool running from its pendulous lips, the rheumy eyes dancing about as if it were laughing at her. A gigantic hand suddenly appeared over the treetops and the devil-like visage motioned for her to come to him.

She shuddered and shook her head. She'd never go near anything like that. The sky went black again, and the next sound, a hard banging, brought her around to face the doorway of the dining room. Someone or something had come into the house. She held her breath. What would she do? She had no way to defend herself.

"Boy, is it raining out there," Bart said, suddenly appearing in the kitchen doorway. "Be glad you didn't go along with me. The umbrella wouldn't have been big enough."

Gathering her befuddled thoughts, Sabra knew she couldn't run the risk of telling Bart what she had been thinking. If she were Curt's age, she could get away with blaming an overly active imagination, but she was an adult, 42 years old, and she was beginning to question her own sanity. Whatever she had seen had to have been a product of her imagination. Things like that simply didn't exist.

Still, she knew she needed something, something from which to draw strength. If it wasn't to be Bart, what would give her the necessary strength to handle her thoughts?

She looked at Bart and said, "I want to go to Mass on Sunday when you go."

Chapter Sixteen

Bart stared at Sabra. "Say that again."

"I said I want to go to Mass with you and the children Sunday. Is that all right?"

"Of course it is. What brought this on?"

Sabra shrugged. "I don't know. I guess I feel that now is the time to make up with God."

Bart shook his head. "Just like that. Well, I'll—" He stopped and stared at his wife for a moment. "Nothing happened while I was gone, did it? I mean—"

"What do you mean, Bart?" Sabra knew full well what he meant. He thought that she had had a vision or something like that. She couldn't tell him that she saw a huge dinosaur and dragon along with the face of some sort of creature motioning to her outside while he was gone. He'd not hesitate a second in calling Rose for advice.

Bart shot a quick glance at Marcy. "You'd better get to bed, honey. It's late."

When they were alone, Bart said, "You know what I mean. Did you have a vision or dream while I was out? Are you going back to the way you were and are afraid of the consequences? Is that what prompted you to say you want to go to Mass with us?"

For an instant, Sabra said nothing. The last thing in the world she wanted to do was lie to her husband. Nor did she want to be adamant and wind up in the same kind of silly argument. She reflected on the images she had seen beyond the trees. She had not experienced a vision; of that she was positive. She knew how the visions began. This one was not like that at all. Nor had she been dreaming. Bart had been gone no more than 20 or 25 minutes, and she had not slept during that time. Consequently, it was not a dream.

She turned to her husband, to find him studying her intensely. "I'm not going back to the way I was—I can assure you of that, Bart—nor did I have a vision. I simply want to go to Mass. Is that such a big deal?"

Bart's shoulders slumped, showing his relief. "I guess it is in one way, if you believe everything the Church teaches. Now, we'll be a family in every respect, even going to church together. On the other hand, it could—"

"Forget your other hand and let's go to bed. I'm exhausted."

Bart smiled and turned out the kitchen light. They went through the living room turning out lamps and pulling shades. After they were upstairs, Bart quickly undressed and got into bed. When Sabra joined him, he propped himself up on his elbow and looked down at her.

"You know I love you very much and would do anything in the world for you."

Sabra looked up at him, puzzled. "I know, darling. What brought that on?"

"It's just that I'm concerned about you and your health and overall welfare. I'd be wiped out if you suddenly started having visions again. You are all right, aren't you?"

Sabra reached up and pulled his head down closer to her. "I love you, Bart Narman, and yes, I'm fine." She kissed him lightly on the mouth.

Bart responded and obviously wanted to make the kiss grow into something more, but the idea of sex wasn't on Sabra's mind.

"Maybe tomorrow night, darling," she murmured and released her hold on his neck.

They said their good nights, and Sabra reached over and turned out her nightstand lamp. She lay on her back, staring into the darkness while Bart turned over, his back toward her.

Picturing the monsters in her mind once more, she shuddered mentally and said a long-unused prayer, asking that she be delivered from any more visions or sights such as the ones she had witnessed that night. She closed her eyes and drifted off to sleep.

After a while, she turned onto her side and fell into a deeper sleep. Her mind, exhausted by the earlier ordeal, refused to be quiet, reaching out to be heard, to arouse her.

At first, when the voice came, she didn't move.

"Sa-a-a-bra-a-a."

The musical voice crying her name made no impact.

"Sa-a-a-bra-a-a."

The sweet tones finally penetrated her sleeping armor and she turned in bed.

"Sa-a-a-bra-a-a?"

She rolled onto her back and opened her eyes. "Who's there?" she whispered hoarsely.

No answer.

"Who's there?"

Still, no answer.

She sat up in bed and reached out to awaken Bart. His side of the bed was empty. Bart was gone.

Bart drove along the quiet, deserted streets of Cascade. He had awakened and gotten up without knowing why. After dressing and leaving the bedroom, he had gone downstairs and out to the wagon, which was still parked in the driveway. He had driven into town and now was slowly prowling the street that ran parallel to Main.

The Curse

He pulled over and parked. After getting out, he looked up at the one lighted window and then searched out the ground-level entrance to the apartment on the second floor.

The steps made no sound as he mounted them, and when he stood in front of what he knew was the entrance to the apartment with the light still burning, he knocked gently.

The door swung open immediately, and the figure of Veloy Delmonica confronted him. She wore a white see-through gown and nothing else. Her flame-red hair flickered in the dim light.

A seductive smile played on her full lips. "I've been waiting for you. Come in."

Bart smiled back and walked into the apartment, the door closing behind him with a quiet click.

Sabra tried to focus her eyes on the alarm clock but couldn't make out the time. Where was Bart? Where could he have gone? She had to get up and find him. Maybe he was ill or something and he might need her help. She tried to get up and shrank back in bed when a resonating crash of thunder rolled directly over their house. The yard lit up, bright as noonday, and she looked out through the window and shrieked. The dinosaur and dragon and the figure of what appeared to be a demon dancing were all in the front yard. She blinked her eyes. It couldn't be real. Things like that didn't exist.

"Bart? Where are you?" she whispered and sobbed.

She reached for the crucifix around her neck and fell back onto the bed.

Sabra opened her eyes and blinked at the bright sunlight streaming in through the windows. She nestled her back into Bart's embrace, and then she suddenly recalled that she'd found his side of the bed empty last night, when she had awakened and—

The dinosaur and the dragon and the—what was it? It almost had looked like the devil. They had been in the front yard and not just shadowy outlines as she had seen them earlier beyond the trees. The brilliant flash of lightning had spotlighted them, and they had had depth and shape and seemed solid. They had *not* been figments of her imagination. But how could she explain something like that? She didn't want to have to explain it to anyone—especially Bart.

And where had Bart gone last night? Maybe to the bathroom or maybe downstairs to get a bite to eat. No. That wouldn't be typical of Bart to snack in the middle of the night. His overall physical condition was very important to him and he seldom if ever did anything that would jeopardize it. She'd ask him. But would that be wise? If she told him she had awakened and found him gone, why had she simply gone back to sleep? Or had she fainted? Why had she awakened in the first place?

The voice. That was it. She had heard the voice again. Had she heard it before? She racked her memory but couldn't think of an instant when she had. No matter. She concluded she'd have even more problems if she asked Bart where he had gone. It would probably be wiser to remain silent.

After the breakfast dishes had been washed, Bart said he and Marcy were going jogging. Curt and Ginger wanted to play indoors after they did their homework, and Sabra announced she was going to the market.

"I'll be back in an hour or so," she said. "Is there anything special any of you want for dinner during the week?"

She jotted down Bart's suggestion of baked salmon and Marcy's of a casserole and cassava. She ignored Curt's suggestion of greasy hamburgers, greasy french fries and malted milks. Ginger had no ideas.

When she found herself driving toward town, Sabra leaned back and smiled. She felt she had made the right decision in not telling Bart about the things she had seen in the yard. Nothing but trouble would have resulted if she had.

Slowing for the 25 mile-an-hour speed limit, she saw people running toward the intersection ahead. Cars lined both sides of the street and, her curiosity aroused, she turned the corner to see what was going on.

When she turned the second corner, she

slammed on the brakes. Hundreds of people milled about in front of Holy Martyrs Church. What could be going on?

Pulling over to the side of the street as best she could, she turned off the motor, got out and stopped a man walking away from the church.

"What's going on?"

Without a word, he turned and pointed up toward the steeple of the church.

Sabra looked up and gasped. The steeple was almost gone. "What happened?"

"Darned if I know, lady."

"Was it struck by lightning?"

He shrugged. "If it was, it's gotta be the cleanest hit in the history of mankind."

"Why do you say that?"

" 'Cause there ain't a splinter of wood on the ground 'tall. No sir. Not even enough for a toothpick."

"But what happened to the steeple?"

"Listen to what I'm sayin', lady. It's gone. Just like somebody snipped it off with a big pair of shears or something." He turned and walked away.

Sabra made her way through the onlookers and finally stood in the front ranks. From where she stood, she thought the steeple looked like it had been sheared off or maybe bitten off.

Bitten off? Good Lord. The dinosaur. The dragon. Were they real? Were they something more than figments of her imagination? Had the monsters she'd seen in their front yard last night come here and done this? She shook her head. She had to be losing her mind to give credence to such wild, fantastic notions.

"Please, people, go home. You aren't helping matters here."

Sabra turned at the sound of the voice and saw Father Wisdom walking along the rows of people, all of whom had their necks craned upward staring at the jagged edge of the remaining steeple. When he saw Sabra he came over.

"Good morning, Sabra."

"Good morning, Father. What in the world happened here?"

"Good question. It was only discovered a while ago."

"What? How could people not have seen it?"

"Quite naturally, I suppose when one stops to think about it. No one looked up."

"I don't understand, Father."

"It's Saturday morning and people sleep late if they don't have early obligations. When I went to the church at six o'clock to open up for Mass, I didn't look up and missed it completely. There aren't that many who attend mass on Saturday morning and none of them looked up."

"Who spotted it first?" Sabra looked beyond the priest at the church and shook her head in wonderment at the fact no one had seen it right away.

"The paper boy. He was delivering around seven-thirty and he saw it first. He knocked at the door and told me, and then he must have spread the word. Bad news seems to travel very fast, especially in a small town."

"I suppose you're right about that, Father."

"Do you have a few minutes, Sabra?"

"A few minutes? What for, Father?"

"I'd like to speak to you in private, if you'll go into the church and wait for me. I think I saw Sheriff Haselton pull up. I want him to get these people away from here, and then I'll be right in." He smiled. "I'll be in just as soon as I talk with the sheriff."

Sabra looked at the church and asked, "Is it safe to go in there? I mean from a structural standpoint."

"There's nothing to worry about, Sabra. We held Mass in there and everyone was all right. Go ahead. You'll be safe in there."

When he turned and walked away, Sabra walked slowly toward the church, her right hand clutching the crucifix around her neck.

The inside of the church was cool and had the same smells of wax and furniture polish mixed with incense which she had detected on her other visit. Without looking at the altar, she sat down in the last pew and slowly looked up. There were no paintings on either side of the altar, and she breathed easier.

Seconds later, the door opened and she saw Father Wisdom. He genuflected and sat down in the pew in front of Sabra. Turning he rested his arm on the back and studied her for several minutes.

Sabra felt ill-at-ease suddenly. Why wasn't he saying anything?

"You have the most unusual color eyes I have ever seen, Sabra. I hope you don't mind me saying that, but one rarely if ever sees blue eyes as pale as yours. They're practically white, aren't they?"

She nodded. He didn't ask her to come in here just to comment on the color of her eyes. "What was it you wanted to talk about with me, Father? By the way, I'll be in church with Bart and the children Sunday. I thought you might like to know."

Wisdom smiled weakly. "That's fine, Sabra. That's fine." He looked away and then said, "Do you know anything about the church being desecrated within the last week or so?"

Sabra gasped. "What?" Her stomach felt as if it had turned over. What did he mean? How could he suspect her of doing something evil toward the church? Because she didn't go to Mass on Sunday and had no valid reason as to why she didn't?

"Father, I have no idea what you mean? Do you mean the steeple?"

Wisdom shook his head. "Of course you don't even know what I'm talking about. Forgive me if you concluded that I thought you might."

"What are you talking about, Father?"

He told her how he had found the church desecrated and vandalized. "The women who regularly clean the church every week helped me clean it up and I swore them to secrecy about the incident," he said. "I only hope that by keeping it quiet, we can eventually find whoever was responsible."

"Why did you think I would know, Father?"

"First, I asked the question all wrong. I guess I thought that you might have heard something that would be helpful to me. I'm sorry if you thought I was under the impression that you might be responsible. I meant nothing like that at all. As to the steeple—well, I think you probably don't know anything about what's going on in Cascade right now."

Before Sabra could answer, the door opened again and Sheriff Pat Haselton walked in.

Excusing himself, Father Wisdom got up and walked over to the lawman.

Sabra felt she shouldn't eavesdrop and closed her mind to the whispered conversation going on a few feet behind her. Fixing her attention on the altar she studied the Gothic lines of the decor. She first tried to figure out why the two statues on either side of the altar might be covered. She shifted to two spire-like extensions behind the altar which gave the impression that the altar had ears.

The extensions slowly shrunk and turned into the rounded ears of the dragon she had seen the previous night. The face formed on the altar and then shifted, melding into that of the ugly demon she had seen in her notebook and again outside during the storm last night.

The Curse

The demon danced in front of the altar and then began defecating on the floor. Scooping it up, he smeared it on the walls of the church. After dirtying the walls, the thing turned its attention to the Stations of the Cross and went through the motions of drawing, holding its face very close to each picture. Suddenly, it turned and looked at Sabra who sat transfixed, her attention riveted to the awful scene.

The demon smiled at her, drool running from his mouth, and motioned for her to come to him. He turned and pointed at the statues of the angels and the covers flew off. The genitals that had been added wiggled up and down and slowly moved in a circle in front of the statues. The demon turned, laughing silently, again motioning for Sabra to come up.

She shuddered. What was going on? Was this a vision, or was it something more threatening? Only once had she felt herself in danger during a vision and that was when the man who had been raping a woman came at her. But this? The thing in front of her suddenly changed and looked like the man who had wanted to rape her.

"No!" she whispered. She didn't want to see him or the demon or the monsters ever again.

The demon reappeared and made a sweeping gesture with one arm.

Sabra suddenly found herself outside and above the church, its steeple intact. It was night and it was raining. The sound of an unearthly roar shook her, and understanding that it wasn't thunder, she turned, not quite knowing what to expect but almost sure of what she would find.

The dinosaur lumbered down the street, looming over everything. While it resembled Tyrannosaurus Rex, it appeared to be three times the size of what she had been led to believe was normal for such a reptile.

The beast paused at the church and turned toward it. Opening its huge mouth, it snapped off the steeple and devoured it. Then the image was gone and she was back inside Holy Martyrs Church.

The demon waved to her and smiled grotesquely, its broken teeth failing to hold back the thick lolling tongue for any length of time. Then the thing faded and disappeared.

Sabra didn't want to respond to the shaking someone was giving her. A warm friendly hand on her shoulder continued to rock her back and forth in a gentle movement.

She didn't want to awaken from whatever it was she was experiencing. If she did, she'd have to tell whoever it was shaking her that she was all right. She was tired of lying and deceiving people—especially Bart. She wasn't all right. Something was wrong.

She wanted to do something different other than awaken. She felt a warmth she had never before experienced embrace her, and she felt safe. She would be safe as long as the warmth was with her. She closed her eyes and settled into a cocoon of security.

Slowly tipping over, she lay in the pew, and Father Wisdom bent down to revive her.

Her eyes fluttered and she attempted to sit up. Wisdom helped her and she looked around. Where was she? The church. Of course. What had happened? She had felt so comfortable, so relaxed. Why had Father Wisdom awakened her? She would have liked to have spent an eternity in that place—wherever it was—because it felt so safe, so comfortable, so absolutely right. For an instant, she wondered if she'd ever go back there. Would she be able to find it again?

"Are you all right, Sabra?" Wisdom leaned down and studied her. "You look a bit on the pale side."

"I . . . I think I'll be all right." Sabra shook her head as if to dislodge the cobwebs that had formed. "What happened?"

"I'm no doctor, but I think you fainted. How do you feel?"

"I feel fine. Really, I do. I fainted?"

"That's what it seemed like to me. Have you ever fainted before?"

Sabra thought for a moment. She couldn't recall a single time she'd even felt as if she might faint let alone actually pass out. Of course, there had been last night when she awakened and found Bart gone. But all of that could have been a dream.

Shaking her head, she said, "No, Father. I wonder what caused it?"

The priest shrugged.

"What was I doing here in the church?"

"I asked you to come in so we could talk for a moment. It had to do with something that had happened in church. Remember?"

Their conversation slowly drifted back, and she nodded.

"I think we'd better talk further on this," she said softly. "Can we go to your house? I think I know what happened to the steeple and who caused the mess in your church a few days ago."

Father Paul Wisdom's eyes widened, and he slowly nodded. Reaching out, he helped Sabra stand, and they walked out of the church together.

Chapter Seventeen

Father Wisdom said nothing while Sabra told him what she had seen in the church minutes before during her vision. When she finished, a thick silence hung over the living room of the rectory where they sat.

After several minutes passed, Wisdom said, "I hope you're not making fun of me or the Church or the awful things that have happened to Holy Martrys recently."

Sabra felt a knot form in her stomach. Why was he doubting her? Why would she lie about something like this? "Father," she said quietly, "I have no reason to lie to you about these things. I'm telling you what it was that I saw.

I believe that what I saw is what happened to your church."

"And you said that it was all a vision. Is that right?" The priest stood and paced back and forth.

Sabra nodded and reached for her crucifix. She rubbed it gently, seeking whatever strength she could derive from it. "You must believe me, Father. There have been times ever since we moved here when I thought I was losing my mind."

"You mentioned someone, a Rose Allan, before. What is she to you?"

"She was my psychologist. She helped me with my problem of visions and dreams. It was her idea that we seek a different place to live." Sabra went on to explain to the priest the incidents that had led up to the decision to move.

Wisdom rubbed his chin and walked across the room, a skeptical expression covering his face. When he reached a table, he turned and half-sat on it. "I find it all very strange, Sabra. You claim to be Catholic but don't attend Mass. And then you—"

"I'm coming tomorrow, Father." Sabra tried to sound normal, but she knew she was somehow running out of time. The expression, "running out of time," gave her pause. Whatever was bothering her had to be recognized and confronted or there would be some awful consequence to pay.

"That's another thing," the priest said and

recrossed the room to take an easy chair opposite Sabra. "What suddenly prompted you to decide to attend Mass?"

"When I saw the monsters in our yard the first time, I suppose. I was alone, and when I saw them I guess I thought I can't handle anymore of this alone, so to speak."

Slowly nodding his head, Wisdom cleared his throat. "Why are you telling me all of this? I'm not qualified to help you mentally. At least not in the way Rose Allan was. When was the last time you went to confession?"

Sabra thought. It had been quite a few years. In fact, she couldn't remember if she had gone to confession since Curt's birth or Ginger's birth. In either case, it was too long. "It's been a terribly long time, Father. Maybe I should go. I—"

"As the old saying goes, 'if there's no pain, it can't hurt.'"

Sabra forced a smile. "Let me do this in my own way, Father. I'll go to Mass tomorrow and then I'll think about confession."

"Very well. Will you answer my question now?"

"Question?"

"Why are you telling me all this?"

Sabra stood, walked over to a window and looked out. Father Wisdom's Camry was parked in the garage, but the door stood wide open. "The visions, the dreams, some feelings I've had—they're suddenly scaring me to death. Everything that's happening to me, what might happen to my family—" She turned to face him. "Father, I need your help and prayers."

Wisdom didn't speak immediately and waited for several seconds before he did. "Do you feel your faithlessness, where your duties as a Catholic are concerned, has anything to do with it? Do you know why you've fallen away from the Church?"

Sabra wrung her hands and returned to the couch where she had been sitting. "That's just it, Father. I feel I love God and Jesus more than I ever have. I seem to sense His love for me. As to why I haven't gone to Church—well, I just can't explain it. In some ways, it bothers me, and in others, the idea of going to Church every Sunday seems so trivial and inconsequential, so unimportant in the scheme of things, that I haven't really thought about it."

"Your answer is anything but enlightening, Sabra. Perhaps God has some sort of grand plan for you, something that none of us, including you, can see right now. If that's the case, I certainly wouldn't interfere. But I am delighted that you are planning to attend Mass in the morning. How does Bart feel about it?"

She told him how her husband had reacted when she made her announcement and how he had suspected that she had had another vision and was scared of it.

"And what about the children? Do they know about any of this?"

"I don't think so. I've never told them and I don't believe Bart has either."

"And how do you feel right now, after telling me all of this?"

Sabra leaned back on the couch and inhaled deeply. "Believe it or not, I feel somewhat relieved. Maybe confession is good for the soul after all." She looked at him and found him smiling broadly. She hadn't really confessed anything of a sinful nature but she did feel somewhat better in having told the priest about her problems.

"Well, I'm going to have to cut this short, Sabra. I have to set up a meeting for Monday night with the church board of directors and several contractors to get the wheels in progress to restore the steeple."

"What are you going to tell them? Will you tell them what I saw in church this morning?"

Wisdom stood and ran a freckled hand through his red hair. "No, I don't think that would be too wise. I'm afraid that would make too complex a kettle of fish."

Sabra got to her feet and started for the door, then stopped and turned. "The kettle. How are you coming with the translation?"

Wisdom's eyes widened. "How do you know about that?"

"Why, the kettle's ours. Our youngest daughter found it while she was playing outside."

Wisdom paled, his voice trembling slightly when he said, "The translation is almost finished. I had no idea that the kettle came from you and Bart."

Picking up on his hesitancy, Sabra looked at him closely. "Father, is something wrong? You seem shocked that Bart and I took it to Jerry Pendergard."

Wisdom put a hand on her shoulder and guided her toward the front entrance. "Something just dawned on me where the translation is concerned. I should be finished with it by Monday or Tuesday, I think. Until then, you'll just have to be patient. Tell you what, Sabra. I'll see you in church." He forced a laugh and opened the door.

"Very well, Father. Good-bye." He closed the door behind her without saying anything else. What had happened to make him change so suddenly? He had been friendly and helpful right up to the point of her asking about the kettle. Then he had changed for some reason.

She recalled how she had reacted when Bart had brought that damned thing into her house. She had almost screamed at him, engulfed in that pervading sense of evil.

Sabra opened the door of the Taurus and got in. A frown crossed her face. If the kettle had caused her to feel like that, why hadn't she sensed the same thing when she came home and found Bart cleaning it in the yard? If the kettle were in Father Wisdom's house while she had been there, why had she felt nothing?

Reaching out, she turned the ignition key and

the motor roared to life. The answer was simple. The kettle had nothing to do with what she had felt.

She pulled away from where she had hurriedly parked and drove down the street without looking at the few stragglers who continued gawking at the bitten-off steeple. She would have to hurry or Bart and the children might worry if she were too late.

An hour later, she drove out of the supermarket parking lot and headed for home.

Sunday morning dawned not unlike a spring day instead of the 20th of September. A few white, puffy clouds populated the azure blue of the sky, and birds chirped their wake-up songs.

Sabra was the first one up and was finished showering when Bart entered the bathroom. Within the hour, the children had gotten up and were dressed for church.

They chatted about nothing in particular until they got to Holy Martyrs Church and Ginger leaned forward across the back of the front seat.

"I'm glad you're going to church with us, Mommy."

"I'm glad, too," Curt added.

Sabra said nothing and took her daughter's proffered hand in hers. She squeezed it and smiled. A lump had risen in her throat, and she thought her voice would crack if she tried to speak.

After they were all outside the car, they took a moment and looked at the remains of the steeple. She had told Bart about the steeple but had not mentioned what had happened inside the church.

They sat about midway up the aisle on the right-hand side of the church. The church seemed to be about half full, if that. She wondered how many masses Father Wisdom celebrated each Sunday. She knew there was one Saturday evening. Maybe the other one would have more people in attendance. Why was she thinking about things like that?

She recalled Father Wisdom had said that Holy Martyrs was a poor parish. She wondered if that meant poor in attendance or money or that poor people were in the majority.

The sanctuary bell rang and the congregation stood. Father Wisdom began the service by leading the people in reading the entrance antiphon. Sabra followed the prayers in one of the missals she found in the book rack attached to the back of the seat in front of them.

When he finished reading the gospel, Father Wisdom held up the book and said, "This is the gospel of the Lord."

"Praise to you, Lord Jesus Christ," the congregation intoned and sat down to receive Father Wisdom's homily.

"There will be no homily today. Instead, I will tell you what will be done concerning the mystery of our missing steeple. The sheriff has no idea as to what might have happened, and neither do I."

The priest's eyes locked momentarily with those of Sabra's when he made his declaration of ignorance where the steeple was involved. Her expression remained unchanged. Of course, he couldn't get up and tell his parishioners that a stray sheep who was returning to the fold told him that an oversized Tyrannasaurus Rex had nipped it off like a tender shoot of grass. One of two things could happen if he did. He'd be locked up in a straitjacket or the people of Holy Martyrs would collectively panic if they happened to believe him.

Sabra mentally smiled to herself. In one way, the thought of the dinosaur, no matter how big, walking down the street and biting off the steeple seemed almost humorous. But how humorous would it be if it actually had happened that way? What else could happen to pro—?

The cattle! The cows that were in the pasture, which abutted their property, had had their heads and parts of their bodies taken. The sheriff had no clue in that case either. There had been no blood or any sign of footsteps. Maybe the footsteps had been there but the lawman failed to recognize them for what they actually were.

She tore her eyes from the pulpit and looked at one of the stations of the cross. If a Tyrannosaurus Rex could walk down the street, unseen and unheard, and bite off a church steeple, the same beast could take on three cows just as easily.

Refocusing her attention on the priest and what he was saying, she listened intently. He continued explaining that there were no clues as to what might have happened to the steeple and that the biggest mystery of all was why there was no debris around the church itself.

"Surely there would be some splinters, some pieces of board or shingles that should have been left behind," he continued. "However, there will be a meeting of our board of directors tomorrow night in the church hall. I have contacted several contractors who will look at the damage tomorrow and give their reports and estimates to repair the damage to the board at the meeting.

"I don't want you to think there is an unsolvable mystery here. While the sheriff has nothing to go on, I happen to believe there is an explanation and that explanation will be uncovered sooner or later. All I'm asking of you, as members of Holy Martyrs, is to be patient. The board and I will do our best to bring all of this to a satisfactory conclusion.

"Please stand for our profession of faith. We believe . . ."

The people stood and prayed along with the priest. Sabra's mind wandered. Would the truth, as she knew it, ever come out for everyone to know? She doubted it. How could it? How could something like that be explained and accepted? It was impossible.

Once the offertory collection was made, Mass continued, proceeding to the most sacred part of the service, the consecration of the host.

Father Wisdom held the host in his hands and said, "Before He was given up to death, a death He freely accepted, He took bread and gave thanks. He broke the bread, gave it to His disciples and said: 'Take this, all of you, and eat it. This is My Body which will be given up for you.' "

The priest held the host up for the congregation to view while the altar boy softly rang a small bell.

A reverent silence fell over the church and Sabra looked up, along with the others.

"Sa-a-bra-a-a?"

She winced when she heard the voice. Where had she heard it before?

"Sa-a-a-bra-a-a?"

Without moving her head, she glanced at the people about her as best she could. No one appeared to have heard anything out of the ordinary. She looked toward the altar again and saw Father Wisdom still holding the host up. Then she swallowed hard and felt her head spin. She could no longer see the host but the image of Christ. The gentility of His face, the softness of His eyes, the serenity of His mouth were fixed on her. Christ smiled and then faded from her view, replaced by the host. Sabra suddenly felt pain in her right thumb and looked down to find she was holding her crucifix so tightly that it was cutting into the flesh of her thumb. The indentation looked not unlike a brand.

The rest of the Mass held Sabra entranced. Had she seen what she thought she'd seen? She had to be going insane. First she saw strange lands and people, then monsters and demons. Now she could claim she had seen Christ. She had to be losing her mind.

Toward the end of Mass, she decided against telling Bart about her vision of Christ. She might possibly tell Father Wisdom one day, when she felt the time was right, but for now it was definitely not right to confide in anyone about it.

When Father Wisdom finished the last prayer of the Mass, he blessed them and finished by saying, "The Mass is ended. Go in the peace of Christ, to love and serve Him and one another."

The people answered, "Thanks be to God."

While they walked out of the church, Sabra decided she felt good. She'd finally come back to Mass with her family but couldn't remember why she had stayed away for so long.

"Well?" Bart asked, when they walked along the sidewalk toward where their car was parked.

"Well, what?" Sabra asked.

"How do you feel?"

"I feel very good. Right now I feel very close to God."

He took her hand in his and squeezed.

The Curse

"Jerry," Father Wisdom called from the altar as the old man was about to leave church. The priest had hurriedly taken off his vestments, knowing that Jerry Pendergard always waited for a few minutes after the service was over before leaving.

"Yes, Father?"

"I have the translation finished. The only problem is I won't be able to meet with you and the Narmans until Tuesday evening. Can you call them and arrange for a meeting to be held at your home Tuesday evening?"

"Of course, Father. What time?"

"Is seven good for you?"

"That'll be fine. About the translation?"

"I don't want to go into it here. I will say this much though. If it is what I think it is, we may have a problem on our hands. A very big problem. Do you still have all the information on Brendan?"

"Yes. I'll have it out if you'll need it."

"That'll be fine, Jerry. I have a call into a friend of mine at the Catholic University in Washington. I should have some additional information to share Tuesday night."

"And you don't want to say what this is all about, Father?"

Father Wisdom looked around the church and then refocused his attention on the old man. "No. You'll find out soon enough, and when you do, you may wind up hating the Narmans for having brought the kettle to you."

"I didn't tell you that the Narmans owned it. Who told you?"

"Apparently you told them that I had it and Mrs. Narman happened to ask how I was coming with the translation."

"I see." Jerry wore an inquisitive mask but said no more. If Father Wisdom wanted to wait until Tuesday evening, then he'd have to wait as well. "Until Tuesday evening then, Father." He smiled and genuflected before turning to leave.

Father Wisdom returned to the sacristy.

When Jerry reached the back of the church, he dipped his finger into the holy water and blessed himself. Pushing open the door, he tried to shake the echoing words of the priest from his mind.

"If it is what I think it is, we may have a problem on our hands. A very big problem."

Chapter Eighteen

Once the children had gone to school and Bart was sequestered in his office, Sabra spent Monday morning cleaning the house. After lunch, she went upstairs to better organize the drawers in her lingerie chest and fell to wondering about the voice she had heard in church the previous morning. It had sounded sweet and mellow. She tried to recall having heard a voice like it before but couldn't think of any instance when she had.

She absently folded and rearranged her slips and nightgowns. When she came to the hosiery drawer, she stopped and went to the window overlooking the hill. Jim Recton's crew had come back that morning and were busy finishing the job of leveling the hill. The broad expanse of land that would open on that side of the house would be much nicer than having the hill mar the landscape.

Suddenly, she fell on her knees, her hands folded in a tight lock, her knuckles turning white from the pressure. "Oh, God, what do you want of me? Tell me so that I may accept your directive and get on with it. Don't make me wonder any longer. I—"

She looked up. What was she saying? Directive? What made her think that God wanted anything of her? She got to her feet and shook her head. She had to be going mad. What other explanation could there be?

Tuesday afternoon, while Sabra was checking Curt's jeans for holes, Bart suddenly burst into the room.

"I've put everything on hold for a few minutes. You don't look very busy." He paused and grinned lasciviously. "I want you."

Sabra looked up, startled. "You what?"

"You heard me. Get your clothes off. I want you right now." He unbuttoned his shirt and opened his trousers. After stepping out of them, he looked at his wife. "Get your goddamned clothes off. I want to fuck you."

Shocked, Sabra glared at her husband. What was wrong with him? He never used gutter language like that. Nor was it like him to shut down the business for a few moments of pleasure

What could be making him do this?

"Get outta your clothes now, or I'll rip 'em off you." He took a step toward her, a threatening expression on his face.

Sabra got to her feet. What was going on? She stepped back defensively and forced a smile. "Can't this wait until tonight?"

"Not on your life. We won't have time tonight. Get 'em off."

Resigned to the fact that they were about to make impromptu love in the middle of the afternoon in their son's bedroom, Sabra reached down and opened her jeans.

"Come on. Hurry up. Kick it into passing gear, for Chrissakes!"

She pulled the T-shirt over her head and fluffed out her hair before taking off her bra. Her breasts jiggled when she unzipped her jeans and quickly got out of them.

"Do you want to do it here?" she asked, pointing toward Curt's bed.

"Of course not. Go to our room. I'll be there in a minute."

Scooping up her clothing, Sabra hurried down the hallway to their bedroom and pulled the bedspread down. Lying back on the bed, she waited.

Why didn't Bart come immediately if he were in such a hurry? She got up and went to Curt's room. It was empty. She looked in the girl's room and found no sign of her husband. The bathroom door stood open and she could see it was deserted. Where had Bart gone?

She returned to the master bedroom and found it as empty as the rest of the upstairs rooms. How could he have walked past their bedroom door, which had been open while she lay on the bed, without her having seen him?

"Very funny," she muttered, pulling on her jeans. After slipping into her bra and pulling on her T-shirt, she went downstairs and could hear Bart talking on the telephone. She eased open the door and heard him saying into the mouthpiece, "No problem, Mr. Schneider. I'll route that shipping and get right back to you. I'll call within the hour and then fax it to you. Good-bye."

He looked up and smiled at Sabra. "Well, well, well. Visiting the slave labor camp today, are we?"

She said nothing. Why wasn't he at least hinting at what he had demanded upstairs a few minutes before?

"How much do you have left to do today?"

She looked at him. "I'm almost finished. Why?"

"I don't want anything to hold us up tonight after we finish eating. The kids can do the dishes and we'll go to Pendergard's home at seven." He turned his chair toward his computer.

What as going on here? Sabra couldn't understand it. A few minutes before he seemed determined to have sex in the afternoon. When they made love it was gentle and reassuring and rewarding, but Bart had come on like a thug upstairs, demanding that she lie down and spread her legs for him that instant.

"Ah, Bart, have you been busy all afternoon?"

"Not just this afternoon—all day." He half-turned to face her.

"You didn't shut down and put everything on hold a little while ago, did you?"

He looked at her as if she'd suddenly lost her mind. "Not when things are going the way they have been today. I don't shut down for anything, you know that. In fact, I almost called you in a while ago. Why do you ask?"

What should she say now? There was some guy upstairs who looked just like you and wanted to screw me? He'd never understand.

She coughed to buy a precious second during which she could think. Then she said, "I thought I heard you come upstairs for something."

Bart shook his head. "Not me. Must have been your boyfriend." He chuckled, turned back to the computer keyboard and entered an order.

Knowing he wouldn't talk to her until he had finished routing Mr. Schneider's request, she turned and left the office, a perplexed and almost helpless expression on her chalk-white face.

The Taurus's headlights cut through the dusk. The time of day made the lights seem unnecessary, but without them the gloom of approaching night seemed all the more imminent. When

Bart pulled up behind Father Wisdom's Camry, the thought that the priest purposely had come early occurred to Sabra. Were the priest and the old man going to make certain their stories jibed? How silly of her to think such things.

They hurried up to the front door and rang the bell. As if he had been keeping an eye open for their arrival, Jerry Pendergard immediately opened the door and greeted them.

"Good evening. Come in, come in. Father Wisdom is already here."

Bart and Sabra walked into the entry way of the mansion and followed their host to the library.

After the Narmans had greeted the priest and everyone had taken a seat, Jerry held up the small cauldron and said, "The inscription is conclusive in one way and inconclusive in others that this was really brought here by Saint Brendan. It seems conclusive that someone buried it here, probably many hundreds of years ago. On the other hand, there is no proof that whoever buried it did so at some time in the far distant past."

Bart sat forward. "Aren't you contradicting yourself, Jerry?"

"I suppose I am in one way or the other. Father, why don't you tell them what you have translated?"

The priest nodded and sat forward. "First, let me say that at the outset the translation seemed just so much nonsense. Now that I've translated it, I'm not certain how the inscription and what it seems to mean ties in with the cauldron or anything. First, let me read to you what the inscription says." He pulled a folded piece of paper from his inside jacket pocket and opened it.

Sabra and Bart sat patiently, waiting for the priest to read the message written on the old kettle.

"All right. Here it is:

'Strike not the cauldron with iron three times for fear he who is not outside but within will be freed. Flar has lain waste to our land and made our people sin grievously against our Lord God Almighty. Flar is he who commands monsters and is held only by the trickery of Brendan. May our Lord God never allow it to be set loose on man again. Only the anointed who, not unlike Brendan, sees with white can conquer Flar.'"

The priest said no more, looking up at the Narmans and Jerry Pendergard.

Sabra found her palms wet, perspiration slowly running down between her breasts and from her armpits. She felt shaky inside and knew that if she had to stand at that instant she would be dizzy and probably faint. What was wrong with her? Had the reading of the translation affected her in some way? To her it sounded like so much gibberish. She made herself turn away from Wisdom when Bart spoke.

"What's all of that mean, Father? I don't understand any of it."

"I'll let Jerry tell you a little about the language involved."

Jerry settled back in his easy chair.

"What Father Wisdom has just read is translated from Latin and was originally spoken or written in Celtic, I believe. The Celts, almost without fail, always spoke in the most oblique of ways. They—"

"Oblique, Jerry?" Bart asked. "I don't understand."

The octogenarian smiled. "You and I, as well as most people who speak different languages, would simply say: 'For fear he who is within will be freed.' The Celts in their roundabout oblique way of saying things have to say more than that. 'For fear he who is *not outside but* within will be freed.' It sounds confusing, and who knows? Maybe that's why they spoke like that—they wanted to confuse. A Celt would know what another Celt was saying, but a foreigner might wind up confused."

"So what we have here then is an English translation of a Latin inscription that began as Celtic writing?" Bart asked, his eyes darting between the old man and the priest.

"Basically, yes," Jerry said.

Bart stood and walked over to the chair in which his wife sat. Sitting down on the arm, he said, "So what does it mean?" He stared first at the priest and then the old man, waiting for an answer.

"I'll be brutally honest with you," Father Wisdom said. "At first I was almost completely in the dark. The other day, when I spoke to Sabra in church, I suddenly realized what the one phrase meant."

Bart glanced down at Sabra. She could feel his eyes on her. She hadn't told him everything she and the priest had talked about. Now she tried to remember what she might have said that would have given the priest a clue as to the meaning of the translation.

"What was that, Father?" Bart asked, a note of suspicion in his voice.

"I will answer that question and any others the two of you might have, but later. First, I must tell you that until I understood that Flar was a proper name and that the use of the name seemed to indicate some sort of demon I had never heard of him. I called a friend of mine who teaches at the Catholic University of America in Washington, D.C., and had him do some research. I finally got an answer yesterday. Flar was written about in ancient scrolls but for some reason did not make it, so to speak, into the Bible or other books concerning devils and demons. About the sixth century A.D. he just seemed to disappear from the face of the earth and the minds of men."

"That's interesting, Father," Jerry said, sitting up to pay strict attention. "How did your friend explain that?"

"He didn't have an explanation. However, this Flar is an exceedingly powerful devil, even more powerful than Lucifer in many ways."

"More powerful than Luc—?" Bart said and stopped. "Are you kidding?"

Wisdom didn't crack a smile. "In no way am I kidding or making light of this, Bart. If it sounds as if I am, I'm sorry. I'm deadly serious about it. This devil controls monsters of bygone times." Wisdom looked at Sabra.

She knew exactly what he meant. The gigantic Tyrannosaurus Rex. The dragon. She'd seen them. But why had she seen them when no one else had? What was going to happen? Were they to be inundated by giant reptiles and beasts from the past?

"What do you mean by monsters, Father?" Bart asked.

"Dragons, griffins, dinosaurs, prehistoric beasts, and—"

"Dinosaurs? Dragons? Come on, Father. This is us you're talking to here, not some impressionable children," Bart said, sarcasm dripping from each word.

Father Wisdom waited to see if Bart was going to continue. When a thick, uncomfortable silence filled the library, the priest cleared his throat and said, "I know all of this sounds preposterous, but let me give you a few examples. Are you acquainted with the Ford Thunderbird logo?"

Bart nodded but said nothing.

The Curse

"That fanciful image of a bird was copied quite closely from the Indians of the southwestern United States. Did you know that?"

Again, Bart nodded and waited.

"The Indians worshipped their Thunderbird god and held it in high esteem and respect. Do you have any idea as to how or where such an idea for an entity or deity like that might have originated?"

This time, Bart shook his head and waited.

"Anthropologists and paleontologists and archeologists have concluded that during severe thunderstorms hillsides would be washed away and the bones of pteranodons and pterodactyls would be exposed in their entirety. Now think about the Ford Thunderbird emblem and the bony outline of one of the flying dinosaurs. Pretty close, aren't they?"

"They certainly are," Jerry said.

"All right, so they look something alike. So what?" Bart asked. "What's that prove?"

"Just that man, American aborigines in this instance, had been exposed to dinosaurs long before scientists ever heard of them. The same might hold true of such fanciful animals as dragons and griffens and what have you."

Bart smiled slyly. "You mean that dinosaurs were introduced to the Indians the way you said and that the Chinese learned about dragons in the same way?"

"Not at all, Bart. Dragons are known universally, not just in the far east. Think of Saint

George and the Dragon. The Chinese, along with the Japanese and the other far eastern races, have always had dragons in their cultures. In the east the dragon is looked on as a symbol of good luck, while in western cultures dragons are thought of as harbringers of evil and bad luck. But, and I must ask you to take this question in a serious way, if dragons are mere figments of man's imagination, why are they so universally known unless there was some type of exposure to such creatures at one time?"

Bart frowned. "Are you saying that dragons existed, and this devil, Flar, is going to bring them back along with dinosaurs and griffins and whatever?"

"I can't answer that one way or the other. I would like to give you one more example of similar mythic beasts that are known in different parts of the world. You know of the Loch Ness Monster, I assume?"

Bart nodded. "I've heard of it and read about it."

"Did you know that there is a very similar beast that is supposed to exist in the waters of Lake Okanagan in British Columbia? The Indians there called it *Ogopogo*. According to the native's drawings of this beast, it resembles quite closely the Loch Ness Monster."

"What are you trying to say, Father?" Bart asked.

"What I'm trying to say, Bart, is that there is conclusive proof that seem to indicate a certain universality of certain myths and legends. The dragon seems to be one of these. That's all."

"All right, then," Bart said, "what about this Flar? You say you've never heard of him."

"That's right. Not until I talked with my friend after he did some research. Beyond the control of monsters, without effort or without the act of possession Flar could make anyone into a sinner and a monster."

"Then, accordingly," Jerry said, "this Flar is quite powerful."

"Flar is very powerful."

Bart leaped up. "I don't believe I'm hearing any of this. It's ridiculous. It's all like a fairy tale."

"It's not a fairy tale, Bart," Father Wisdom said.

Sabra sat up. "Just what is the tie-in? We have a kettle with an inscription and Flar is mentioned. I don't understand the point you're trying to make, Father."

Wisdom turned his attention to Sabra, a look of hopefulness on his face. "For whatever reason Brendan or someone brought the kettle to these shores and buried it in an attempt to keep Flar imprisoned. As the translation of the inscription states: 'Flar has lain waste to our land and made our people sin grievously against our Lord God.'"

"Of course," Jerry said suddenly. "I should have thought of it before. There was much chaos in Northern Ireland or what was to become

Northern Ireland until the eighth century. The Celts brought the old Gaelic language and the iron age with them to that part of the world in the fourth century. There was much fighting, and needless killing went on much of the time until it slowly died out in the eighth century. It could have been the influence of this Flar that caused it. Lawlessness and havoc was the order of the day. Of course, of course."

"You're all nuts if you believe this stuff, you know. The next thing you'll be telling us is that we have to fight Flar and his monsters," Bart said and forced a sardonic laugh.

Father Wisdom turned to him, a sad, laconic look on his face. "Not us, Bart. Your wife."

Chapter Nineteen

A heavy silence pressed in on them until Bart finally broke it.

"I'm not trying to be disrespectful, Father," he said, forcing a little, embarrassed laugh, "but I'll have some of whatever it is your having."

A sense of relief spread over them and all except Sabra seemed to relax.

What did the priest mean by implying that she would have to fight the demon? What kind of nonsense was that? She was no more equipped to do something such as that than she was to perform brain surgery successfully.

"What did you mean by that, Father?" Bart sat straight up and fixed his stare on Father Wisdom. "What did you mean when you said

Sabra will have to fight this devil?"

"I wish it could have been broken to you more gently," Wisdom said, turning to Sabra. "There are other things that must be discussed before we talk of that."

"I want to know *now*, Father," Bart said, standing.

Sabra looked up at her husband. "Bart, please sit down and let Father continue. I'm sure he'll explain himself in due time." Turning to the priest, she said, "You will, won't you, Father?"

He smiled reassuringly and nodded. "Of course, I will."

Bart sat down again and leaned back into the easy chair, his hands gripping the arms until his knuckles turned white. "I really don't like the direction this conversation is taking. I'm not certain now what the hell you're going to say next. But go on. Do it your way. I'll listen."

"Thank you, Bart," Wisdom said. He stood and held up the paper with the translation. "I'd like to decipher the inscription from beginning to end. That way, I think you'll both understand the severity and gravity of everything."

Bart made no move to object, and Sabra looked at the priest with an all-encompassing stare.

"Very well, then," the priest said, running one hand through his hair. "The first phrase: 'Strike not the cauldron with iron three times for fear he who is not outside but within will be freed.' We have to assume that the lid was secured on the kettle when it was found. Was it? Bart? Sabra?"

Bart shot a quick look at Sabra and nodded. "I tried to open it when I found it but with no luck."

"But it's open now. How did you get it open?" Wisdom pointed to the cauldron standing next to Jerry's chair. "Or did you open it, Jerry?"

While the old man shook his head, Bart said, "That happened in a strange way, Father. I was cleaning it up with a hose and brush. The phone rang and I dropped the kettle to run answer it. The call was one I was expecting and was very important. Come to think of it . . ." Bart paused as if replaying in his mind the event as he was describing it. "Yes. I heard the kettle strike something and it made a ringing sound. You know, like metal on metal?"

The two men nodded and waited for him to continue.

"When I came back out, the kettle was open. The lid was just lying there on the ground."

"What had it struck?" the priest asked.

"There was an old boot jack the hose had started to uncover. Yes, that's right. And—Oh, my God. It was a wrought-iron one." He looked at the priest and then at Jerry. " 'Strike not the cauldron with iron three—' But I heard it hit only once. How do you explain that, Father?"

Wisdom puckered his lips in thought. "Perhaps it had been struck twice previously. You said your daughter found it, Sabra?"

Sabra nodded but said nothing. She was listening to everything being said, but none of it made too much sense to her. Yet, for some reason, she felt she was on the threshold of learning something about herself. She had no idea why she felt that. The priest had mentioned that she was to fight Flar, but that seemed ludicrous at best. Still, she could not help but admit to herself that somehow this whole thing was going to center around her.

"There you have it. It was accidental, I'm sure, that the kettle was struck twice before you found it, Bart. It was an unfortunate occurrence that your phone call came when it did. When you dropped it, the lid came off."

"You mean that you believe this demon or devil called Flar was inside the pot?"

Wisdom shrugged. "What else could it mean? ' . . . for fear he who is not outside but within will be freed.' No one else is mentioned in that way other than Flar. Yes, Flar was contained within the cauldron in some way by Saint Brendan. The translation is: 'Flar is he who commands monsters and is held only by the trickery of Brendan.' I wish whoever wrote that had included the trickery Brendan used. It would make me feel a lot more secure."

Bart shook his head. "I know you believe this stuff, Father, and I'll admit that I'm a little apprehensive myself now that I've cooled down. Forgive me for blowing up like that, Father?"

"There's nothing to forgive, Bart. We're not talking about a Sunday walk in the woods here. We're talking about a devil who, according to my friend in Washington, is more powerful than Lucifer. If that be the case, then we may be facing the most powerful demon ever known to man."

Bart stood and crossed the room, before turning to face the two men and his wife again. "Wasn't there something about laying waste to the land?"

"Yes," Wisdom said and held up the paper once more. " 'Flar has lain waste to our land and made our people sin grievously against our Lord God Almighty.' "

"Well," Bart said, smiling at Sabra, "he hasn't started that yet, has he?"

"The church steeple," Wisdom said and turned to Sabra. "Tell him, Sabra."

Sabra told of her experience in Holy Martyrs Church without mentioning that she had a vision as such or had told the priest of her past.

When she finished, she quickly added, "I also thought of the fact that the cattle that had been killed and mutilated in the pasture next to our land might have met the same sort of fate."

"Did you have a vision in church?" Bart asked pointedly.

Sabra slowly nodded. "It's not something I can control, you know. Maybe all of the trouble I've had in the past has something to do with all of this."

"Don't be preposterous, Sabra," Bart said and looked up to find the priest nodding. "What are you agreeing with?"

"With what your wife just said. Remember the last sentence? 'Only the anointed, who not unlike Brendan sees with white, can conquer Flar."

"What does that mean, for crying out loud?"

"Your wife's eyes are most striking, Bart. The irises are practically white, not your ordinary run-of-the mill shade of light blue. Apparently, Saint Brendan had eyes of the same color."

"Now, wait a minute. Why would Sabra have eyes like this dead saint? Just so she can battle this Flar? Come on, Father, who're you kidding?"

"I'm not kidding, to use your word, Bart. I'm dead serious. 'Only the anointed can conquer Flar.' The inscription says so."

"And you believe it?"

"When I consider the church steeple, the cattle and the fire in which someone saw a demon dancing, according to Sheriff Haselton, I know that Flar is at work. For all we know, he's been making people sin as well."

"If he's so damned powerful, why hasn't he done something really big, really stupendous?" Bart asked, failing to control his anger.

"I suspect," Wisdom said, "that he is gaining power by the minute after his long confinement in the cauldron."

Bart clenched his hands into fists. "This whole thing is looney tunes, you know that? Why would Sabra be anointed? What the hell does that mean anyway?"

"Anointed means to have been consecrated by the use of oil. The Anointed is Jesus Christ himself. Someone who is anointed is a consecrated or sacred person."

"And you're saying Sabra is an anointed person?"

Father Wisdom said nothing and merely looked at Bart, then at Sabra, then back to Bart.

"Just when in hell did this take place?" Bart asked.

"Hardly in hell, Bart." Wisdom forced a smile. "If Sabra is truly an anointed person such as Saint Brendan, then she was not anointed by an earthly power but one that came from heaven, from Jesus himself, from God."

"I'm sure because she's anointed was the reason she stayed away from the church for so long. Right, Father? Or have you forgotten that?"

"That's hardly relevant, Bart. I can understand that you're upset with this. It's so out of the ordinary that it seems almost fanciful. Still, if Sabra is an anointed person, and I believe she is, then who are we to question the ways of God? I'm sure there was some reason He had in mind for your wife not attending Mass all that time. You know that old saying: 'The ways of the Lord are mysterious, His wonders to behold.' I feel very strongly that that is what we're witnessing here."

"Let me tell you about my wife, Father. She's had visions and done all sorts of crazy things. Why, she—"

"I know, Bart. She told me."

Bart stopped short and fell silent. He looked at Sabra who nodded almost imperceptibly. "You told him? Why?"

"I had never talked with a priest about it, and it just sort of seemed the right thing to do at the time—especially when I saw in my mind the gigantic dinosaur bite off the steeple of Holy Martyrs."

Bart turned to Father Wisdom. "Well, now that the cat is out of the bag, what do you think of all the visions and dreams?"

"I feel they fit in with what is going on around here."

Bart looked at Jerry Pendergard who had a peculiar expression of disbelief on his face. "Jerry, you've been around longer than any of us. What do you make of all this?"

Jerry coughed and appeared to Sabra as if he didn't want to get involved in the discussion going on between Bart and Father Wisdom.

"I'll only say that, all things considered, I won't argue with any of the points being made by Father Wisdom. The whole situation is out of the ordinary and we can't expect to have ordinary solutions for extraordinary problems. I feel we are faced with an extraordinary problem, even though it hasn't surfaced completely yet."

Bart turned away. "I think I'm the only one here who has his brains in place."

Father Wisdom stood and walked over to Bart. Laying his hand on Bart's shoulder he said, "I want you to think about something for a moment, Bart. Why are you and your family here in Cascade?"

Bart frowned at the strange question. "Here in Cascade? Because—well, because of Sabra, I guess. Rose Allan suggested we make a move, and well, here we are. That isn't so difficult, is it?"

"You're right in saying that that is what brought you here to Cascade, but I asked you why. Why aren't you in Poughkeepsie or Peaseleeville or Buffalo? Why didn't you and Sabra consider any of those towns? Do you know?"

"Well," Bart said, his voice patient but strained, "we had begun going on weekend outings to look over towns. We did the same to Cascade." He turned to Sabra. "Didn't we, honey?"

Sabra looked up at him and frowned. "It wasn't exactly like that, Bart." She got up and walked over to where her husband and the priest stood near Jerry's chair.

"What do you mean?" Bart said, turning to his wife. "Yes, it was."

"No, it wasn't. Remember? We came to a junction in the road after we left the interstate. You were going to go the opposite way, away from Cascade, and I asked you to turn and drive here. At first, none of us liked the town, but then, when we saw our house was for sale, we went through it and made an offer. It was all so quick.

I couldn't even remember what the town looked like until we came back earlier this month."

Bart nodded. "I never once thought about it but you're right. That *is* the way it happened. We just sort of did it all spontaneously."

"That then is why you're here. God more or less directed you to come here for the reason He had in mind all along. If that isn't the answer, how else would you explain your purchasing the home you did whereon was located the very same cauldron, buried by another person who obviously had eyes quite like Sabra's?"

Sabra returned to her chair and sat down heavily. Bart and Father Wisdom did the same. She looked up when they were all seated.

"You know, over the last few days I've asked myself more than once if I were losing my mind. I thought I was going crazy."

"What made you think things like that, hon?" Bart asked.

She explained about the incident earlier that day when she thought Bart had confronted her upstairs. She held back the overtures to have sex but told the rest.

"That must have been Flar at work," Father Wisdom said.

Bart turned to the priest. "What do we do next? I think we should get out of here and away from this Flar. Sabra's undoubtedly in danger."

Wisdom slowly shook his head. "That's not in God's plan, the way I see it. I only wish we had more time, but I feel we don't. If we did, I could go to the bishop and seek his advice, but who knows what will happen when? I'm not certain if there are procedures to follow in this situation or not. I know that in the case of out-and-out demonic possession doctors and psychiatrists must be contacted and the person suspected of being possessed examined very carefully. The examination, especially the psychiatric one, can take weeks. I don't think we have weeks here. Besides, Flar does not possess souls in the same way that Lucifer does, according to my friend—and he's the leading expert in demonology in the world."

"So what are you suggesting, Father?" Bart asked.

Sabra tried to focus on what the priest said but her thoughts raced wildly from dinosaurs to the possessed Bart who had wanted to have sex with her that afternoon. She shuddered at the thought. What about the children? Had they been affected in any way? She recalled the morning when Curt and Ginger had had an argument. That had been completely out of character for them, but to blame a demon named Flar seemed a little bit on the bizarre side.

Sabra settled back in her seat and closed her eyes. As a parent she wanted nothing for her children but safety and success. At that moment, it seemed as if her offspring were headed in that direction.

Her own parents had been passive at best, when it came to raising her. She had been made to stay at home when she wanted to go to social events at school. Her parents had been too strict in their attempts to make her a "good" girl. No wonder she had entered a convent right out of high school. It had been the only way to escape their domination.

At first, the convent had seemed right, but then something began nagging at her, eating at her mind like a cancer. She bore the doubts and questions forming in her mind for almost three years, and then, right before she said her final vows, she had told the Mother Superior that she wanted to leave. The cloistered order was too demanding of her, she had told the nun. She didn't want to serve God in that way. What had made her say those things then? The devil? No. It must have been God putting his plan into action. Maybe the time spent in the convent was to prepare her in some way for whatever lay ahead.

She thought of her refusal to attend Mass. There had never been any reason why she hadn't gone now that she concentrated on it. She loved God. Maybe she was closer to Him right then than she had ever been before in her life. She didn't know.

She settled back farther into the chair. It felt warm and comfortable. Was she so sleepy that she was about to doze off? Her body felt languid, her strength virtually nonexistent. How could she fight a devil feeling as weak as she did at that instant? She felt as if she were slipping away—

away from Bart and Father Wisdom and Jerry Pendergard.

Off in the distance, she could still hear Bart's voice. She loved Bart, but there was something she had to do before their lives would be normal. Had their lives ever been normal? What did she have to do? Something—but what?

A whiteness rose slowly from around her, closing in on her. A vision? Was she going to have a vision now? Not with the others present. Were they close to her? She didn't know, but she didn't want a vision now. The whiteness closed in completely around her, and she relaxed. There was nothing she could do about it.

She tried to move but was unable. The voices were barely audible and seemed to be drifting away from her. Or was she the one who was drifting away? Where was she?

Her head fell to the side, and her hands, which had been gripping the arms of the easy chair, relaxed and went limp as she sunk further and further into a comatose state. She heard what sounded like the clanging of a heavy metal door, and then a nothingness closed in on her until she heard the sound of waves and the voices of men.

"I tell you, Father, it's insanity to think that Sabra would be up to facing this devil. I'm totally against it," Bart said and turned away from the priest.

Jerry stood and patted Bart on the shoulder. "I wish I could help you make a decision. But the way I see it, it isn't your decision to make, Bart."

"Are you siding with Father Wisdom, Jerry?"

The old man nodded and smiled benignly. "I have to go along with what is logical."

"That's just it. This isn't logical. It's sheer madness."

"Perhaps, Bart, we can have this night yet," Father Wisdom said, "to examine the situation. Maybe I can have the time to contact the bishop tomorrow if God sees fit."

"You're going to need a lot more time than that, Father, to convince Sabra and me that what you're proposing is the right thing to do. My God, Father, she's—"

"Father, look at Sabra," Jerry said, pointing a wrinkled hand toward the woman in the easy chair.

The other two men spun around and Bart was the first to move.

"Sabra, what's wrong?" He crouched next to the chair, picking up her hand. He slapped it gently when he saw that she was sleeping deeply.

Father Wisdom went to the far side of the chair and crouched down next to Bart.

"I can't bring her to, Father. What's wrong with her?"

Wisdom picked up her other hand and placed his fingertips on her wrist. After several seconds passed, he looked up. "Her heart is beating at a normal rate. In fact, it's a good strong heartbeat, slow but strong."

"Why won't she wake up?" Bart asked.

Wisdom leaned forward and held his fingertips under her nose. "She's breathing quite steadily as well." The priest studied her closed eyes for a moment. "Her eyes are remaining fixed. No rapid eye movements."

"We should call a doctor," Jerry said.

Bart looked up. "Will you, Jerry? Please?" What difference did it make about demons and devils now? Sabra needed help and needed help desperately. What could be wrong with her?

"Sabra!" Bart called loudly.

No reaction.

Father Wisdom stood up and went to the desk. He returned with a letter opener and knelt down. He looked at Bart. "I want to see if she'll react to a little pain—not much."

"You talk like a doctor, Father."

"I was a good student in Monsignor Gannon's psychology classes. That's all. I never thought I would use it this way."

"What are you going to do?" Bart asked.

"The doctor will be here as soon as he can," Jerry said, returning to stand nearby.

"I want to jab her with the point of this letter opener. I want to see if she'll react." Wisdom held the sharp point of the letter opener over the back of Sabra's left hand and jabbed at her lightly.

No reaction.

He did it again.

Nothing. No reaction of any kind.

"Let's wait until the doctor gets here, Bart," Father Wisdom said. "I think Sabra has entered a comatose state."

A perplexed and worried look crossed Bart's face when the priest's words sunk in. Why would Sabra have gone into a coma?

Chapter Twenty

Sabra was afraid to open her eyes. She felt as if she were in some place other than Jerry Pendergard's library. She could hear men's voices on occasion and the sound of waves. Where were the waves coming from?

When the men's voices began shouting, and to Sabra it sounded as if they were shouting for joy, she forced herself to open her eyes.

She gasped. Below her, floating on what she knew was the Atlantic Ocean, were three oblong boats. They almost appeared to be rubber life rafts. As if on some unspoken command, she zoomed down closer to the crafts.

When she neared the one craft, she took the opportunity to wave to the men aboard. She

341

quickly counted them and then realized that none of the 14 men had acknowledged her salutation. They seemed intent on looking at a flock of birds that flew around their small fleet. The sailors were overjoyed, knowing that the birds meant they were close to land.

"Hello?" she called out.

They ignored her.

"In the boat. Hello. Where are you going?"

Again, there was no sign that they had heard her. Could it be that they didn't hear her? Or that they *couldn't* hear her? She moved in closer and stopped. How was she able to do that? It hadn't dawned on her before but she was hovering in midair without any support.

When she had first opened her eyes, she had seen the craft far below. Then, by merely thinking it, she moved down and took a close look at the one boat. What was going on? Was she—could she be—dead? No, that wasn't likely. She knew nothing of death, but she felt certain that, considering what had been going on in Jerry Pendergard's library, she was most definitely not dead.

But if that weren't the situation, what *was* going on? Who were the men in the—? Of course. She was for some reason witnessing Saint Brendan's voyage to the North American continent. Now that she looked closely, she could see the small boats were made up of animal hides, stretched over a framework. Water beaded on the skins, and she recalled what Jerry had said about the boats in which Brendan would have made his voyage. What had he called them? *Curraghs?*

High above the boats, she watched as the men leaned into the oars, pulling the *curraghs* ahead. Looking to her left, she could see the outline of a land mass. A thrill of excitement shivered through her body. The men would soon see it, but for the moment she felt as if she herself had discovered North America. She knew what the land mass was as well as the purpose of the three boats below. For some reason she could not comprehend, she was being allowed to see what had happened almost 1,500 years ago.

When she looked down, the boats were gone. Where were they? She looked off toward the coast and saw three tiny specks in the vast wasteland of water.

Within the span of a thought, she was immediately over them once more. The men had seen the land and were shouting. She dove toward them and could hear their voices more clearly. Astonished, she realized she could understand what they were saying.

"How long, Brendan?" one shouted above the others.

"We should touch land before the sun leaves for the day."

"Pray God, that we have made it thus far. Our mission is not yet over," a huge man said.

Sabra noted they were, for the most part, all dressed alike. She frowned. She had seen men

dressed like this before but where? Her vision—
the one in which the rape took place. The monks
had come over a hill and had chastised the people for their sinful ways, then had continued on
their journey The men in the boat were dressed
exactly the same as those in her vision.

"We are safe from his evil power as long as
we control him. Do not do anything but pray,
my friend Liam," Brendan said. "The Almighty
Lord God shall protect us on our errand of
salvation."

Sabra watched as they quietly pulled on their
oars, moving the tiny crafts closer to the land.
Off to the north, she could see the mouth of a
large river. She knew that it had to be the Saint
Lawrence River.

When she looked down again, the three
curraghs were gone. Searching for them, she
found nothing on the ocean. Soaring higher to
get a better view of what lay below, she spotted
them already on the Saint Lawrence River. She
smiled. In one way it was like fast-forwarding
a VCR to view certain parts of a recorded program.

She looked to the west and saw the sun balancing on the edge of the horizon. Would the three
boats pull into land for the night, or would they
continue ahead? Certainly they had not had the
opportunity to stop on the ocean. Perhaps they
would continue in the dark.

As if in answer to her unspoken question, the
three boats turned and made their way toward

the shore. When she hovered nearby to see what they were doing, they had already established a fire and campsite. They huddled around the fire and were praying when Sabra grew aware that someone or something was watching them from the confines of the surrounding forest. She peered intently into the gloom of the trees and saw the dark-skinned bodies of aborigines hiding behind trees, spying on the monks.

She held her breath. Would they attack the monks? What if they did, and what if they killed the intruders? What would happen? No, it couldn't happen that way. Brendan had to bury the kettle. The kettle? Where was it? She moved to the boats that sat on the shore and looked inside. In the third boat, she found it. They somehow had to get it to the place where she and Bart and the children lived. How far away was that? She pictured in her mind the upper New York state region and the approximate distance from where they lived to the Saint Lawrence River. They would have to go overland and portage their boats to Lake Champlain.

She went back to where she had seen the natives hiding behind trees. They were gone. Had they left to bring reinforcements so they could attack the party of monks? Would the monks fight? Why wasn't there something she could do to warn Brendan that they were in danger?

Her heart weighted heavily. What was in the future for her? If Brendan failed, maybe she wouldn't have to confront Flar. Still, she knew he must have succeeded because the cauldron was found on their property and it was still in existence and Flar was loose. She would have to fulfill her destiny. She knew that now. There was no way not to face the devil and fight him. She had no choice.

It all seemed so unreal to her. Sabra Narman, devil fighter. Sabra Narman, the anointed one. Sabra Narman, chosen by God. She wasn't prepared for anything like this. At least Brendan had been a monk, a holy man, ordained and anointed by God himself. What was she? Nothing. She was no more prepared to confront and fight a powerful demon like Flar than Bart was prepared to carry and give birth to a child. It was an impossible situation. She couldn't do it. Still she knew she must. It was obviously preordained that she would one day do this.

She settled in for the night and watched the monks sleep and take turns to stand watch and tend the fire.

The next morning, after eating some berries they found, the monks pushed off and continued paddling up the Saint Lawrence River.

Sabra shot up into the sky and hovered, looking down at the earth below. She could see the shortest portage the men would have to face if they were going to wind up on Lake Champlain. Watching something like the burying of the cauldron unfold was depressing to her. Once the kettle was buried in that hill, she knew the die was cast for the future. But what would happen to her in the meantime? She knew she was seeing the things below her and that they had happened some fifteen centuries before. But what was happening to her right at that instant?

She looked down at her body, but was it really her body or was her physical self still back in Jerry Pendergard's library? It must be. She was breaking every known law of physical science ever known to man, and she was paying no price to accomplish her feats. She felt unaffected by flying around. She wasn't the least bit hungry. She could see but not be seen. She would have to be patient and see what lay ahead. For some reason, she did not feel fear. She was anxious but not afraid of what the future might hold for her.

Later that day, Sabra watched the monks pitch a more permanent camp. Hovering in the trees above, she could hear everything being said.

"Liam," Brendan said, "take Timon and two others with you and search to the south. We must find a place where we can secrete the cauldron and keep it from man for the rest of eternity. If you find water that can sustain our *curraghs*, we will carry them and go as far inland as possible."

"Very well, Brendan," the huge man said. "Timon, get two others who can travel fast."

The next day, before the sun rose, the four monks started out. Brendan dispatched others to gather berries and hunt for small game.

Sabra wondered how long it would take the party that went south to find whatever it was they would find and come back to the campsite. A flickering of light distracted her for an instant, then the bush surrounding the campsite suddenly parted and Liam and the others entered the clearing.

They couldn't be back already. Sabra thought for a moment and concluded the flickering she had experienced was actually a passage of time.

"Less than a day's walk without *curraghs*, there is what appears to be another waterway. With the *curraghs*, it will take most of one day."

"You have done well with God's assistance, Liam. On the morrow we shall go that way."

After eating and praying, the monks retired, and Sabra fixed her attention on the shadowy figures of the dark men who had returned to hide among the trees. They did nothing but watch. Perhaps that was all they would do. She certainly hoped so.

She smiled sadly. She knew she was the one who would fight Flar in the end. Was she capable of succeeding or would Flar with his evil power annihilate her? She knew nothing of what might happen. Still, the one thing she did know was that she had no power whatsoever to resist the events that were forming here and would culminate in the future.

The Curse

The next day found Brendan and his entourage making their way across land. By mid-afternoon, they came to the edge of the water. After launching their boats, they began paddling downstream. By nightfall, they reached the edge of a large body of water.

Sabra knew it was Lake Champlain and that the monks would proceed inland and find the spot near her home where they would bury the kettle. A fit of melancholy swept over her. If it could only be some other way—but she knew better.

When Brendan and the others beached their *curraghs*, two monks were left behind to make any necessary repairs on them. They were to gather food for the long voyage home when they finished with the boats. The other monks would go inland, following Brendan to dispose of the cauldron.

Sabra followed, her heart feeling heavier with each step the monks took. When they reached a small valley, Brendan signaled a stop.

"Here," he said, pointing to the ground. "This is the place where God shall not be." The monks went to the trees, came back with branches and began scratching at the ground. Half of them began weaving long grasses and branches together, making containers that were more flat than curved to hold whatever was to be held.

Sabra noted that the natives still hung back in the trees, watching as the monks dug a hole and constructed the mysterious baskets.

When the hole was not progressing the way Brendan wanted, he held up his hand. "We will have to cover it instead of burying it. Are the baskets ready?"

"They are, Brendan," Liam said.

"Then begin." Brendan picked up one of the baskets and walked to where others had loosened the ground by scratching it with branches. Scooping loose dirt onto the woven mat, he picked it up, walked to the cauldron and dumped his load onto it.

Each monk in turn did the same, and they worked the rest of the day. When the sun went down, they had built a small mound five feet high. Making camp, they ate a meager meal, prayed and retired.

Sabra watched the natives in the trees fall back and disappear. She knew they'd return the next day.

The aborigines did return and continued to do so each day. For the better part of the next three weeks. Sabra watched the monks resolutely build the mound over the kettle that had long since disappeared from view that first day. The mound required the monks to climb to the top in some instances while at other times the loads were planted at the base. The hill continued to grow. She suddenly recalled what the landscape man had said about not finding very many rocks when he and his men were demolishing the hill behind the house. Brendan and his monks mostly had built the hill with dirt to cover the cauldron.

Sabra shook her head. She didn't think it possible but she had actually witnessed it happening. The men had moved about 1,200 pounds of dirt each trip, and they made four trips in an hour. The monks worked over 12 hours a day and had been at it for ten days. Sabra did some quick mental math. There were over half a million pounds of dirt in the hill covering the kettle.

On the eleventh day, Brendan knelt at the base of the hill he and his men had built and prayed. "Oh, Lord God Almighty, keep this mound untouched and keep imprisoned the devil, Flar. He has done enough to your people. Keep him here for the rest of eternity. Let no man uncover his prison—ever."

The monks stood and followed Brendan as he walked toward the trees. They passed within 15 feet of the natives but failed to see them as they slowly made their way back to the lake shore.

Sabra held her breath for fear that either the monks would see the hiding men or the aborigines would attack. But Brendan and the monks passed on without incident, and then Sabra saw the natives file from the trees and walk toward the mound. The mat baskets still lay where the monks had discarded them, once their work was finished.

The leader, a tall, angular man, leaned down and picked up one of the mats. He folded it in two as he had seen the monks do and then walked toward one of the places where the monks had gathered earth. The rest of his men did the same, and they began carrying dirt to heap onto the hill that to them had become a sacred spot.

Sabra watched and wondered. Could this have been where the mound-building Indians of North America got their initial inspiration?

She followed Brendan and the others back to the lake shore. They launched their boats and paddled northward.

Sabra shot up into the clouds and hovered. What should she do? Why was she still here? Hadn't she seen everything she was supposed to see? Where were Bart and Father Wisdom and Jerry Pendergard? Were they concerned about her? That was a stupid question. Of course they'd be concerned as to her safety and well-being. But what was actually going on? Was she in some sort of trance? Was Bart trying to bring her back to consciousness? Would they have called a doctor? What was she to do?

She was surprised by a sudden stabbing pain in her arm. It had felt almost like a bee sting, but there were no bees in the clouds where she hovered.

She felt tears well in her eyes. Where did she turn now? She didn't want to fight some devil, but she knew she was going to have to whether she wanted to or not.

She wiped away a tear.

"Sa-a-abra-a-a?"

The Curse

Sabra looked around in jerky movements. Who had called her? She had heard that voice before. But where? In her dreams? In one of her visions? In—? Church! Of course. She had heard it just last Sunday when she went to Mass with Bart and the children. She had heard it during the elevation of the Host, when she had seen Jesus' face.

The sweet, mellifluous voice called to her again. *"Sa-a-abra-a-a?"*

"Who's there?" she asked timidly. "Who's calling me?"

The voice called once more. *"Sa-a-a-bra-a-a? Come to me."*

The clouds disappeared and were replaced with a seething whiteness that engulfed Sabra. She felt herself being transported someplace—but where? And to whom?

Chapter
Twenty-one

While Sabra could not see anything passing by, she nevertheless felt as if she were moving at tremendous speed. After several seconds, the sensation of motion stopped and she knew she was standing still. But where was she?

She looked around and at first was unable to discern anything other than a brilliant whiteness that surrounded her. Then, little by little, her surroundings took shape. She stood in what appeared to be a small alcove of some sort. Three walls were solid and had writing in bas-relief, a writing she did not recognize. The fourth wall was open. She suddenly became aware that the other three walls had disappeared and she was enveloped in the seething whitness of clouds once more.

For some reason, she felt compelled to walk, but where would she walk in what was nothing more than a white fog? She could see nothing. She could hear nothing. Her footsteps made no sound. When she concentrated on her breathing, she couldn't even hear that, much less her own heartbeat. It was as though she were in a vacuum, cut off from all human endeavor.

Shadows began forming in the folds of the clouds surrounding her, and she stopped short. The shadows now were taking on form—human form. There were two of them off to one side. She peered intently but felt that whenever she was about to focus on them, they would slither out of shape and become something else.

She moved forward and slowly approached the shadows. They wiggled and moved about, as if by doing so they would not be recognized. When she stood within five feet of the forms, Sabra reached out and said, "Who are you?"

The forms stopped moving and slowly took on the definite shapes of a man and a woman. The last things to clear were their faces. Slowly taking on the countenance of an older man and an older woman, the shapes stepped forward and stopped, facing her.

They opened their eyes and Sabra felt tears forming in hers. "Mommy? Daddy?"

The man and woman nodded, the movement barely perceptible.

"Mommy? Daddy? Where is this place? Where am I? Where are you?"

Her mother made a slow, sweeping gesture with her left arm. "It is where we are. On the other side. We are on the other side."

Sabra swallowed and almost choked. "The other—? Am I—am I dead, Mommy?"

Her father reached out to her but did not touch her. "No, Sabra, you are not dead. You are only here temporarily. You will go back. You must go back. Your work is not finished."

"My work? You know about—?"

"We know everything now," her mother said. "Can you find it in your heart to forgive us, your father and me?"

"Forgive you? I don't understand."

"Forgive us for the way in which we treated you while you were growing up," her father said, pulling back his hand.

Sabra reflected on the years of her childhood. Neither of her parents had been overly demonstrative in showing their love for her. When she had reached her teens and was going to high school, they had held on to her, refusing to let her associate with others her own age. For years she had felt socially inadequate. For that reason she had welcomed the hard life of sacrifice and prayer she had encountered in the cloistered convent. There, she had to have no social skills, to speak of, no ability to carry on an intelligent conversation, no need for interaction with her fellow human beings. And she had been miserable, so miserable that when her parents had both died, she had asked to be allowed to leave the order three weeks before her final vows.

"Mommy? Daddy? I don't know what to say." Her voice broke and she sobbed.

"Forgive us, Sabra," her mother said. "You must forgive us or we will never see the beatific vision. We have been told that our way of treating you was not all of our fault. In a way it was part of a plan. But we must have your forgiveness to see God. You must give it to be free of any petty evil when you—when you . . ." Her mother's voice trailed off.

Sabra stared at her mother. "When I what, Mommy?"

"When you face your ordeal, Sabra," her father said.

"My ordeal? You know what's going to happen? Tell me. Please?"

"We do not know what the future holds for you, my darling child," her mother said. "Only God knows that."

"But," her father said, "you must be rid of anything that can be used against you. You must forgive us and then you will be that much safer. Do you understand?"

"All I ever wanted from you while I was growing up was to have you love me. I felt so alone, so worthless."

"Did you ever hate us for making you unhappy?" her father asked.

Sabra shook her head. "Never. You were my parents. I couldn't hate you. There's nothing to forgive. I love you now as I did then. There were times when I resented what you had done to me, but that was nowhere near the hate that you seem to think I held for you. I love you."

Sabra wiped tears from her eyes, and when she looked up she found herself alone. Where had her parents gone? She wanted more time with them. Now that she knew their indifference had been part of an overall plan involving her, she wanted to make up for times lost with her parents. Where had they gone?

She turned and continued walking. The silence crushed in on her as she looked around at the clouds. They were of such a sheen that it was unthinkable a speck of dirt might exist anyplace in the universe.

Off in the distance, she could see a pinpoint of light forming, slowly growing larger as she approached it. The brilliance of it magnified, and she squinted as she neared to it. When she could make out the shape of it, she saw that it was in reality a doorway through which she could see a landscape of some sort.

She stopped, looked to her left and saw a corridor that was foggy like the hall in which she stood. A desire to see what was in that direction overwhelmed her desire to go through the door and bask in the brilliant sunshine she would find there. Turning, she started walking toward the fog. It seemed darker than that of the other corridor where she had seen her parents. The clouds darkened even more, and when she turned around to see if she should retrace her steps, the way behind her was as dark and forbidding as that which lay in front of her. She wished she had gone through the doorway.

Continuing to walk slowly, she saw what appeared to be a dim light off to her right. She walked toward it and stopped when she saw a large glass partition separating the hall from the room inside. She pressed her face to the glass and looked in.

She gasped. Marcy, Ginger and Curt were strapped to crosses inside a large glass tank. Water that appeared to be almost two feet or so in depth covered the floor of the glass cage. Off to her left, Sabra found Bart, chained to a treadmill. He was walking, his head hanging while he struggled to keep moving.

Sabra pounded on the glass window and the three children looked in her direction. Their fearful expressions changed instantly into broad smiles of recognition. She couldn't hear their shouts but she could read their lips. "Daddy! It's Mom! It's Mom!"

Bart looked up, a grin on his face, and stopped walking. Instantly, water gushed into the tank where the three children were strapped in place. Bart began walking, and the water stopped.

Sabra screamed. What was going on here? Was she actually seeing her husband and children? Who had devised such a devilish scheme as this? How long could Bart continue walking and keep the water out of the tank?

The looks of fear and horror on her family's faces tore at Sabra. She turned away, weeping, wanting to scream out her frustrations. Who could have done this? She turned back and the window was gone.

Sobbing, she continued walking along the foggy hallway. Another window opened to her left and she looked in, fearful of what she might see this time. The sight of her parents had been good. She and they had come to an understanding, one that she would have to wait to enjoy after she reached the other side in her own way, in her own time. But the horrible scene she had just witnessed with her family in jeopardy had been almost too much.

Had the scene been real? Did it have a meaning? Or was someone simply torturing her now? Was Flar responsible?

Sabra turned and ran into the fog again, stumbling but maintaining her balance while she moved along the passageway. When a third light appeared, again to her right, she stopped and walked directly to it. Inside, she saw a bedroom. A woman, a voluptuous red-haired woman, stood naked at the foot of the bed. She fingered her clitoris and her huge breasts rose and fell in rhythm with her growing passion. She held out a hand toward the shadows to one side and a naked man walked out.

Bart!

The Curse

Sabra turned from the window and ran. Her heart pounded, her breath coming in short gasps. Why was she being treated this way? What had she done that was so wrong?

Another window opened and she looked inside. Curt. Her ten-year-old son was kicking a boy who lay in front of him. A sadistic look twisted Curt's handsome features. He continued kicking, and Sabra turned away, sobbing. Was she going mad?

Another window opened, and she saw Marcy astride a boy on the ground, pumping her hips in the age-old rhythm. The boy struggled, his face a mask of pain, while Marcy continued her unrelenting attack on him. Sabra covered her eyes. None of this had happened. It couldn't have happened because she'd know if it had.

She turned away and walked slowly. When another window opened, she kept on walking. To hell with it. She wanted no part of any of this. What did any of it mean?

Because she felt her entire being out of control, she turned back to the window and saw a classroom. Ginger stood near the teacher's desk and was looking at a purse. She dumped the contents out, then picked up something and ran to one of the student's desks. She opened it and threw whatever it was she had taken into the desk. Then Ginger ran out of the room.

Sabra stood rooted to the spot when the window dimmed and disappeared. What had she just seen? Before she had seen the last window, she felt none of what she had witnessed could have happened, but this last one—Ginger had come home and told how one of her classmates had stolen money from the teacher's purse.

Sabra turned around and continued walking. Had Ginger actually taken the money and put it in the other child's desk? If that were true, then had the other things she'd seen actually happened as well?

Wait. It made no sense to think that the children were tied up in a water tank that only Bart could keep empty by walking on a treadmill of some sort.

If all of this was some sort of trick on her imagination, had she actually seen her parents? What significance did their presence have in the scheme of the other awful scenes she had witnessed? Where had her parents gone when they left?

"They've gone to see God," a man's voice said from her side.

Sabra jumped and turned to find a man walking with her. Where had he come from? Who was he?

"What did you say?"

"They've gone to see God. You made it possible."

"Who's gone—?" She stopped. She recognized the man's voice. She had heard it before. She had heard him calling her name. She was sure it was the same voice. She had heard it in church and also when she had left Brendan and his fleet of three boats.

A peculiar sensation passed through her, and she suddenly felt whole. It was as if she had never before felt complete, as if she had never been anything but a partial something which existed for no reason at all. She felt whole for the first time in her life.

"Who—who are you?"

"You have done a fine thing, Sabra. Your parents now will enjoy the beatific vision. They will see the face of God, Himself."

Sabra could feel the shocks of electricity wending their way down her back with every word the man uttered. She had never before heard such a voice, so soft and sweet and musical. A voice that would never shout in anger. It was a voice that could only sing praises to others and speak of goodness.

"You do not have much time here, Sabra. Come, walk with me for a while." He held out his hand.

Sabra reached out, tentative to do so. She had no idea who the man was or what he wanted of her or where they would go for their walk. Still, something deep within her knew she would be safe. From him, she could very well draw the strength that she would need later, when she faced—it seemed almost sacrilegious to even think of demons or devils much less one named—she couldn't bring herself to think the name. What sort of man was this who could influence even her thoughts by his mere presence?

She thrust her hand at him and he took it, wrapping his warm fingers around it. The thumb of her hand trembled, and she looked at it, half-expecting to see it convulsing.

They walked on but said nothing. Sabra could feel strength growing in her soul and body. What did he look like? She turned, but as she did so he turned away as well. She'd try again in a moment.

Suddenly, the picture of her three children being drowned with Bart collapsed at the treadmill exploded in her mind. She gasped and began weeping.

"Don't weep, Sabra," the man said. "What you saw was what could happen unless this demon Flar is done away with. He must be confined again or man will loose any gains that have been made in the last fifteen centuries. Wars will be waged unceasingly, fathers will fight sons, brothers will rape sisters, mothers will become whores. There will be chaos with complete anarchy and lawlessness spelling the doom of mankind."

"Can't God stop it?"

"Yes, but man has a free will. He can choose to comply or not comply with Flar and what he wants. And Flar is powerful."

"My family. Have they been—? Did they do—? I don't know how to say it."

"You want to know if Bart did what you saw, if

Marcy did what you saw, if Curt and Ginger did what you saw them do. The answer is yes. Flar is the one responsible. Your family is made up of good people, but good people alone cannot win out against the likes of Flar."

"Why can't that happen?" Sabra asked, turning to see the man's face. He had sat down on a rock and had his back to her.

Sabra waited breathlessly, but when he turned, he pulled up a hood that concealed his face. Disappointed, she repeated her question. "Why can't that happen?"

"Because man has no defense against Flar. You do. Lucifer and his followers have caused much havoc on earth, but there are prayers and religious rites against them that are effective. But there are no such prayers, no such rites to be exorcise Flar."

"Why did God create him then?"

There was a long silence. "God, my Father, did well when he selected you. Flar was created to love, honor and worship God like all creatures. He subsequently followed Lucifer but then gradually grew away from the fallen angels as well. He is alone but so powerful that it took trickery on the part of Brendan to get him into the cauldron wherein he lay for hundreds of years."

"What was the trick? Perhaps it can be used again."

The hooded figure shook his head. "I think not. Brendan wisely appealed to the devil's ego and said that Flar could not do something. Brendan challenged Flar to fit inside the cauldron. When he was within, Brendan sealed the pot and cursed it as far as opening it was concerned. His curse will carry over if he is recaptured.

"If Flar was safely locked up and no longer a threat to man, why was he permitted to escape?" Sabra asked.

The man chuckled. "You have keen perception and will be a worthwhile weapon for God, Sabra. Currently on earth there is a minimum of strife. The bear has weakened and fallen prey to itself, and the eagle has triumphed. Those of the same blood, but different cultures, have made attempts to heal wounds that are thousands of years old. Flar must be dealt with now."

Sabra wondered if "dealt with" meant eradicating him or simply reimprisoning him in the cauldron.

The man stood and held out his hand. Sabra took it, and they walked toward a brightness that rivaled that which she had seen before turning away from it into the foggy corridor.

"If Flar is dealt a death blow, which will come from you and your weapon, or if he is merely confined again—either will be satisfactory. If he is confined, then he and the cauldron must be held in water until the end of time, if possible."

Sabra nodded, understanding what it was the man meant.

They passed through the portal and stood in

sunshine the likes of which Sabra could not recall ever having experienced before. Lush, verdant hills rolled toward the horizon in the distance, while at their feet wildflowers grew in such profusion that she felt they would not be able to move without stepping on some. Trees abounded, and birds flitted from one to another, singing their songs. An air of complete joy filled her.

Sabra relaxed. Never had she seen such beauty, and the peacefulness of the countryside swept over everything in such a way that she felt she could almost touch it. She turned to the man again. "Is this—?" she said and stopped.

The man pulled back his hood, and she recognized his face when he turned to her. "Heaven?" he asked. "Yes, Sabra, this is a small corner of heaven that we decided to show you. Now you know what you will be protecting when you fight Flar. You are gaining the strength necessary to wage mortal combat with him. There is one more to whom you will speak and it is from him that you will gain insight into the ordeal that lies ahead for you. Good-bye, Sabra. I will be with you."

Sabra watched the man turn and walk away, His robes barely grazing the flowers. She had seen Him before in church, when His face replaced the host the priest held up for the congregation to view. She had walked with Christ and talked with Christ and had His promise that He would be with her.

"But that will not be enough, Sabra," a voice said from behind her.

She whirled around and faced a handsome young man who stood at least six and a half feet tall. His flowing dark hair surrounded his face, and he smiled at her. Then she saw the wings.

"Who are you?" she asked, unable to tear her attention from the wings at his back.

"I am Michael, the archangel."

Sabra's head swam. How much more could she stand? Now that she was with the angel and Christ was no longer to be seen, the full truth of what had been happening closed in on her. What would the angel say to her?

"You, Sabra, are about to face the most severe test that any human being has ever faced. Because I have had much to do with fighting Satan, I have been instructed to tell you of the dangers involved. You have been chosen by God to confront Flar, and while there is much I could tell you, most of it you already know. He will use your family against you, and because he is almost at full strength following his imprisonment, he will be a vicious foe. Your goodness, your love, your devotion to God Almighty will be among the strongest weapons in your armory. In the end, it will be the most insignificant tool that you have that will spell the difference between victory and defeat."

"What do you mean? I understand little of what you say," Sabra said and stared at Michael.

"I cannot say it any more clearly."

The Curse

Sabra felt a tug at her shoulder and turned. No one was there. She looked to Michael for an explanation, but he was gone.

Who had tugged at her?

She felt a hand on her right hand but could see no one. What was happening? The hills and flowers, the trees and birds began fading from her view. She didn't want to leave. To leave was to have to face Flar and possible death. If she lost her life in this battle, she might wind up back in heaven. That would not be so bad. But she still didn't want to leave now. She thought of dying. She wasn't ready to leave her family and her husband. They needed her, and she needed them.

The pull on her hand grew stronger, and she thought it felt familiar. The pastoral scene disappeared completely, and she was whisked through the white cloudy hallway. She felt a tremendous pressure on her body and opened her eyes.

Chapter Twenty-two

It took a moment for Sabra's eyes to focus, and when they did, she saw the off-white of her bedroom ceiling. She was back. She was home. Looking downward, she saw the top of Bart's head resting next to her side. He held her right hand in both of his.

"Ba-Bart?" she managed to say, her throat dry, her voice hoarse.

At first, he didn't react, and then the realization she had spoken struck home. He raised his head, tears filling his eyes. "Sabra? Sweetheart? You're conscious. How do you feel?"

Sabra struggled to sit up and felt a tug on her left arm. She turned and saw the tube running from her arm to an IV bottle hanging next to the bed. She recalled the sensation of pain she had felt while she was—Where had she been? She had not merely been unconscious. She had gone someplace, seen something, done something. What?

"I feel—I guess I feel all right. What happened?"

Bart wiped the tears from his eyes and sat up on the edge of the bed. "You went into a coma last Tuesday night at Jerry Pendergard's home. Do you remember being there?"

The evening slowly reformed in her mind and she nodded. They had been discussing the writing that had been inscribed on the cauldron. She vaguely remembered sitting back and relaxing and then—and then she had gone into a coma. Had it really been a coma, or had she actually experienced the things she remembered? She'd have to think on that for a while, sometime when she was alone.

Sabra managed a nod. "I remember. What happened after I went into a coma?"

"We called a doctor, and he said that you were in a coma. Father Wisdom had suggested the same thing after looking at you."

Sabra shivered. "It seems strange hearing you say things like that. I feel so detached from the whole situation. How come I'm here at home? Didn't the doctor take me to a hospital or anything?"

"He did. You were given electroencephalogram tests, three of them to be exact."

"What was wrong with me?"

"Nothing the doctor could find. Your brain wave activity was high, so he began doubting his own diagnosis. He swore you were conscious due to the waves rolling around on the paper the way they did. He showed them to me, but I couldn't make head or tail of what it was he was trying to tell me. I was too worried about you."

Sabra reached out and took Bart's hand in hers. "I love you, Bart."

"And I love you more now than I ever have before, Sabra. I don't know what I would have done if something had happened to you." He clamped his free hand around hers and squeezed.

"So why am I home and not in the hospital?"

"That was the doctor's idea. He felt you were in no danger, so he suggested bringing you home."

"Who is the doctor?"

"Doctor Steven Welbes."

"Is he from Cascade?"

"Peaseleeville. But he's been here at least three times each day."

"Speaking of day. What day is it?"

Bart smiled. "September twenty-ninth, your birthday. Happy birthday, darling." Bart leaned down and kissed her lightly on the cheek. "I'd better go call the doctor. He wanted to know the instant you became conscious." Bart turned and left the room.

The Curse

Sabra snuggled back into the bed. Her birthday. What a grand gift. To have seen her parents, walked and talked with Christ and been instructed by Michael, the archangel. She smiled. It was Michael's feast day as well. Michaelmas. She stared at the ceiling. Some gift, all right. She had to confront Flar. She wondered what Bart would say when she told him. Maybe she wouldn't tell him and just let it happen. She felt positive that he would find every objection he could manage to dissuade her from the task, but she knew she must face Flar. She must confront him for the sake of mankind. She must fight him and win, or life on earth would become hell on earth.

Several minutes later, Bart came back. "I called Father Wisdom, too. He's delighted that you're all right again. So is Jerry Pendergard."

Sabra nodded. Of course, they should have been notified. They had been there when she became comatose, and they had an interest in her welfare because they knew what it was she must do.

"I find it hard to believe I was in a coma for seven days."

Bart smiled. "Almost seven days to the minute. It's almost eight-fifteen, which was just about the time we found you. Father Wisdom pointed something out to me." Bart's voice dropped on the last sentence, as if he had remembered something unpleasant.

"What was that?"

"Michaelmas is the same day as your birthday."

Sabra smiled inwardly. She knew that but couldn't tell him she had spoken with Michael. He'd think her crazy. "Is that important?" she asked, feigning ignorance of its significance.

Bart explained that Michael was God's foremost weapon against the devil. "He gave me a prayer card," Bart said, handing it to Sabra.

Sabra turned it over in her hand and looked at the short prayer.

"Saint Michael, the archangel, defend us in battle. Be our safeguard against the wickedness and snares of the devil. Restrain him, O God, we humbly beseech Thee, and cast him into hell along with the others who roam the world, seeking the destruction of souls."

The doorbell sounded and Sabra looked up at Bart. He turned to answer the door.

"It's either the doctor or Father Wisdom," he said over his shoulder.

"Well, I feel that a few days rest and you'll be back to normal in no time, Sabra," Dr. Welbes said, his attention fixed on her eyes. He said nothing about them and turned to Bart. "See that she rests and takes it easy, Bart. She's in remarkably good condition from what I can tell right now. Why don't you plan on bringing her into my office on Friday? I'll give her a complete physical then, and she can have her walking papers at the same time."

"Very well, Doctor." Bart opened the door for the doctor.

Welbes stopped and turned back to Sabra. "You probably feel real good right about now, but you follow my advice and rest for the next couple of days, young lady."

Sabra nodded. She did feel good but a little tired. Father Wisdom had been there before the doctor arrived, and as far as she knew he was still downstairs.

A smile, almost bitter, crossed her face when she recalled the doctor's statement about being normal. What the hell was normal? She had no idea. She'd be committed to an institution of some sort if she mentioned what she had experienced while she was in her so-called coma.

The door opened to reveal Bart and Father Wisdom.

The priest entered first. "I thought I'd say good night, Sabra. It's getting late for you and you should get some sleep. I'll stop by tomorrow if you'd like and we can visit."

She wanted to ask him what they could visit about, but she knew. She wasn't sure if she wanted to talk about her upcoming confrontation with Flar or not. If Bart found out, she knew he'd do everything in his power to stop her, but it was not within his power to stop her. It was beyond everyone's power, even hers now. She had to do battle for God, for Christ, for mankind.

A low rumbling outside brought her attention to the window. What had that been?

Bart walked over to the window and pulled the shade. "It's supposed to storm tonight, sweetheart. Don't let it bother you." He smiled reassuringly and wiggled her toe when he passed the foot of the bed again.

"I'd better get going or I'll get soaked," Wisdom said. He moved toward the door. "Good night, Sabra, pleasant dreams." He left the room and walked down the hallway.

"I'll be back as soon as he's gone," Bart said and followed the priest from the room.

When they reached the bottom of the steps, Bart said, "You had a raincoat, didn't you, Father?"

"Matter of fact, I don't. I left in such a hurry that I forgot about the possibility of it raining. I'd best hurry."

A loud crash of thunder overhead and a sudden onslaught of rain pelted the windows of the kitchen.

"You'd best wait for a while, Father."

"Good idea. By the way, I meant to ask you something, but with the doctor here and the excitement of Sabra's regaining consciousness and all, I didn't have a chance. Did she say anything about what we were discussing at Jerry's home when she went into her coma?"

"Not a word, other than she wanted to know what had happened."

"She didn't mention the kettle or the inscription or anything?"

"Nothing."

"She'll remember in time, I'm sure."

"Would you like some coffee, Father. It sounds from the way it's raining that you'll be here for a while."

"That would be nice, Bart. You'd better tell her I'm going to be here for a while yet."

"Good idea, Father. I'll be right back."

Bart raced up the steps two at a time and went to the master bedroom. He found Sabra lying on her back, her golden hair spread out on the pillow. Her white nightgown seemed to emphasize her coloring, and when she looked at him with her white/blue eyes, she smiled.

Bart returned the smile. "Father Wisdom's going to stay a while until the rain lets up. I'm making some coffee for him. Try to get some sleep and I'll be up as soon as he's gone."

"I never once asked how the children are," she said quietly.

"They're fine. They're in their rooms. I've told them that you're all right. Do you want to see them now?"

Sabra shook her head. Now was not the time. She felt that her meeting with Flar might be drawing close. She didn't want the children involved. "Why don't you tell them that I love them and I'll see them in the morning. I probably should get some rest, just like the doctor said."

Bart turned out the ceiling light, leaving just the glow from the bedside lamp. He closed the door quietly and left.

Sabra listened to the rain pounding on the windowpancs. The thunder rolled again and lightning flashed, brightening the room despite the drawn shades.

Thunder crashed directly overhead, and Sabra sat up in bed. It sounded as if her name had been called.

It happened again. *"Sa-bra!"*

She looked around. Had Bart or Father Wisdom or the children heard? She waited for what seemed an eternity, but no one came to the door. Had she imagined that she'd heard her name called?

"Sa-bra!"

Her eyes wide, she went to the window and raised the shade. She winced when she saw the dragon and gigantic Tyrannosaurus Rex in the yard, their tails angrily lashing in the storm. Where was Flar?

As if answering her question, the devil suddenly appeared in a blaze of lightning. He stood between the two monsters and laughed. He pointed at the house and the window through which Sabra looked, making a gesture with his arm, motioning for her to come out.

She reached up and grasped the crucifix around her neck.

It was time.

The Curse

She turned, walked to the door and opened it without making a sound. Treading quietly down the steps, she entered the dining room and could hear Bart and Father Wisdom talking in the kitchen. If she went outside through the door in the dining room, they might not hear her, but they would feel the cool air and hear the wind and rain.

Something caught her attention and held it. The cauldron sat near the living room door.

She picked up the kettle, went to the living room and opened the door that led to the front porch. Stepping through quickly, she closed it behind her and went to the screen door.

She hesitated before opening it, looking at the place where Flar and the monsters had been. They weren't there. That meant nothing. He was ready for her. Was she ready for him? She'd soon know. Her fingers caressed the crucifix for a moment, and then she pushed open the screen door.

"I'm coming, Flar," she said quietly and stepped into the rain.

Chapter Twenty-three

Lightning and thunder cavorted overhead through the Stygian night. Sounding not unlike crescendoing welcome for the white-clad figure of the blond woman walking through the rain, the thunder reached its peak directly over her and crashed, sending a reverberation through the air that shook buildings and trees alike.

Sabra looked around. Where was Flar? She knew he was out there someplace, but where? Why did she have to seek him out? Why didn't he show himself? Would he strike at her from behind, hoping to rid himself of God's champion? Or would he and his monsters confront her openly and try to devour her? She had no idea as to what she should expect, much less how to prepare for it. Questioning God's judgment in choosing her, she walked around the house toward where the hill had been all but removed. She felt as though she should be slogging through the mud and, looking down, was startled to find her feet and gown virtually dry.

A roar of thunder sounded, and she stopped. She realized it hadn't been thunder she heard but the roar of the dragon. The beast stood in the middle of the meadow that lay beyond the hill site, lashing its tail through the muddy soil. Its eyes glowed in the dark, swords of flames jetting from its open mouth. The huge scales covering its body glistened in the light of the fire.

As if seeing her for the first time, the monster roared again and sent a tongue of flame 50 feet long toward her.

Sabra, in a reflexive, defensive move, swung her right forearm up to protect her face and the flame disappeared. She caught her breath. If only she could rid herself and the world of the dragon as easily as she had the flame.

"I wish you didn't exist!" she cried and stepped forward.

The dragon glared at her for an instant, then disappeared.

Sabra looked at the spot where the beast had stood, a sense of astonishment holding her fast. What had happened? Where had the dragon gone? Had her silly wish been granted? Would the dragon return?

Clutching the kettle in her left hand, she continued walking away from the house. Maybe she should wish for Flar and the giant dinosaur to vanish as well. If it worked, she would be finished and the world would be safe. A sense of irony crossed over her. The world would be safe? Would it really be safe? She thought back to the words Christ had spoken about the bear no longer being a threat, about the eagle being triumphant, about those of the same blood but different cultures talking of peace. The last one had bothered her in a way, not quite certain what it meant. Her conclusion was that the Arabs and Israelis sitting at the peace conference might be a sign of something greater to come in the future.

But Flar could ruin everything, and she had to stand in his way. She looked heavenward and struck her breast in a supplicating way. "Must it be me, Lord?"

As if in answer, a crash of thunder sounded and lightning grazed the clouds. Another roar sounded and Sabra turned. There, between her and the house, the gigantic Tyrannosaurus Rex stood balanced on its two hind legs. The smaller claws of the forelimbs flexed open while the animal's mouth hung agape. Another screeching roar peeled through the night, and it charged. The head, almost 70 feet over Sabra, savagely whipped back and forth, its cavernous mouth opened wide. Its 100-foot length quickly covered the distance between them, and Sabra fell back, astounded at the quickness of the monster. Her foot caught on a rock and she fell down in the mud.

"I—I wish you didn't exist!" she screamed.

Nothing happened.

"Bitch of God!" Flar screamed.

The dinosaur stopped, its huge mouth opened right above Sabra, its 18-inch-long teeth dripping a smelly reptilian saliva onto her. The beast's head swooped down. Sabra pressed against the earth, throwing her own head back and exposing her throat. The teeth swept to within a fraction of an inch of her skin. One tooth caught the gold chain and the crucifix flew into the night.

She scooted backward and then got to her feet. She had heard Flar, but where was he? Backing away slowly, she looked about the darkness.

"I will destroy you. You're nothing but a woman, a weak woman. Didn't God have anyone else to send but his whore?" Flar's voice rang out through the rainy night. His peculiar, high-pitched laugh changed and plummeted to a deep-throated roar that mingled with the thunder so that the two became indistinguishable.

"Where are you, Flar? Show yourself if you do not fear a mere woman!"

"Don't worry, sucker of holy cocks! If my pet doesn't eat you, we will find each other when I'm ready."

Sabra kept her eyes on the Rex. He stood perhaps 30 feet from her now. She couldn't possibly hope to outrun such an animal. One of its strides would match 30 or 40 of hers. She had to hold her ground, but she had no weapons with which to fight.

The words of Christ exploded in her mind. "If Flar is dealt a death blow, which will come from you and your weapon, or if he is confined again—either will be satisfactory." But what weapon? She had no weapon. She remembered nodding as if she had understood what He had said. She should have asked Him about the weapon. She had no idea what she should do.

The Rex stepped forward, its mouth again hovering directly above her. She cowered and wanted to vomit. Why hadn't Christ told her about the weapon? She had nothing. She had no weapon.

Staring up at the Tyrannosaurus Rex, she covered her ears when it roared. After it stopped, it snapped at her. Once again, the teeth barely missed her, clamping together with a loud crash. It snapped again, and she ducked to one side. If she stopped moving, she'd be killed instantly.

The scene she had witnessed with Bart having to walk on a treadmill to keep water from rushing in to drown their children suddenly flashed in her mind's eye. What would happen to her family if she failed? Would they fall under Flar's spell? She hated Flar. She hated this monster trying to kill her.

When she glared up at the beast, a bolt of blood-red lightning streaked from her blue-white eyes, striking the monster in the throat. The tip of the bolt slashed through the leathery skin, ripping it wide open. Blood rained down on her, but she somehow remained untouched by it.

The dinosaur roared its death throes, falling back toward the house.

Realizing she did after all have a weapon, she pursued the beast, glaring at it with all the hatred she could muster. The beast collapsed and fell in a heap. She recalled being told that her children and husband had been made to sin by Flar and her hatred intensified even more.

The Rex continued thrashing about, its screams growing fewer and farther between. The diminishing cries turned to grunts, and when no more sounded, a heavy silence fell over the scene. Sabra's eyes continued blasting the monster, turning it to ashes, and when the last bit had been consumed, she stopped. Her shoulders slumped and she heaved a sigh of relief. Where had the lightning come from? How had it happened? She closed her eyes and rubbed them. Lightning shooting from her eyes? It didn't make sense. It was all unbelievable. Impossible.

Opening her eyes, she found the ashes turning into a muddy pile from the rain washing it away in small rivulets. If only it was Flar who lay at her feet.

She straightened up and shook herself. She had no idea if her eyes could kill Flar or not. She could do nothing more than try.

The wind picked up, whipping the trees and long grass on the hillside in a weaving dance. The rain fell harder, lashing at Sabra but not touching her. Her long blond hair flowed about her while she fought to control her breathing, her breasts rising and falling.

A crash of thunder announced Flar's arrival. His voice boomed from behind Sabra.

"Now you must deal with us!"

Not knowing what to expect, Sabra turned slowly. What would she face? More of his beasts and monsters? More devils like Flar himself? She wondered what he might look like and recalled the incident in the bedroom when she had found her missing sketch pad. There had been an ugly sketch of something that had glared at her—thick jowls and fat, pendulous lips, drool dripping that had turned blood red in the wink of an eye. The rest of the face had colored itself, too. A mauve-colored complexion with open sores and pustules surrounded the one nostril in the broad nose that half-covered its awful countenance. The slanted, feline eyes had stared at her, and she shuddered at the memory.

Keeping her eyes on the ground, she completed the half-circle and raised her head. Flar stood some 50 feet away from her, his long muscular arms around his reinforcements—Bart, Marcy, Curt and Ginger.

She gasped. It couldn't be them. He had to be playing some sort of trick on her, a loathsome hallucination that was meant to take her off guard. She had to be strong or she would fail. She winced when she thought of the fact that Flar had made all of them commit sins—sins they wouldn't normally have even thought of, much less perform. She knew it hadn't been their fault. Christ—or the man she thought had been Christ—had told her that. What was Flar up to with this ploy? She couldn't be seeing the real Bart, the real Marcy. Ginger and Curt had to be figments of her imagination. How could she hope to be victorious against an entity that was capable of doing something such as this?

"What do you hope to accomplish with this move, Flar?" she demanded. How had she found the courage and the strength to ask such a question?

Flar laughed and closed his thin fingers around the shoulders of Marcy and Ginger who stood at the outside of his troops. His talons caressed the flesh on their bare arms. "Give up now, you slut, or you'll never be the same when I show you what they can do." His gutteral voice mixed in with a roll of thunder.

Sabra had to be hallucinating. She was seeing a mirage. She was seeing what Flar wanted her to see. Why didn't Christ or Saint Michael intercede for her?

Bart and the children danced about Flar, pointing at her and laughing.

"You're a goody-two shoes, Mom. You're too good to be true."

"Little Miss Sin-free! Mother never commits a sin."

Bart glared at her. "Bitch of God!"

Marcy bared her breasts. "Whore of Christ!"

Sabra wept at the insults and taunts. Why were they saying such things? None of this was fair. If Flar wanted to lock with her in mortal combat, she'd do it. If he wanted to name the weapons, she'd do her best and fight him. But this was going too far. He was using her loved ones against her.

"He will use your family against you!" Michael's words bounded back to her. She closed her eyes. No matter what Flar made the creatures who resembled her family do, she would resist having the desired reaction. They weren't real. Her children were good children, and Bart loved her as much as she loved him. And right that second, she knew she loved him more than she had ever dreamt possible.

"Flar," she yelled and opened her eyes. She said nothing more. A look of disgust and horror crossed her face, turning it into a twisted, contorted visage of itself.

Marcy was on her knees in front of Flar, licking his huge penis. Bart had lifted his daughter's skirt and was copulating with her from behind. Off to the side, Curt had Ginger pinned to the ground, trying to rape his younger sister. Ginger, instead of fighting him off, helped him.

"None of this is real," Sabra screamed. "Those are not my children and husband! Do you need tricks, Flar, to fight a mere woman?"

The look of pleasure that had held the devil's face turned into a frown. He snapped his fingers, and the images of Bart and the children disappeared.

A sense of victory teased Sabra, if for no reason other than the ugly scene had been taken away. Sabra felt almost confident. She had made Flar do something he apparently didn't want to do. That was the way Brendan had imprisoned Flar in the cauldron, but she couldn't use trickery on him. Christ had said so. The same sort of tactics wouldn't work twice.

Flar stepped toward Sabra, lightning shooting from his cat eyes. Bolts shot at her, but she lithely sidestepped them. Then, one caught her on the shoulder and she reeled backward before falling to the ground.

Flar roared, his evil, contemptuous laughter mixing with the storm's thunder. Lightning etched surrealistic patterns across the roiling clouds overhead, and the wind picked up, sounding for all the world like cheering to Sabra.

She got to her feet and looked up. Flar appeared to be twice again as big as he had been. She didn't care what he did. She would not quit without a fight. Too much depended on her to see this confrontation through to its end. She drew herself up to her full height and found she matched Flar in size.

"Bitch of God! I'll kill you and eat you." Flar glared and sent a bolt of lightning at her.

This time, instead of trying to sidestep it, Sabra met it head on and deflected it with the palm of her left hand. She glared at him but nothing happened. She tried again. Nothing. No lightning, such as had eradicated the Tyrannosaurus Rex, burst from her eyes.

Flar's laughter roared, shaking Sabra. He stopped laughing and fire erupted from his mouth. His pendulous lips hung loosely, the flames seething through broken teeth.

Acting instinctively, Sabra blew her breath at him and fire shot from her mouth. The two flames met, stopping each other. Dazzled by her actions, Sabra wondered how she could do these things. How could they be? It could only be the work of God, allowing her to fight Flar with his own weapons. Her right hand shot to her throat. Where was her crucifix? A sense of panic struck at her, wounding her self-confidence.

Lightning flashed and thunder followed immediately as if encouraging the rain and wind to attack the earth and the combatants more savagely.

Where before she had seemed immune to the rain and mud and blood, Sabra found herself being soaked to the skin. Her gown clung to her body, outlining her breasts and nipples. Wind tore at her wet hair, thrashing it about her head.

Flar shot up to a new height and wiggled his cock at Sabra. She instantly grew as big as he.

"Let's forget this foolish fight. I want to fuck your holy body. You'll never have it so good." He waved his huge penis like a sword until she turned away.

Hiding her eyes from his ugliness, Sabra whispered the prayer to Saint Michael. "Saint Michael, the archangel, defend me in battle. Be my safeguard against the wickedness of the devil. Restrain him, O God, I humbly beseech You, and cast him into hell with the other—"

Sabra stopped. She shouldn't whisper this. She should shout it as loud as she could. "Cast Flar into hell along with the other evil spirits who roam the world, seeking the destruction of souls."

Flar screamed when he heard the words, the thunder drowning out his cries.

Had her supplication been heard in heaven? "Help me, Jesus! Help me. Make me strong enough to rid the world of this filthy demon!"

She stopped when a voice, the same soft, sweet voice she'd heard before said, "You are strong enough, Sabra."

Flar doubled his size again, standing over 100 feet tall. "Fuck you, Christ! Stay outta this! This is between me and your cunt!"

Sabra shot straight upward and started toward him. She was bound and determined to fight him to the death.

"Forget fighting, bitch. I want you. You'll be the biggest fuck I've had in centuries." He threw his head back and roared his laughter.

The storm continued unabated and seemed to grow in intensity.

Sabra tried breathing fire at Flar but nothing happened. It was gone. She glared at him, hoping to strike him with lightning. Nothing. She wished for him to be gone, to exist no longer. Again, nothing happened. What was wrong? Didn't she believe enough? Was her faith suddenly suspect? Had Christ and Saint Michael abandoned her?

Flar laughed. "What's the matter? Out of everything?" He walked toward her, his erection standing straight out in front of him, waving from one side to the other as he moved. His taloned claws reached out for her.

Sabra fell back and held up her hands to ward him off.

"Jesus! Help me!"

A stream of pure light in the shape of the crucified Christ shot out from her thumb where she had pressed her cross during the elevation of the host at Mass.

The image of Christ struck Flar and, branding itself on his face and chest, seared the mauve flesh deeply. A stink arose.

Flar instantly shrank until he stood no more than six feet tall. Sabra found herself growing smaller as well, and when she stood on the ground opposite the branded devil, the words of Saint Michael about the most insignificant weapon being the deciding factor rang in her ears.

Sabra advanced toward Flar who groveled and continued shrinking. He screamed out in pain and obeyed Sabra when she motioned for him to back up.

She steered him toward the cauldron, and when she was near enough, she set it upright. Lifting the lid, she pointed to the inside.

Flar screamed out his objection but obeyed.

Once he was inside, she clamped the lid on, praying to God that he never be set free again. "Please, Lord Jesus, I beg of you. Let Brendan's curse hold him until the crack of Judgment Day."

The wind suddenly died down to nothing and the rain stopped. Overhead, the clouds were breaking apart and she could see stars twinkling in the heavens.

She was exhausted. Picking up the cauldron she walked toward the house.

Sabra opened the door to the kitchen and walked in, carrying the kettle. Bart and Father Wisdom stopped talking and stared.

"It's over," she said simply.

"What's over?" Bart asked, rushing to her.

"The battle. Flar has been vanquished. He's a prisoner once more. But you must help me."

"Flar is in—?" Wisdom asked, pointing to the small kettle.

She nodded. Turning from one side to the other, she repeated, "You must help me dispose of the cauldron. Will you?"

"What has to be done?" Bart asked, peering intently at his wife. "Are you all right? You're supposed to be in bed." He stared at her. "Your eyes! My God! They're deep blue. How—?"

"I'm fine. The whole thing is over, except that the kettle must be put in deep water now. As for my eyes, I don't know. Maybe it's God's way of saying I'm finished. The water will better hold Flar imprisoned forever, and there's no chance of iron striking it there.

"We could go to Lake Champlain," Father Wisdom said. "We can charter a boat and—"

"No, that's not deep enough. Nor is it far enough away. If we could, I'd say we take it to the middle of the Pacific Ocean and drop it in." Sabra sat down on a stool and put the kettle on the floor.

"Where do you suggest?" Bart asked, moving nearer his wife.

She took his hand in hers. "Can we take it to Lake Ontario? We could charter a plane, fly it out over the water and drop it in."

Bart looked at the priest. "Would you go with us, Father?"

The Curse

Without hesitating, Wisdom said, "Of course. I think we can be back in time for me to say Mass. It's not that late yet. What about your children?"

Sabra stood. "We can tell Marcy that she'll be baby-sitting for the night until we get back."

Bart shook his head. "What'll we tell them when they ask where we're going?"

"You'll have to forgive all the lies we'll be telling tonight, Father," Sabra said, smiling benignly. "Tell her, Bart, that I have to go see the doctor. She'll believe that. Go ahead. I'll change into something more presentable, and we can be on our way."

Twenty minutes later Bart backed the Taurus station wagon out of the driveway and headed toward the highway. Another 20 minutes passed before they turned onto Highway 3. In less than two hours they'd be in Watertown. There they either would hire a plane or a boat to take them out far enough to rid the world of the kettle.

"What story will you tell whoever you hire?" Father Wisdom asked.

"I hadn't thought of that," Bart said. He turned to Sabra who sat next to him, her head back, her eyes closed, "Any ideas, Sabra?"

"We'll tell them the kettle contains the ashes of a dear, departed one. It was his or her wish to be buried in Lake Ontario at night."

Father Wisdom chuckled but said nothing.

"Because Father Wisdom is with us," Sabra continued, "the story will ring that much more true."

They fell silent, each locked into his or her own thoughts, and the minutes dragged into hours. Shortly before two o'clock the next morning, they pulled up in front of the police station.

Their request for a pilot's name was granted, and following the directions given by the officer, Bart drove toward the airport where the pilot was to meet them at 2:30.

The Cessna 172 lifted off the ground effortlessly and sped into the night. The pilot, Joe Zwack, banked to the right and flew toward the dark expanse of water that was Lake Ontario.

When they were out far enough to commit the "last remains" to the waters, Sabra, who sat next to the pilot, turned to Father Wisdom and said, "Should we say a prayer, Father?"

"I think enough prayers have been said, Sabra. Whenever you're ready, you may commit the kettle and its contents to the water. I might suggest that if you want to pray, you do so silently."

The pilot reached across Sabra and opened the door. She pushed the cauldron through the opening. Immediately, the door slammed shut. A heavy, almost tangible silence filled the cabin despite the roar of the engine.

"Take us home, Joe," Sabra said.

The Cessna banked in a 180-degree turn and headed back toward Watertown.

HELL -O- WEEN

DAVID ROBBINS

On Halloween night, two buddies decide to play a cruel trick on the class brain...but the joke is on them.

They only want to scare their enemy to death...but their prank goes awry and one of their friends ends up dead, her body ripped to pieces.

Soon seven teenagers are frantically fighting to save themselves from unthinkably gruesome ends...but something born in the pits of hell is after them—and they have no hope of escape.

___3335-6 $4.50 US/$5.50 CAN

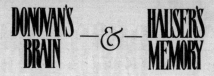